# *PLASTIC GODS*

To my daughter,

Maryanna Manchee

# PLASTIC GODS

## A Rich Coleman Novel

Volume 2

by

## WILLIAM MANCHEE

Top Publications, Ltd.
Dallas, Texas

PLASTIC GODS

Plastic

They came from everywhere
Over here, over there
The mail, the phone, the mall
Unsolicited, one and all
Get them one, two, or ten
Don't wait—just grab a pen

It's a simply wonderful game
All you do is sign your name
Now jump for joy, and yell hooray!
Cause baby they're on their way
Dillards, Penneys to name a few
Visa, Mastercard, and Amex Blue

You can live the American dream
Stand up now and let out a scream
Buy it now, no money down
You've got credit all over town
Sit back and watch your dreams come true
Don't worry, only pennies due

For Moses it was manna provided by the Lord
No need to sit around the house so bored
Now its silver, gold, and platinum too
Macy's, Sears to name just two
Cars, clothes, a ten day cruise
Gambling, clubs, and lots of booze

You've got it all and then some more
Until the bills flood in the door
It cannot be, I didn't spend that much
Just a few odds and ends and such
Eighteen, twenty, twenty-four
Interest, interest, bills galore

Oh my God, it's all a scam
To steal my life, I'm in a jam
Collectors calling day and night
My balances clear out of sight
I can't sleep or think
Go to work, eat or drink

My lover scorns me, yells, and screams
God, what happened to my dreams?
Letters come demanding blood,
Tears from my face do flood
My lovers's gone, couldn't take the heat
I'm here alone, tired and beat

Is all that's left bankruptcy?
What was my sin? Idolatry
I see it now, clear as glass
I fell in love with cold, hard cash
Visa, Mastercard, Amex Blue
Lucifer got his due

# 1

Love, at first sight, must run in the family. My son Matt had just revealed to me his plans to marry a girl he had just met. Matt and Lynn fell in love just hours after meeting at a New Year's Eve party at the Hotel Continental in Dallas. It was January 2004, just 22 years since Erica and I had been married. We had fallen in love almost immediately too. However, our circumstances were such that we had to keep our love a secret. The illicit affair was eventually discovered, and the consequences were severe.

We survived somehow and were still deeply in love. I'd been practicing law as a sole practitioner in North Dallas. I had started my career with a small firm and made partner in record time. My life was perfect until my wife died in a car wreck. I was devastated and quickly turned to alcohol to forget my loss. Fortunately, a friend helped me get through those most difficult times, and I put my drinking behind me. The loneliness persisted, however, and I frequently fell into a deep depression.

This loneliness made me vulnerable to Erica, and perhaps it was the emptiness in Erica's life that drew her to me. Her mother had deserted her when she was fifteen and, when she was just beginning to adjust to that loss, her father was killed in a skiing accident.

Erica was indeed an extraordinary young woman—smart, sexy, confident, and determined to get whatever she wanted. Our illicit affair led to my expulsion from the firm, the death of Erica's Aunt Martha, and Erica's trial for murder. We are still very much in love and, despite everything, have few regrets.

Erica and I have two children, Matt and Ryan. Matt was the eldest, and during his childhood he never indicated any desire to be an attorney. We were shocked during his junior year in college when he announced he was applying to law school. It's not that I wasn't delighted, as any father would be, to have his son follow in his footsteps, it was just so unexpected. Matt always said he would never become a lawyer because he didn't want to have to work as hard as I did. There had to be an easier way to make a living with less stress and more time to spend with the family.

I couldn't really argue with him about that since I was working eighty hours a week trying to keep up with more than a hundred cases. So what was it that changed his thinking? In my mind, it was the money. Money had always been the most important motivating factor in Matt's life. He inherited that mind set from his mother. When he was young, she would bribe him with a quarter here, a dollar there, in order to get him to do what she wanted with the least amount of resistance. It worked very well; in fact, so well that he began to expect a cash reward for almost everything he did. At some point, we had to put a stop to that practice. It was at age eighteen when he went off to college that I jolted him with the fact that someone else would have to reward him in the future for his hard work.

It took a little adjustment, but when he entered Southern Methodist University in Dallas, his clear objective was to get a business degree and then go to graduate school to get his MBA. In his mind, once he got his MBA he could find a lucrative job where he could live high with the least amount of effort. Unfortunately, the business classes were difficult and tedious with no immediate reward, so he soon switched his major to political science, something that came naturally to him and required only a modest effort.

I don't know where he got it, certainly not from me or his mother, but Matt was very fortunate to acquire a tremendous thirst for knowledge. I'm no psychiatrist, but I always thought it came from his high ego and competitive spirit. He couldn't stand for anyone to be more knowledgeable than he. He loved to spout off esoteric facts to people and watch their expressions of surprise or dismay. He'd spend countless hours reading books and devouring magazine articles—fascinated by the world in which he lived and anxious to tell everyone what he had learned.

Matt loved to argue and debate with anyone who dared to do battle with him. He rarely lost, which made finding opponents difficult. His brother Ryan was his fiercest adversary. Ryan was as intelligent as Matt but had completely different values. He cared little about money and material things. Needless to say, dinnertime conversation often got very intense.

The one thing they had in common, however, was their love for fantasy, warfare, and science fiction. They spent countless hours engaged in mock combat, whether it was Risk, Dungeons and Dragons, Civilization, or countless other games. To get an advantage over the other, they studied the theories and exploits of Machiavelli, Alexander the Great, Genghis Khan, Napoleon, and Rommel. Although Ryan held up better than most, Matt almost always prevailed, not so much due to his ruthless, relentless attack, but more on account of his thorough preparation for battle.

He liked to dazzle his friends with his incredible knowledge of history. He loved the reactions he got when he spouted off some detailed facts about historical events or ancient rulers. He would exaggerate at times, which hurt his credibility. As a result, many of his young opponents were lured into thinking him a charlatan and thus dismissed him as a serious threat. This usually gave him a competitive advantage as he wasn't seriously challenged before his armies were mobilized, fully equipped and ready for battle.

His mother and I were usually amused when he'd bring a new friend home to play one of his games. They'd be smiling and giggling when they arrived but invariably would leave with long, sullen faces.

Despite what I've said, those who got to know Matt would tell you he had a good heart and would go to great lengths to help his friends. He was very sociable, loved to talk with anyone, and never forgot a name. He seemed to need approval and acceptance and would go to great lengths to get it. Although he had a tough facade, he genuinely cared about people and wanted to help them.

After hanging out my shingle, I decided to specialize in financial and estate planning. The publicity I had received from Erica's trial had gotten me a lot of exposure and made me a hot commodity. Unfortunately, when the economy cratered after the big banking scandal in the mid-eighties, so did my practice. After that debacle, I decided I needed a second specialty that would do well when times were bad. The obvious pick was bankruptcy. The hedge worked very well, and my bankruptcy business grew to the point that it now comprised more than 45 percent of my annual billings. Most of this growth came as the result of quick and efficient handling of the vast amount of paperwork needed for the average bankruptcy. This was made possible by new computer software that took care of the math and preparation of schedules. While most attorneys needed two or three appointments to finish a bankruptcy, I did it all at the first appointment.

I learned early on that 80 percent of the bankruptcies that came through the door were nearly identical. This allowed me to have substantial portions of the paperwork preprogrammed on the computer before the client stepped into my office. This quick processing delighted clients and baffled my competition. With efficiency came volume and with volume came nice profits.

My office was located on the 18th floor of One Main Place just two minutes from the Earl Cabell Federal Building where the United States Bankruptcy Court for the Northern District of Texas was situated. This was an ideal location for a bankruptcy practice and made it easy for me to run to court or attend creditor meetings held by the trustee. Matt didn't like the location since he lived in Carrollton, which was 15 miles away. It was late January, and Matt had come into my office to tell me he'd fallen in love.

"She's a senior at SMU, a marketing major—we met at a party."

"Sounds interesting. Tell me about her."

"She's a brunette, medium height, great body, and she's got a head on her shoulders. She wants to go into advertising. You and Mom are going to love her."

"That's a good field. What's her name?"

"Lynn . . . Lynn Lakey."

"So when do I get to meet her?"

"In just a few hours. She's coming by to go to lunch. Why don't you come along?"

"No, you guys go ahead. I've got to get ready for a mediation tomorrow morning."

"We'd really like to talk to you."

"About what?"

"About what in the hell I'm going to do with my life."

"Why would you want to discuss something like that with a girl you just met?"

"It's going to affect her too."

"How do you mean?"

"She's the one, Dad."

"But you just met her."

"I know, but I've never felt this way about a woman before. You know how sometimes you're looking for something, but you don't know exactly what it is? All you know is you hope you recognize it when you see it."

"Yes, I do."

"Aside from all the sexual feelings I was getting from Lynn, there was something else. I couldn't figure out what it was until it finally hit me."

"What was that?"

"*Relief.* For years I've been looking for the right woman without success, but after twenty-four hours with Lynn suddenly I felt calm and contented. I think the search is over."

"That's how I felt when I met your mother. . . . I hope it's true. I can't wait to meet this woman. She must be something else."

"She is—she's dynamite."

"Good. . . . Well, I've got a client waiting for me, but I will definitely see you for lunch."

Matt went into his office and started to work on some discovery that he had to get out. While he was working, he found himself looking out his window toward SMU. He could see Moody Coliseum on a clear day, and he wondered where Lynn was and what she was doing. The morning dragged on, and he had trouble concentrating.

Finally, it was time for lunch. Matt and I met Lynn at the Peking Palace in the underground city beneath One Main Place. It was crowded, so we had a drink while we waited. Matt excused himself to make a phone call.

"So you two enjoyed the New Year's Eve party, huh?" I said.

"Yes, it was wonderful," Lynn replied. "I've never seen so much confetti. I think it was knee deep."

"Really?"

"Yeah, the hotel had an atrium, and they had it loaded in nets high above us. I didn't notice it until they dumped it on us at midnight."

Rich shook his head. "Well, it's going to be an exciting year, I think, with technology advancing as rapidly as it is. It seems like every day I pick up the newspaper and read about some incredible new invention."

"I know."

"Just today I was reading about the new Smart Card. I guess we won't be using checking accounts much longer."

"That's right; we've been learning about that in one of my finance classes. Everything's going to be automatic. No checks or deposits. On payday, you just run your Smart Card through the company scanner, and it credits your account. All transactions will be instantaneous. No more hot-checks or overdrafts."

"I hope I don't ever lose my card. What a disaster that would be."

"Really."

Lynn looked toward the phones and saw Matt returning. She smiled at him as he approached and sat next to her.

"So have you made a decision about what area of the law you want to practice?" I asked.

"As a matter of fact, we have. That's what I wanted to talk to you about. I've been telling Lynn how I planned to be a PI attorney until Congress and the state legislature spoiled that idea."

"You can still make a living practicing personal injury law. It's just not as lucrative as it used to be."

"Well, I want to make a ton of money. I didn't spend seven years busting my ass to become an attorney just to make a living. I want to be financially independent. A lot of lawyers manage to do that, so there's no reason why I can't do it too."

"You just graduated from law school, for godsakes. Don't you think it's a little unrealistic to think you can get rich overnight?"

"Maybe," Matt replied. "But you gotta think big, particularly if you love money the way I do. I plan to have a lot of it."

Matt's obsession with money bothered me, but there wasn't anything I could do about it. Erica had come from a wealthy family and was used to living well. Matt had acquired all her tastes and desires. Erica had an appreciation for the finer things of life. This had cost me plenty, but it was the price I had to pay for the woman I loved.

I said, "Are you listening to this, Lynn? You sure you want to get involved with such a greedy young man?"

"Actually, I like Matt's thinking. Why not make as much money as you can?"

"Yeah, Dad. You always quoted the Bible to us: 'Seek, and ye shall find, ask, and ye shall receive, knock and the door will be opened onto you.' Am I wrong?"

"No," I said. "That's what the Bible says, but I don't think it applies to obtaining wealth."

"Why not? Haven't you noticed people who demand a lot usually get it? So why put up with anything but the best?"

"He's right, Mr. Coleman," Lynn said. "The law of concentration. You get what you focus on most. We studied that in psychology."

"Jesus, you two were meant for each other," I said. "So what area of the law is going to propel you to financial independence?"

"This will probably surprise you, but I'm thinking I'll go into bankruptcy law."

I chuckled. "Bankruptcy? There's no money in bankruptcy."

"I don't know, Dad. Lynn and I have been talking and doing some research, and it seems to us that bankruptcy is the most promising of any field of the law."

"How do you figure?"

"I've been studying the market," Lynn said, "and what's amazing is that more than 10 percent of the population is insolvent and delinquent on one or more of their debts but less than 1 percent file bankruptcy every year."

"Is that right?"

"Yes, so we have an incredible market. All we have to do is identify those people who are insolvent and get them to face reality. That's going to be my job, to get these people into the office so we can make them realize bankruptcy is their best move."

"People are proud and naturally optimistic. It's not easy to convince them to file bankruptcy," I said. "Believe me. I've been playing this game for years. A lot of people say I'm the best damn bankruptcy attorney in Dallas, but I certainly haven't got rich from it."

"That's because you're not trying to get rich, Dad. You're just trying to make a living. You don't do any advertising with the exception of the Yellow Pages and you don't solicit business. That's why you only do two hundred or so bankruptcies a year. We think we can get a thousand with the right advertising campaign. That will give us gross revenue of more than one million dollars a year."

I shook my head and replied, "You're right. I'm not a damn TV Guide lawyer, if that's what you mean. I'm a professional and I try to act like it. It's not right to peddle the law like a used car salesman."

"I disagree. As long as I provide competent services, which I will, then it shouldn't matter how I get my business. I think tasteful ads, whether they are in the TV Guide, on the radio or on television, are quite appropriate."

"Well if you've got it all figured out, why do you need me?"

"You know bankruptcy practice as well as anyone in Dallas. If we start bringing in a high volume of clients, we're going to have to gear up for it. We'll need a good staff and a system for getting the cases in and out as quickly and efficiently as possible. This is where we could use your help, Dad. Will you help us set up our operation?"

I frowned and said, "Why should I help the competition?"

"Because I'm your son."

"I'm not sure you understand how much paperwork is involved in bankruptcy practice. You can't just rush clients through. They all take a certain amount of time and attention. You have to do your due diligence to be sure everything you file is correct. Handling a thousand bankruptcies would be a colossal nightmare."

"We know that. That's why we need you to show us how to handle them as efficiently as possible. General

Motors puts out a shitload of cars, but that doesn't mean they're all a pile of junk. You can have high volume and good quality at the same time if you're geared up for it. We need you to show us how to do that."

"Okay, okay," I sighed. "I'll help in any way I can."

"Good, we really appreciate it, Dad."

"So what's the game plan?" I asked.

"Well, once we have our systems and support staff ready, we'll launch our advertising campaign. I'm going to let Lynn explain what we have planned."

Lynn smiled and began explaining their plans with great eagerness and excitement. "Okay . . . There are ten local telephone books, three area books, and then the main Dallas directory. We plan to get in all of them but since they all come out at different times, it will take a full year to do it. To get us some immediate business, we plan to advertise in TV Week in the *Dallas Morning News*."

"Oh God, are you really going to do that?"

"Yes," Matt replied. "It's the only way to get some immediate business, and since our overhead will be high, it's absolutely necessary."

"I can't believe the Coleman name is going to be in the TV book."

"Oh come on, Dad. It's no big deal. A lot of good firms advertise in TV Week," Matt said.

"Anyway, after a few months, if the cash flow is sufficient, we'll do a few radio and TV spots," Lynn continued.

"It sounds expensive. Have you done a cost analysis?"

"Yes, it will be expensive, but our revenue should be at least five times our advertising dollar. It will all work out."

"Maybe eventually, but you may have negative cash flow for a while. How do you plan to fund the initial startup?"

"We can do some short-term financing if we need to," Lynn said. "We've got good credit."

"If you're wrong about this, you may be filing your own bankruptcy."

"Sometimes you've got to gamble," Matt said.

"I can understand your gambling, Matt, but I don't think you should drag Lynn into this. You've only known each other a few weeks. What if things don't work out between you?"

"I want to be in on it," Lynn said. "It's exciting, and I want to be part of it."

"Lynn doesn't have to do this," Matt added. "No one is twisting her arm. She wants to do it and I'm glad she wants to be involved. It will make it that much more fun, and with her expertise, it will be more likely to succeed."

I leaned back, smiled, and said, "Well, I hope it works out."

"It will, Dad. Don't worry."

The waitress finally took us to a table, and we sat down and studied the menu. Matt watched me intently, wondering if I was angry. I wasn't—just frustrated because he was so naive and wasn't being realistic. Unfortunately, being like his mother, he was stubborn, and once he got an idea in his head, there was no dissuading him.

"So, I want to bring Lynn home to see Mom sometime."

I looked up and smiled, "Sure, your Mom would like that, I'm sure. Why don't we all go out to dinner Saturday night?"

"Saturday?" Matt said and then looked at Lynn.

"That's fine with me," Lynn said.

"Good then, it's settled," I said. "Come by the house, and we'll all go together. Do you like Italian, Lynn?"

"Oh, absolutely."

"Good, we'll go to Antonio's in Addison. How's that?"

"Good," Matt said. "That's a great place."

After lunch, we went back to the office. It was cold, and a light snow was falling. Lynn didn't have an overcoat, so Matt held her close to him as we walked.

"Do you have classes this afternoon?" I asked.

"Just an ethics class at two."

"Ethics? I didn't know there were any ethics in advertising."

She laughed. "That's why they developed the course. Anybody who's a marketing major has to take it."

"I bet it's an interesting class," I said.

"It is. We get into some very heated debates sometimes."

As we approached the lobby to our office building, Matt said, "Well, I'm going to walk Lynn to her car."

"Okay," I replied. "It was very nice meeting you, Lynn. I'm looking forward to going out with you for dinner."

"Yes, I can't wait to meet your wife. Matt has told me so much about her."

"Yes, Erica will be anxious to meet you too."

"Bye," Lynn said.

I watched them walk to the elevator still in shock over Lynn's sudden appearance in Matt's life. She was a delight, and I could understand how Matt fell in love with her. I wondered what Erica would think of her.

***

On Saturday night we all went out to dinner as planned. Erica and Lynn hit it off from the start. Erica wanted to know all about her and Lynn didn't seem to mind telling her. She told us about her family and growing up in

13

Bonham, a small town northeast of Dallas near the Texas–Oklahoma border. She had only one sibling, an older sister who had just graduated from the University of Texas at Austin with a degree in English. They were very close. Lynn's dad was a dentist and her mother, besides being a homemaker, was on the local school board.

It was a very impressive family resume. I was certainly convinced she would be a great catch, but I wondered if they would actually ever get married. Before I married my first wife, I had thought I was in love more than once. You just never knew about those things. As the girls talked, Matt and I kept busy dipping our bread into the olive oil the waitress had left for us. It was good, and I kept telling myself to stop before I was too full to eat the entree.

"So, Rich tells me you're going to help Matt out in his new law practice," Erica said.

"Yes, I'm going to be his right-hand woman, so to speak."

"I was really surprised to hear you were going into bankruptcy law, Matt," Erica said.

"I'm surprised too, Mother. I never even considered it until Lynn pointed out to me how lucrative it could be if we handled it right."

"So, when will you start?" Erica asked.

"Well, that's a good question," Matt said. "But before we answer it there is something we need to tell you."

"What's that?" I asked.

"Well, Lynn and I are getting married."

A big smile came over Erica's face. "Oh my God. What a surprise."

"Yes, we're kind of in shock too, but now that we've found each other there's no reason to wait."

"Congratulations," I said. "I was worried this big lug would die a bachelor."

"Well, that's not going to happen now, Dad."

"Good."

"So, have you set a date?" Erica asked.

"Not exactly, but we're thinking the middle of June," Lynn said.

"That's not too far off. So, where will the wedding be?"

"We're not sure. All our friends are here," Matt said. "But Lynn's parents may want to have it there."

"Well, Bonham isn't too far away," Erica said. "If you have it there, it wouldn't be so bad. . . . This is so exciting! Have you told your parents, Lynn?"

"No, you're the first to know."

# 2

The limousine pulled up in front of St. Monica's Catholic church and an usher opened the door. It was a warm, sunny day in June and a large crowd had already gathered inside the magnificent edifice. Lynn took the usher's hand and stepped out of the limousine. She wore a long, short sleeve silk gown with a long train. Two of her bridesmaids held the delicate fabric as she walked up the steep steps. Her mother and father watched joyfully as she entered the church. After her mother was seated, the bridesmaids and ushers each proceeded to the altar and Lynn and her father waited for *The Wedding March* to begin.

Finally, the music started, and the crowd came to their feet. Lynn, on her father's arm, walked proudly down the aisle to the altar. Matt watched her intently as she walked. Their eyes met, and she smiled radiantly. When she finally reached him, Matt took her arm and stood proudly, ready to be wed. The priest began the mass, and when he got to the homily, he turned his attention to the bride and groom.

"Matt and Lynn, you are getting married at a very difficult time. I know the world is at peace, the economy is good, and all seems well, but there is still great danger, especially to a young couple just starting out. You see, never in the history of the world have there been more distractions and temptations set before you by the fallen angel, Lucifer. What are these temptations? They take the form of money, fancy cars, lavish foods, liquor, drugs, gambling, and promiscuity, just to name a few.

"The last two decades of the twentieth century were an abomination. In just twenty years the morals of our country quite literally fell into the gutter. Divorce has become a tragic reality for 60 percent of marriages today. Why has this happened?" He opened the Bible and began reading," *For the love of money is the root of all evil; which while some coveted after, they have erred from the faith, and pierced themselves through with many sorrows.'* The love of money, this is the sickness that festers in our society today, and this is why I say you are getting married at a difficult time, indeed a perilous time."

Matt looked over and glared at me. I had suggested to Father Bob that money might be a good topic for his homily. We had a long discussion about materialism and the decay of the family. Matt shook his head and looked at Lynn who was rolling her eyes.

"Matt and Lynn, listen to my words. Your only hope of survival is your love of God and each other. Turn away from the temptations that surround you and keep your sights on the Lord. Live a modest, happy life . . . Avoid the lavish lifestyle that will lead you ultimately to the house of Satan."

Following the marriage ceremony there was a reception at the Dallas Country Club and then the newlyweds flew off to Cancun for a brief honeymoon. When they returned, they set in motion their plans for Matt's new bankruptcy practice. They incorporated the practice as Debt Relief Centers of Texas, P.C. They planned to open three offices initially in Dallas, Arlington, and Fort Worth. Each location had a staff of one attorney, a secretary, and a paralegal. Matt and I worked hard for several weeks setting up their systems and getting ready for the commencement of business. Finally, in mid-July they opened their doors.

Business was slow the first few days but picked up quickly as people began to spot their ad in TV Week. By the end of the month, they had done twenty-one bankruptcies which were just four shy of their first month's target. In August they did thirty-two which would have been good for most practitioners, but it wasn't enough to cover the overhead of three offices. One afternoon in September, Matt, Lynn, and I met at their Dallas office to discuss the situation and to determine what needed to be done to ensure their survival and future success.

"We seemed to have leveled off at thirty to thirty-five bankruptcies. I really don't understand why," Matt said.

"That number should jump when the Dallas phone book comes out in December, don't you think?"

"Right, but that's nearly two months off. At the rate we're going, we'll lose another twenty grand by then."

"I warned you two you were moving too fast," I said. "Bankruptcy is a tough business, and there's a lot of competition. I'm sure the other bankruptcy firms have beefed up their advertising to keep you from stealing their business."

"That's the problem," Lynn said, "we're competing for the same amount of business that has always been out there. Somehow we've got to increase the number of bankruptcy filings and capture the new business, so the existing firms won't feel threatened."

"How do you propose to do that?" I said.

"I'm working on some TV ads, but it's going to be expensive to air them. We don't have the money right now to do it."

"Don't look at me, I'm not going to invest in the competition," I said.

Matt shook his head and replied, "I guess I'll have to borrow some money from the bank. They've offered me a $50,000 line of credit."

"Do you have any idea how hard it will be to pay back that kind of money? If the TV campaign doesn't work, you'll be sunk."

"It will work," Matt said, and then looked at Lynn. "Won't it, honey?"

"I think so, but obviously there are no guarantees."

"I'm not looking for guarantees, just a good probability of success."

"Have you got the TV ads approved by the state bar?"

"We've submitted them, but we haven't heard back yet," Matt said. "They're supposed to make a decision within thirty days, so we should be hearing soon."

"Well, it's your call," I said. "I don't think I can add much to what has been said, so I'm going to go."

"What's your hurry?"

"I've got to get ready for a §727 trial tomorrow."

"Really, why is the trustee objecting to the discharge?"

"My client started a cosmetics business. It was one of those multi-level marketing deals. Unfortunately, he neglected to get it properly licensed, and the Attorney General shut him down. A lot of people lost their shirt."

"Was it like a pyramid scheme?"

"Kind of like that. Basically, the first guy signs up three or four people to sell product. They each have to buy some product themselves, of course. Then those people, in turn, sell to three or four other people. Each time the number of new salesmen multiplies. After six or seven levels there are literally thousands of salesmen in the down line. As a result, sales soar and profits increase geometrically."

"Pretty slick. Well, good luck at the trial."

"Thanks, I'll need it," I said, and then embraced Matt. Lynn smiled and gave me a hug.

Lynn said, "Thanks for your help, Dad. We really appreciate it."

Over the next thirty days, the situation didn't change. Matt acquired his fifty-thousand-dollar line of credit so he could pay his bills and Lynn readied her TV commercials for airing. On Sunday night they cuddled in bed in front of their bedroom TV to watch the first commercial which was scheduled during the 10 o'clock news.

The first shot they saw was of a man at his desk paying bills. The camera focused on the huge stack of bills and the obvious distress of the man trying to pay them. Suddenly the man let out a cry of despair and with one swipe of his hand, sent the bills flying. Then he turned to the camera and said, "What's the use! There just isn't enough money to go around."

The scene changed to Matt's office where he is seated at his desk working. As the camera pans in on him, he stops what he is doing and addresses the audience. "If you've got more bills than you can possibly pay, it may be time to consider bankruptcy. The law says you have a right to a fresh start. Most people who finally file bankruptcy complain that they waited and suffered too long before they filed. You shouldn't make the same mistake. Give us a call for a free consultation to see if you're eligible to file."

The scene changed back to the man who was seen earlier. Now he is calm and tranquil, and only a few bills are left on his desk. He looks up and says, "Since I filed bankruptcy, everything has been so much better. The phone has quit ringing, my wife and I are talking again, and we're actually starting to save some money. What I keep asking myself is: why did I wait?"

Finally, the camera shifts back to Matt, and he concludes, "If you can't pay your bills as they come due you're probably eligible to file bankruptcy. Call for a free consultation, and we will be happy to tell you if bankruptcy is the answer for you. Give us a call at any of the three Debt Relief Centers from nine to five, Monday through Saturday. We're looking forward to helping you get out of debt and back on the road to financial security. Thank you."

At the conclusion of the commercial, Lynn looked over at Matt and smiled. "Well, what do you think?"

"It looked good to me, but I guess tomorrow morning we'll really find out how good it was."

"I'm scared, what if it's a bomb?" Lynn said.

"Then we'll punt and try something different."

"Yeah, but you'll have lost all of your savings and with all your student loans and the $50,000 you just borrowed. . . . You'll owe more than $100,000."

"I know, and I couldn't file bankruptcy. That wouldn't be an option. I could never look my father in the eye again. It would be too humiliating."

"No, no way. You couldn't do that. We just have to make it work. We don't have any choice."

Matt and Lynn watched the rest of the news and, when it was over, shut off the TV and the lights and tried to go to sleep. It was a restless night for them both, tossing and turning, dreaming of success and failure until the first rays of sunlight entered their bedroom window. They were exhausted before they got up. At breakfast the conversation was brief; they just looked at each other wondering what the day would bring.

They got to the Dallas office at 8:45. The staff was just arriving, and a fresh pot of coffee was brewing. Matt started sorting through his mail and faxes, and Lynn chatted with the receptionist.

"So did you see the ad?" Lynn asked.

"Yes, I loved it," the receptionist said. "Rob, my boyfriend, watched it with me and he said he was thinking about filing."

"Really," Lynn laughed and then looked down at her watch. "Better take the phones off forwarding. It's nearly nine o'clock."

The receptionist picked up the phone, hit seven-three and then put the receiver down. Matt walked into the reception area and smiled at Lynn. She looked at him anxiously. The phones were quiet.

"A watched pot never boils. Let's just get to work."

Lynn sighed and then walked into the kitchen and pulled two cups out of the cabinet. Matt followed her and put his hands on her shoulders and began massaging her back. She closed her eyes and enjoyed his magical fingers. She loved to have Matt rub her back. The kitchen phone rang, she jumped and looked at Matt. They strained their ears to hear what the receptionist was saying. She hung up.

"Who was that?" Lynn yelled.

"Your envelopes are ready to be picked up at the printers."

"Oh . . . shit! I thought the ad was good. It's almost ten after nine, and we haven't got one call."

"Maybe putting them in the 10 o'clock news was a bad idea."

"The station said that would be a good time."

"You know. The first ad isn't going to be enough to convince anyone to file bankruptcy. They're going to have to mull it over, think about it for a while. I bet it will be a few days before the phone starts ringing."

The phone rang again. This time the receptionist buzzed them in the kitchen. "New prospect on line two."

Lynn smiled as Matt picked up the line. As he was talking, the phone rang again. Lynn heard the receptionist refer the caller to the legal assistant. She walked into the legal assistant's office to confirm that it was new business. Satisfied that it was she went back to the kitchen, where Matt was just hanging up.

"Well?"

"He's coming in at two."

"Good. Did he see the ad?"

"No," Matt laughed. "He found us in the telephone book."

"Oh." Lynn said and then went to the counter and poured a cup of coffee. When she turned, the legal assistant was there smiling.

"Well, the guy on the phone said he saw the ad and decided to call us.

"So, is he coming in?"

"No, he just wants a free brochure."

"Oh," Lynn said and then took a sip of her coffee.

"What do you think I did wrong, Matt?"

"Nothing, just try to relax. It's just going to take some time."

The phones were only slightly more active the rest of the week. Lynn's TV ads hadn't even increased business enough to pay for their cost. She didn't understand it. She watched them over and over again, trying to figure out why they weren't effective. Matt was very patient and supportive, but she could tell he was scared. Their money was running out, and it wouldn't be long before they would have to close the two satellite offices. She sat in her office, staring out the window when it hit her. She got up and walked into Matt's office.

"Honey," Lynn said. "I'm going over to SMU to talk to Professor Gray, my marketing professor. Maybe he can tell me what's wrong with the ad."

"That's a good idea, honey. He'll probably spot the problem right off."

"Okay, I'll be back before five."

"Good luck."

Lynn arrived at the SMU campus and parked. It was a warm July day with a light wind from the south. As she strolled past the Student Union, memories of her college days flooded her mind. She loved the majestic SMU campus with its giant trees and luscious grass. It was so shady she barely noticed the sweltering heat. As she neared her destination, she ran into a familiar face.

"Professor Swensen . . . Hi."

"Lynn, is that you?"

"Yes, it is."

"What brings you on campus?"

"I was going to see Professor Gray. I had him last semester for marketing, and I needed a little advice."

"Oh. . . . So, I hear you got married."

"Yes, I met this wonderful guy, Matt Coleman. He's an attorney."

"Yes, I know. I saw him on TV."

"Oh, what did you think?"

"Frankly, I was disappointed."

"Oh, you were."

"Yes, I hate to see the legal profession stoop to such depths. What happened to professionalism?"

"This is the twenty-first century, professor. It's the age of electronics. Everybody advertises on TV."

"I know, but have you ever seen sharks circle a wounded whale, waiting to go in for the kill, and then fighting each other over the carcass? It's rather frightening and reminds me of what I saw Sunday night."

"But that's not what Matt's doing. He's trying to help all those people who are hopelessly in debt."

"But why? Why does he want to help them?"

"Because he cares."

"Ha!" the professor said. "Really, do you think everyone is stupid? Your husband is pleading, begging them to go bankrupt, so he can make a nice fat fee. He doesn't give a damn about his clients. That's one thing that was obvious."

"Is that what it looked like?"

The professor nodded.

"Well, maybe that's why it didn't work. Matt came off as just another greedy attorney trying to get rich off of other people's misery."

"Precisely. He's going to have to convince people he cares about them and not just making money in order to gain their trust. He has to be on a mission for truth and justice. I like the name of the practice, the Debt Relief Center. God knows people need relief from the interest trap."

"What do you mean, interest trap?"

"You know. We talked about it in class. From the day you are born, you are indoctrinated on how important credit is to everyone. You're told over and over again that good credit is the secret to financial success and happiness in life. You're barraged with advertisements for all the expensive luxury items you can buy right now on credit, and nearly everyone takes the bait.

"They get a house they can't afford, a luxury car they don't need, and run up a half dozen credit cards to the hilt. Before you know it you're a slave to the system. Most of your hard-earned money is going to banks and mortgage companies in interest payments. You pay and pay and pay, yet the balance you owe never goes down. Soon the joy is gone in your life—happiness is replaced with constant worry and depression."

"Jesus, that's depressing."

"But, am I wrong?"

"No, now that I think about it, you're right on the money. I can't believe the scam that's being played on the American people."

"Exactly, and if you put your husband on TV to expose that scam, *then* you'll get people's attention."

"Hmm, I'm glad I ran into you, professor. I guess I got what I came here for. I think I'll go back to the office and discuss what you said with Matt. I think he'll be excited. Do you mind if he calls you and discusses what we've been talking about?"

"No, by all means, have him call me."

"Do you have statistics and documentation of all of this?"

"Of course, I've been studying the phenomenon for years. I'd love to share it with Matt."

"Good, thanks again."

"Bye."

***

Lynn watched as the studio crew milled around while they waited for the shooting to begin. She smiled as she watched make-up being applied to Matt's face. Personally, she didn't think he needed any make-up as he was quite handsome and photogenic. He was tall, trim, and had golden brown hair—thick like his father's. She thought he looked at home on the TV set. Finally, the director snapped his fingers and the set became still. Matt got up and walked over to the podium set up before a live audience. The director nodded, and a man stuck a board in front of the camera and said, "Scene two, take three."

Matt looked out into the audience and said, "Good afternoon, ladies and gentlemen. My name is Matt Coleman and what I'm about to tell you is going to make you very angry. I'm here to reveal to you a vicious lie, a deception that has devastated the lives of millions of Americans. Yes, from the day you were born, each and every one of you have been carefully manipulated into becoming slaves. Yes, carefully programmed robots who go to work every day and then religiously send seventy to 80 percent of your wealth to your masters, the big corporate giants of Wall Street and the government bureaucrats in Washington."

"Think about it. From the day you are born, you're told that good credit is your ticket to the American Dream. You can have all the luxuries and modern conveniences of life right now, on credit. Why wait, they say, when you can have it now."

"Think about it. Let's say you're a middle-class family with annual income of forty thousand dollars a year. If you work forty years, you'll earn 1.6 million dollars. If you're a typical family you'll buy a hundred and fifty-thousand-dollar home, a car every four or five years and have a half dozen credit cards maxed out very early in the game."

"Now the enemy here is compound interest. It's common knowledge that you'll pay nearly $315,000 over thirty years for that $150,000 home. The cars will cost you double their initial cost, and you'll be paying the minimums on your credit cards until you're dead and buried."

The camera zoomed in on Matt as he pointed to a chart he had prepared. "Now if you subtract 25 percent of your income for taxes that leaves you with $1,200,000.

Subtract $314,000 for what you actually pay for your home, including all the interest, and now you only have $806,000. By the time you subtract $360,000 for your automobiles you have only $446,000 left to live on for 40 years!"

The crowd broke into excited chatter. Matt paused a second until they quieted down.

"That's only $11,150 a year for food, clothing, utilities, property taxes, insurance, recreation and your kid's education. It's no wonder the average person is broke all the time—barely making ends meet! It's no wonder it takes two bread winners nowadays to survive! It's no wonder the divorce rate has gone to the roof and suicides are at a historical high!"

Someone in the crowd yelled, "That's right! Those bastards have made us their slaves."

"That's exactly right," Matt continued. "But there is a way out. There is a loophole they can't close. There is a way each and every one of you can get free!"

"Tell us what it is!" A lady screamed. "Tell us the way to salvation!"

"It's bankruptcy, my friends. That's right, bankruptcy."

The crowd was silent.

"Now most of you think bankruptcy is a bad word, right?"

"That's right, a bad word," a lady said.

"Who told you it was a bad word? Was it your mother and father? Your teachers in school, perhaps? Did you hear it from your friends and relatives? Well, the men up on Wall Street want you to think bankruptcy is a bad word. They want you to think if you file bankruptcy that you're a failure, a deadbeat, and a loser. They want you to feel this way for two reasons. Number one, if you go bankrupt, you're going to be set free from the tyranny of compound interest. You won't have to line their pockets with your hard-earned cash anymore. And number two, if you file bankruptcy, you'll have bad credit, and that will mean the goons on Wall Street won't be able to put you back on the compound interest treadmill!

"Ladies and gentlemen, bankruptcy is not a bad word, it's a sweet melodious word! It should fill your heart with gladness and joy for it is your salvation!"

The crowd stood up and gave Matt a standing ovation. Lynn ran over, and Matt put his arm around her as they stood and waved to the crowd. The camera focused on their smiling faces, and they panned around the crowd clapping and yelling wildly. After the session was over, the director came over and met with Matt and Lynn.

"That worked out quite well, don't you think?"

"Oh yes," Lynn said. "It was wonderful, but it was too long for a commercial."

"I know. What I would suggest is that we have a five-minute infomercial on Sunday night. Then all week we'll feature ninety-second segments with a short intro beforehand and then flash the name, address, and telephone number of your company at the end."

"Oh, I see," Lynn said. "That should be very effective. What do you think, honey?"

"You two are the experts. Whatever you think. But I don't mind telling you it felt good being out there saying what I did. Did you see how riled up the crowd got? . . . Now I know how it feels to be a politician. I could feel the power."

"Yes," the director said. "I think it will be a dynamite ad campaign. You did a fine job, Matt."

That night Matt and Lynn went out to dinner to celebrate. It was around eight when they were seated at the

Outback Steak House in Addison. A waitress quickly appeared.

"What can I get you to drink?" she said.

"Two margaritas, please. Big ones," Matt said.

"Coming right up," the waitress said with a smile and then left.

"I think you hit a home run tonight, honey," Matt said.

"Me? You're the one that whipped the crowd into a frenzy."

"True, that was a lot of fun, but if you hadn't come up with the words, I wouldn't have known what to say."

"You sounded like you believed what you were saying. Nobody will even guess it was just a script. Everybody's going to think you're some kind of consumer advocate or something."

"Who cares as long as the business rolls in, right? We're going to make a mint. Won't my father be surprised."

"He'll be jealous when he sees you making more money your first year out of law school than he's making after twenty-five years."

"No, you're wrong about that. Dad won't be jealous. He makes a lot of money on the stock market. He'll be glad if what we're doing makes us happy and we're taking good care of our clients."

"Oh, I don't know. I bet he'll be a little jealous."

"Maybe," Matt said and then noticed the waitress coming with their drinks.

"Here you go. Two margaritas."

"Thank you," Matt said, and then handed the waitress a twenty-dollar bill. "Keep the change."

The waitress smiled and said, "Thanks," and then left.

Matt lifted his glass and proclaimed, "I want to make a toast. To the beginning of a very lucrative law practice. Honey, I couldn't have done it without you. I love you."

"I love you too," Lynn said, and then they touched their glasses together and took a sip of their drink.

"Hmmm. These are good margaritas," Matt said.

Lynn nodded and took another sip. "Yes, very good."

After dinner, they went to a nearby club, danced a little, talked, and continued to drink. By the time they got home, around midnight, they were feeling quite amorous, so they went straight to the bedroom. They undressed each other quickly and jumped under the covers. They made love for hours until every ounce of their energy was spent.

When Matt awoke the next morning, Lynn was still wrapped around him. He smiled and took a deep breath. Her smell was so sweet he pulled her up close and squeezed her gently. He had never felt so content—so happy. He had it all now—everything he had ever wanted.

# 3

The phones began ringing before eight o'clock the day after the infomercial ran. The receptionist handed Matt eleven voice mail messages. When the phone came off service, it was all the entire staff could do just to keep up with it. In the afternoon the barrage of calls tapered off and Matt and Lynn began to assess the success of the ad.

"Look at this. We set up seventeen appointments this week. Can you believe it?" Lynn said.

"God, how will I do all these bankruptcies?"

"Hey, if it keeps up this good, you'll have to hire some more attorneys. Eventually, you won't have to see clients at all. You can just supervise the operation."

"I know, but now I've got seventeen bankruptcies to do in the next five days."

"Well, you wanted a cash cow. Now you just have to learn how to milk it effectively. . . . How did the other offices do?"

"The same as us. They're booked solid for two weeks."

"Wow. I should call Dad."

"Good idea."

Matt went to the phone and dialed the number.

"Hey, did you see our TV spot?" Matt asked.

"What was that, anyway? I couldn't tell if it was a campaign rally or a sermon. It certainly wasn't a legal advertisement."

"I know, Dad. Our other ad wasn't going anywhere, so we had to try something different."

"I can't imagine the State Bar Advertising Committee approved the ad."

"They didn't."

"What?"

"We didn't have time, and we knew they wouldn't approve it."

"But Matt, that's stupid. They're going to be all over you."

"The station manager referred me to an expert on legal advertising, and he told me with the format we used it wasn't really advertising. We never once solicited any business. It was simply a community service broadcast protected by the First Amendment."

"Maybe so, but the message was clear that you wanted them to call you."

"No, the message at the end of the broadcast simply gave the name of our firm and our telephone number. We never asked anybody to call us."

"Well, if you think the State Bar is going to let you get by with that, I think you're very naive."

"Maybe so, but I've got the best First Amendment lawyer in Texas ready to respond to anything the State Bar throws at us."

"I hope he's as good as you think he is."

"He is, so don't worry about it, Dad. . . . Now, aside from the unorthodox approach what do you think?"

"It was very persuasive, but I think you've oversimplified the problem. People need credit sometimes."

"True, but the banks and mortgage companies have crossed the line. They've become obsessed the last fifteen or twenty years with milking every last dollar out of the American people at whatever cost. It's time it stopped."

"Maybe so, but to suggest bankruptcy is a solution is rather extreme, if not downright irresponsible. You should go into politics if you feel so strongly about it. Maybe in Austin or Washington, you could help change the system."

"I doubt it. The only way to change it is for the people to rebel. They've got to hurt Wall Street in the pocketbook. That's the only language those people up there understand."

"Be careful, Matt. If they get hurt, they'll be looking for revenge. Don't let this thing get out of hand."

"I won't, Dad. I've got all the business I can handle, so I won't be making any more waves. Lynn and I figure if the volume of business we're getting this week continues, we'll easily gross more than a million bucks. That's plenty. So all we have to do now is maintenance advertising, just a few spots each week."

"Well, I'm glad to hear that. I personally don't know why you need that kind of money anyway."

"Oh, don't worry, Dad," Matt laughed. "We'll figure out how to spend it."

For several weeks it took Matt and Lynn's every waking hour just to handle the business that was flowing in. Matt hired three new attorneys and five paralegals just to keep up with the voluminous paperwork generated by the ad campaign. Then one afternoon Matt got a phone call from the prominent radio talk show host, Mitchell Banks.

"I really love your ad campaign, Matt. May I call you Matt?"

"Sure, everybody does."

"When I first saw your infomercial, I was flabbergasted. I had never realized what a number Wall Street was doing to the American people. What you said made so much sense, it was incredible."

"Well, actually we got the idea from a professor over at SMU. He has been preaching about the compound interest scam to his classes for years. I guess my wife, Lynn, is the first student who paid any attention to it."

"Well, it's very interesting, and I want you to be on the show to explain it."

"Really?"

"Yes, absolutely. You're the talk of the town right now, and I'd like to ask you some questions and let my audience do the same. It should be very interesting."

"Hmm. I don't know. I better talk it over with my wife and my Dad. You know how the State Bar watches everything you do. You can't be too careful."

"Well, that's one of the questions I wanted to ask you. How is the State Bar taking it?"

"I think we threw them a curve by not making any direct solicitation of business in the ad. I haven't heard from them at all."

"Lucky for you. . . . Well, will you do it?"

"I guess it couldn't hurt. It's a free country, and I suppose I have a right to talk about whatever I want."

"Well, I hope so."

"Okay then. I'll do it."

"Fine. My people will be in touch to make the arrangements."

Lynn's eyes lit up when Matt told her about the radio interview. She hadn't expected it. She listened intently to Matt's account of the conversation. She knew it was a dream come true for an ad to be so good it becomes news itself.

"I can't believe Mitchell Banks called you!"

"Why, what's so great about that?"

"He's only the number one talk show host in Dallas, Matt. Come on! Where have you been?"

"I don't listen to talk shows."

"Well a lot of people do, and he's got the biggest audience in the Metroplex."

"He seemed like a nice guy."

"We're going to have to really prepare you for this interview."

"Prepare me?"

"Yes, he's going to ask you some very probing questions. I don't think right now you could pull this interview off. Maybe Professor Swensen will help me get you ready."

"You think so? He's got to be an extremely busy person."

"He is, but you've become his spokesman. For years he's been spouting off this theory, and nobody has taken him seriously. But now you've managed to get the attention of the people of North Texas. He'll be delighted to help; I can assure you. We'll just have to be sure he gets the credit he deserves."

"I already told Mr. Banks about the professor so that shouldn't be a problem. The fact that a college professor came up with the theory should actually add considerable credibility to it, don't you think?"

"Yes, of course. I'm sure he's got lots of documentation and statistics to back up everything you've been saying. I'll call and talk to him this afternoon. I'm so excited. This is wonderful news."

"You know what's funny?"

"What?"

"When I was talking to him, I actually started believing some of the shit I've been preaching."

Lynn laughed. "Well you should, it's true, and it's about time people started realizing it."

The Debt Relief Centers did so well over the coming weeks, Matt and Lynn opened up two new Metroplex offices to help handle the steady volume of business. They also hired a full-time accountant to manage the firm's finances, which had become a full-time job. They were also getting calls from attorneys around the state wanting to utilize the Debt Relief Center marketing approach and inquiring if franchises were available. All of this was a little overwhelming for Matt, but Lynn was eating it up.

As the radio interview with Mitchell Banks drew near, Lynn took Matt to see Professor Swensen. As she predicted, he accepted with alacrity her request for help. For three solid days, the three went over the professor's theories and backup documentation. As the professor shared his data, Matt and Lynn became more and more convinced of the veracity of the professor's theories. When the radio talk show began, Matt was ready.

"All right folks, this is what you've been waiting for. We've got attorney Matt Coleman here with us today. As you recall, Matt recently embarked on a revolutionary advertising campaign for bankruptcy lawyers. Essentially he's saying we should all file bankruptcy. Is that right Matt?"

"Well, no, of course not. What I'm saying is that many Americans are caught in a web that has paralyzed them. No matter how hard they work, no matter how frugally they live, they cannot extricate themselves from this money-sucking-web called *compound interest*."

"Well, interest isn't anything new. It's the price you pay to borrow money. So, what exactly are you referring to?"

"Madison Avenue has done a great job convincing the American people they should buy now and pay later. They told us we can afford the best right now simply by paying for it over time. This has been done intentionally without regard to what's good for the people. It's totally profit-motivated."

"Okay, so now the American people should get even by filing bankruptcy, is that what you're saying?"

"I'm saying if you're hopelessly in debt and realistically can never get out of the compound-interest trap, then you have the perfect right to file bankruptcy. And you shouldn't feel bad about it because you've been the victim of a devious campaign to enslave you economically."

"Wow! That's pretty extreme, don't you think?"

"Not really. I believe it's the truth."

"You're telling us that the banks, mortgage companies, and other financial institutions in this country are consciously formulating and implementing policies to keep Americans in debt."

"Exactly. Look at the flood of credit card applications that come in the mail. They know if they tempt you enough they'll catch you in a weak moment, and you'll fill in the application. They call you at home wanting you to open up an account. They accost you at the supermarket, at the airport, and in the department stores. They know once you have that little piece of plastic, you've been hooked. How long did it take you to max out the last credit card you got?"

"About a week or two," Banks laughed.

"You see?"

"Okay, but these people are over twenty-one. Nobody is putting a gun to their head."

"What they have is more powerful than a gun. It's an addiction. Just like the tobacco industry for years pulled the wool over the American public's collective eye, so have the banks and financial institutions in this country failed to warn the American people of the devastating, debilitating effects of credit and compound interest on their lives."

"Those are pretty strong words; don't you think?'

"No, what do you think is the leading cause of divorce?"

"I don't know—infidelity?"

"Wrong, it's money. Specifically, the lack of money because the government, the banks, and other financial institutions of this country are bleeding the American people dry. Middle-class Americans are literally living lives of poverty while they send billions of dollars to the fat corporations on Wall Street."

"Well, the phones are lighting up, so we better start taking some calls. . . . This is Mitchell Banks. You're on the air."

"Mitchell, this is Ernie from Carrollton."

"Hi, Ernie. What do you have on your mind?"

"I think Matt has hit the nail on the head. My wife and I work our tails off every month trying to make ends meet, and it's virtually impossible. After I heard Matt's commercial, I figured it up, and we're living on $800 a month and paying $1300 on interest payments."

"Well, that certainly doesn't sound good," Banks said.

"And you know," Matt added, "that doesn't even take into consideration taxes does it?"

"No," the caller replied.

"So, you're actually living on five or six hundred dollars."

"Exactly."

"Does that make you mad?"

"Yes, I'm pissed."

"All right, let's hear from another caller," Banks said. "Okay, this is Mitchell Banks, and you're on the air."

"Hi, Mitch, this is Frank from Plano. Listen. I work for a bank and frankly, I'm offended by Mr. Coleman's remarks. I'm not part of any conspiracy to rip off the American people."

"Well, I'm glad we have another viewpoint. Let me ask you, Frank, if someone is hopelessly in debt, do you think they should file bankruptcy?"

"No, we have what's called the *American Consumer Counseling Service* or *ACCS*. This is a nonprofit organization designed to help consumers establish a budget and manage their debt responsibly. Bankruptcy is a ten-year mistake."

Matt chuckled.

"You're laughing, Matt," Banks said. "You obviously don't agree with the caller."

"*ACCS* is a fraud."

"A fraud?"

"You heard me. They're Wall Street's way of dealing with people who have been milked dry. Instead of letting them file bankruptcy like they need to do, they came up with *ACCS* to try to keep them in the system. You see, the *ACCS* counselors show them how they can cut their meager little budgets even more and continue to feed the banks and mortgage companies the 18 to 25 percent interest that they demand. You know, there used to be usury laws in this country and it was illegal to get a second lien on your homestead, but not anymore. The banking and finance lobby is so strong, usury laws are gone, and now lenders can even steal the equity in your homestead. There's no protection at all for the average consumer."

"So, you think it was a mistake to repeal the constitutional prohibition on borrowing money on a homestead?"

"Oh God, yes. Now, every day, consumers are barraged with advertisements for debt consolidation loans. They are loans supposedly designed to get you out of the interest-trap, but they are just new loans that will do nothing but exacerbate the situation. The sad aspect of home equity lending is that many consumers will become homeless when they get to the point they can't make the payments on the home equity loan anymore."

"Wow. Very enlightening. . . . All right, folks," Banks said. "Our time is up. Thank you, Matt Coleman, for a very interesting interview. Good luck with your new bankruptcy practice.

"Okay, everybody . . . Stay tuned for our next guest on the Mitchell Banks Show, Dr. Phyllis Wakefield, to tell us about her new book entitled, *There's No Shame in Lying.*"

Matt got up, shook hands with Mr. Banks and then went backstage where Lynn was waiting. When she saw him, she ran up and gave him a big hug and kiss.

"You were great, honey. I'm so proud of you."

"You think so?"

"Oh yes, everybody in the studio commented how persuasive your arguments were. One of the sound men came up to me and made an appointment to come in to file bankruptcy."

"You're kidding?"

"No."

"Well good, the day wasn't a total waste of time then."

"Hardly, I just don't know what we're going to do if we get any more business, though. We can't keep up with what we already have."

"Maybe we should refer some over to Dad."

"Good idea. I'll tell the receptionist if we get booked too far out to refer clients to your father for a while."

"I'd like to be there to see his face when the phone starts ringing off the hook. He's going to hate me."

"Hate you? He should be grateful for your generosity."

"I know, but he may not see it that way."

"Too bad."

"You know I'm exhausted from all our preparations for this show and everything. Why don't we take the rest of the day off and go home and, you know . . . take a nap?"

Lynn smiled and replied, "You know what we really should do is take a vacation. You've been working fourteen hours a day for the last few months. You need some time off."

"True, but do you think the staff can handle things without us?"

"I should hope so. If not, then we're nothing but slaves to the law practice we've created. I thought the idea was to get rich so we could enjoy the finer things in life."

"Okay then," Matt said. "Where should we go?"

"Somewhere far away where there aren't any telephones."

"Hawaii?"

"Yeah, Hawaii's nice, but it's a tourist trap. My Dad was telling me about a place in Alaska where they fly you into a magnificent lake surrounded by snowcapped mountains. They leave you there all alone for a week and then come and get you. He says it's the most beautiful place on earth and this time of year the temperature is in the sixties and seventies."

"A week all alone, just you and me and no phones. When do we leave?"

"With a little luck, we could be out there by the weekend."

"Good, I'm ready."

# 4
## Houston, Texas

It was early afternoon at the United Mercantile Bank Building in downtown Houston. The weekly board meeting was about to begin. Several hostesses were passing out coffee, cold drinks, and mineral water to the members who were milling around and making final preparations for the meeting. Suddenly the doors opened and MidSouth's executive vice-president, Douglas Barnes, a trim, deliberate man in a gray suit, entered the room with an entourage of assistants. He took up a position near the head of the long conference table and waited stone-faced for the meeting to begin. Finally, the inside door opened and Frank Hill, the chairman of the board, walked in and sat at the head of the conference table.

"Good afternoon, ladies and gentlemen. Let's get down to business, shall we? Are there any corrections to the minutes of last week's meeting?" Hill looked around but nobody said a word. "Hearing none, they are approved. . . . Mr. Barnes, I believe you are first on the agenda."

Hill sat and Barnes stood up to address the meeting. "Yes, sir. I've been in Dallas this last week to find out why bankruptcy filings in the Northern District are up thirteen percent in the last quarter."

"Yes, that's very disturbing. What did you find out?"

"Well, it seems there is a new attorney, Matt Coleman, who has launched a very effective marketing campaign to promote his bankruptcy practice. His wife is a marketing major and, along with a finance professor at SMU, has been helping him."

"What could they possibly be doing to cause bankruptcy filings to increase so much?"

"They're convincing people that they are the victims of a conspiracy by banks and financial institutions to enslave them economically and that the only way out is to file bankruptcy."

"You can't be serious? How ridiculous," the chairman said.

"Obviously, Mr. Chairman, but a lot of people are taking him seriously, and not only is Mr. Coleman doing a booming business, but everyone in Dallas is benefitting from his campaign."

"So, Mr. Barnes, is this just an aberration or do we have a problem?"

"Well, Mr. Coleman is starting to get some press and attorneys around the state are beginning to take notice. Because we have been marketing heavily in the Dallas Metroplex area, we are getting hit harder than anyone. So, yes, I'm afraid we do have a problem. Our default rate is already at 15% and rising at an alarming rate. If it gets over 20%, we'll be in serious trouble."

"What course of action do you suggest?"

"The State Bar of Texas is scratching its head on how to deal with the situation. I think we should put some heat on them to put a lid on Mr. Coleman."

"Good idea. Do you think that will work?"

"Hopefully, but if they fail, then we need to have an alternative plan."

"Of course, what did you have in mind?"

"Well, I can foresee several potential problems for Mr. Coleman in processing so many bankruptcies. With so many people filing just to free themselves from this financial bondage, I would imagine a few people might fudge a little and fail to disclose an asset or two, don't you think?"

"Quite possibly. How do we monitor that situation to make sure it doesn't happen?"

"We've got someone at the bankruptcy trustee's office checking Mr. Coleman's filings very carefully, and they'll keep in close contact with the FBI and report anything suspicious."

"Excellent. What if nothing turns up?"

"Well, since Mr. Coleman is making so much money, he might have trouble keeping track of all of it. In fact, I wouldn't be surprised if he might forget to report all his income on his income tax return. After all, someone who holds financial institutions in such contempt obviously wouldn't like the government much either. I think the IRS should be alerted to keep an eye on him also."

"I presume you can handle that for us."

"Consider it done, sir."

"Thank you. Now, what's next on the agenda?"

At the conclusion of the meeting, Douglas Barnes and his entourage left immediately for the airport to return to Dallas. When they arrived, they went to the Adolphus Hotel, where they had set up a temporary office in the name of American Creditor's Alliance. Barnes was going through his messages when his secretary announced Hans Schultz was there to see him. Schultz was an ex-Marine turned private eye. He had been court-martialed and dishonorably discharged for disobeying his commanding officer in Desert Storm. Barnes told her to show him in.

"Hans, how are you?" he asked, as he stood and extended his hand.

"Just fine, sir," Schultz said as they shook hands.

"Thanks for getting here so quickly."

"No problem, what can I do for you?"

"We've got a little trouble here in Dallas. A young attorney has started a campaign against banks and financial institutions alleging a conspiracy to economically enslave the American people."

"That's very perceptive for an attorney."

"True, unfortunately, a lot of people are starting to listen to him and, as a result, local bankruptcy filings are way up."

"Huh. So what would you like me to do, send him on a long vacation?"

"No, that wouldn't be wise. He's too much in the public's eye right now. I just need you to follow him around and keep an eye on him. We need to know where he is and what he's doing at all times. If he happens to do something compromising, make sure the press hears about it."

"Sure, I understand. No problem."

"We have to bring this guy down hard. And it's got to be done in public to set an example. We don't want to go to all the trouble to get rid of him and then have other attorneys turn around and adopt his marketing plan. We've got to nip this thing in the bud before it becomes a serious problem."

"Don't worry. I'll take care of my end."

"Good. Report back to me every few days, okay?"

"I will," Schultz said.

After Schultz had left, Barnes pressed his intercom button and told his secretary to get Peter Robinson on the line. Robinson was general counsel to the State Bar of Texas.

"Robinson."

"Mr. Robinson, this is Douglas Barnes from the American Creditor's Alliance."

"Yes, what can I do for you?"

"Our organization represents hundreds of financial institutions around the country and, frankly, our members are outraged at the publicity campaign of that young upstart attorney, Matthew Coleman."

"Oh, yes. I can imagine."

"I've been asked to find out what the State Bar intends to do about this irresponsible member of the bar. Surely you can't let him get away with such a vicious attack on our financial institutions."

"Well, we're looking into the situation right now. Technically he's not seriously breaching any ethical duties."

"So what are you going to do?"

"Well, we don't know yet. We're studying the matter."

"Do you realize bankruptcy filings are up 30 percent in the Northern District? You know what that means to the members of our institutions in dollars and cents. This ad campaign is illegal, unethical, and totally irresponsible. The State Bar is supposed to police its member's advertising and make sure it is professional and not misleading. We demand that something be done, and done quickly."

"I totally understand the concern of your members. The State Bar will do something, but it will take a little time to study options and come up with the best strategy. There are a lot of complicated legal issues here."

"I understand, but our members are losing thousands of dollars a day, and they can't wait indefinitely. We'll be forced to take action ourselves if the State Bar doesn't act soon. I know there's been a movement to take control of the bar away from the members and set up a state agency to oversee it. If this isn't resolved soon, our organization may have to throw its support behind that movement."

"That won't be necessary. Just give us a few more days, and something will be done."

"Good. Would you give me a call just as soon as a course of action is adopted?"

"Yes, of course."

"All right then. I'll be waiting to hear from you."

# 5

The Cessna 172 took off from Juneau airport and headed out over the rugged mountains toward Glacier Bay. The young bush pilot taking Matt and Lynn to Paradise Camp had indicated it was about a forty-minute flight from Juneau. As they flew, they marveled at the rugged, snow-covered peaks, vast forests, and raging streams below. They saw deer feeding in the meadows, bears frolicking in mountain streams, and moose running across treeless mountain tops. Time went quickly, and the pilot was soon pointing to a lake on the horizon. He pushed the controls forward, and the plane began to descend toward its watery runway. When it was over Paradise Lake, he pulled back on the throttle, and the plane settled into the frigid water and quickly came to a stop.

The pilot swung the plane around and began to taxi toward a cabin in the distance. As they got closer, Matt saw a small dock protruding out from the bank. The plane taxied up close to it, then the pilot cut the engine and let the plane drift up to the dock. After he had the plane tied up, he waved for them to come on out. Matt climbed out and jumped onto the dock. Then he turned and helped Lynn deplane. Matt looked around wide-eyed at the surroundings.

"Wow! Look at this place, honey. Isn't it beautiful?"

"Oh, yes. This is wonderful. It's like a postcard."

The pilot unloaded the luggage onto the dock, picked up a couple of pieces and started carrying them to the cabin. Matt took what was left and followed him. When they got to the cabin door, the pilot set the luggage down and unlocked the door.

"I came by this morning and restocked the pantry," the pilot said. "You should have plenty of food, and the propane tank is three-quarters full. The water up here is excellent so drink to your heart's content."

"Okay, this is great," Matt said.

"This time of year it doesn't get below fifty at night, so you shouldn't be too cold. If you like to fish, there's fishing gear in the closet. You can fly fish or use lures. This lake doesn't get much activity so either way, the fishing should be excellent. There's a Jon boat if you like or you can fish off the shore."

"What about hiking?"

"I wouldn't wander off too far from the lake as it's easy to get lost up here. If you hike around the lake, it's about three miles so that should give you plenty of exercise."

"Is there anybody up here at all?" Lynn said.

"There's an Indian family about a mile from here. They maintain this place for us. You can contact them in an emergency. They have a shortwave radio."

"Good. I can't imagine anything happening, but it's comforting to know we're not totally isolated out here."

"I'll come check on you a couple of times during the week. Don't leave any food out and put your garbage in the sealed disposal containers in your cabin. There are grizzly bears in the area and, if they smell food, they'll come looking for it."

"Are they dangerous?"

"Only if you provoke them. There's a shotgun in the cabin. If any animal bothers you, just shoot the gun a few times in the air, and they'll leave you alone. Don't shoot at them directly though. If you don't kill them, they're liable to get really pissed off."

"We'll leave them alone," Matt said. "I've camped in the Colorado Rockies many times so we should be okay."

"Good. Most of the time this is the quietest place on earth."

"That's why we came up here," Lynn said.

"Well, I'm going to get along. I'll see you in a couple of days. You two have fun."

"We will, definitely," Matt said.

The pilot smiled and shook Matt's hand. He nodded at Lynn and then went out the front door. Matt and Lynn watched as he climbed back in his plane and took off. When he had disappeared, Matt took Lynn's hand and pulled her to him. They embraced and kissed passionately.

"This is going to be a great week," Matt said after their lips parted.

"Umm," Lynn replied, her cheeks slightly flushed.

"We can catch up on our lovemaking."

"You promise?"

"Absolutely, we'll start right after I go fishing."

"What?!"

"Just kidding," Matt said as he pulled Lynn up close and began to unbutton her blouse. She gave him a wry smile and led him into the bedroom to the big king size bed that lay waiting for them. There was a fireplace with wood neatly stacked, ready to be lit. Matt found a match and lit the fire. Lynn drew the shades, and they finished undressing and got under the covers. As their bodies came together, Lynn sighed.

"Oh God! You feel so good. I love you so much."

Matt kissed her gently and replied, "Me too. This is going to be a great week."

They made love for hours until they were so exhausted they fell into a peaceful sleep in the comfort of each other's arms. They had slept a few hours when they were awakened by the sound of an airplane. Matt got up and looked outside. It was still light, but he didn't see any sign of a plane.

"It sure sounded like the airplane landed, didn't it?" Matt said.

"I thought so, but I guess it just flew by," Lynn replied.

"Are you hungry?" Matt asked.

"Starved."

"Okay, let's go see what there is to eat."

"Go ahead. I'll be right there."

Matt pulled on some boxer shorts and headed for the kitchen. Lynn yawned, stretched, and then put on a T-shirt. For a moment she just stared at the embers smoldering in the fireplace. She wondered if this was the happiest day of her life. She couldn't think of a single moment of her existence that she would cherish more. She sighed and then joined Matt in the kitchen.

Matt was taking a mental inventory of the contents of the refrigerator. It was loaded with meat, milk, vegetables, condiments, beer, and soft drinks.

"How about a steak?" he asked.

"Fine."

"You want a beer?"

"Okay."

Matt brought her a beer and then proceeded to make supper while Lynn watched him from a big stuffed chair across the room. She usually did all the cooking, so it was a great amusement to her to watch Matt fumble around the kitchen.

"You need some help?" she asked.

"No, I've got it under control. You just relax."

"You're so sweet fixing us supper. Are you going to do all the cooking this week?"

He smiled. "Don't press your luck. I'm just feeling grateful after having such great sex."

"Hmm. You enjoyed that, huh?"

Matt winked at her and replied, "Well. I'll just say, I'm glad I didn't go fishing."

Lynn stretched and gave a sexy moan. "I don't want ever to go back to Dallas. Let's just stay here forever."

"You won't get any argument from me," Matt replied.

When supper was ready, they took their plates outside to a picnic table. By this time, it was after nine o'clock, but it was still daylight.

"Boy, can you believe it's still light?" Matt said.

"Yeah, I wish we had all this daylight in Dallas. The crime rate would probably plummet."

"No doubt."

"We should make this an annual ritual; don't you think?" Lynn said.

"Well, once we get our staff properly trained, we should be able to take a lot of vacations. After all, what's the point of being rich if you don't enjoy life, right?"

"Exactly."

After supper, they got some fishing gear out of the cabin and tried their luck off the dock. It was just starting to get dark, and the flies and mosquitos were swarming. Matt cast his line out about twenty yards out and waited. Nothing happened so he reeled it in and tried again. The line sailed gracefully through the air, and the lure hit the water. Immediately a fish attacked the little yellow-and-black fly and was hooked.

"I've got one!" Matt yelled as the fish jumped out of the water.

Lynn smiled and immediately picked up the net. Matt worked the fish in until it was close enough for Lynn to sweep it into the net. He pulled out the hook and held it up. It was bluish green and about eighteen inches long.

"What kind is it?" Lynn asked.

"Some kind of trout, I think."

Lynn picked up her rod and cast it out into the water, and just as quickly she hooked a fish.

"Oh my God! I've got one too!" she said as the much bigger fish jumped out of the water and then fell back, causing a big splash.

"Don't lose it, honey!"

"I won't—it's just so big! Jesus!"

After several minutes, Lynn brought the big fish close enough to the dock for Matt to net it. He pulled it up on the dock and held it up.

"Wow, look at the size of it," Lynn said.

"It must be thirty inches."

"That's good, huh?"

"I *guess* so."

"Hurry up and take it off, I want to catch another one."

Matt laughed at Lynn's enthusiasm and quickly removed the fish. She immediately cast it again to the same spot. Matt looked at the sky which was quickly turning dark. Lynn landed another fish and reeled it in.

"I think we better call it a night. I don't want to be out here in the dark with fresh fish."

"Oh, you're just mad because I've caught more than you."

"No, I'm serious. Grizzly bears can smell fresh fish a mile away."

"Oh. Good point," Lynn replied. "Let's get these fish into the refrigerator then."

Sunrise the following day came very early. Matt and Lynn tried to ignore the bright sunlight that came flooding into their cabin. Lynn finally opened her eyes and gazed at Matt sleeping soundly. She smiled, yawned, and rolled out of bed. Since Matt had prepared dinner, she decided to give him breakfast in bed. She went into the kitchen, opened the refrigerator, and pulled out a carton of eggs and a pound of bacon. She set them near the stove and then pulled out a loaf of bread from the cupboard. After putting on some water to make coffee, she pulled open the curtain over the sink to see what kind of day it was.

"Ahhhh!" She screamed as a man was standing in front of the window looking at her.

Matt sat up and looked around. "What's wrong?"

"Somebody's out there!"

"What?" Matt said, and then jumped out of bed and rushed toward Lynn. "We're supposed to be alone up here."

"I got news for you—we're not."

Matt put on some jeans and a T-shirt and hurried out the front door. He looked around and, not seeing anyone, he circled the cabin and scanned the forest in every direction. Finally, he came back inside.

"He must have run off. What did he look like?"

"He was a tall, muscular man—his head was shaven."

"How old?"

"In his thirties, I would imagine."

"Could he have been one of the Indians up here?"

"No, he was white."

"Damn it! I can't believe this. I wonder where he's camped?"

"Maybe he came in on that airplane we heard."

"Maybe. After breakfast, we can hike around the lake and see if we can find the camp or the plane."

"But we don't know who he is or what he wants."

"He probably means us no harm, but I'll bring the shotgun just in case."

"I don't know. Maybe we should just leave him alone."

"Maybe so, but I won't be comfortable until I know who's out there and what they're doing."

"Okay, whatever," Lynn said and then went back into the kitchen to finish breakfast. Matt went into the bathroom, shaved, and then finished getting dressed. During breakfast, neither Lynn nor Matt had much to say. Each was worried about the unexpected visitor.

After breakfast, Matt found the shotgun, some ammunition, and a pair of binoculars. Lynn did the dishes while he was getting ready for their hike around the lake. As they began their trek, it was a little chilly as a layer of cirrus clouds filtered the sun's rays. Someone had cleared a trail around the lake, so the hike was quite pleasant.

"If the sun burned off the cloud cover it would be a nice day," Matt said.

"You think it will? I'm freezing."

"I don't know. Hopefully."

The trail went up a small hill and at the top they could see the entire north end of the lake. The hikers stopped, and Matt took a look around with his binoculars.

"Do you see anything?"

"Not yet," Matt said as he swung the binoculars slowly around the perimeter of the lake.

"I wonder who that guy was?"

"I'm clueless . . . wait. . . . What's that?" Matt said as he focused on a glistening object at the back of a cove.

"What is it?" Lynn asked.

"It's an airplane."

"Oh, shit."

"Single engine, red and white—a Cessna."

"So we did hear a plane land last night. I wonder who it belongs to."

"Your friend, Baldy, I'm sure."

"Do you think he's watching us?"

"It looks that way. Maybe he's planning to rob us?"

"Rob us!" Lynn said. "We should go back to camp. I bet he's stealing us blind while we're gone."

"Oh, shit! You may be right."

As they turned to head back to camp, they heard an engine turning over. They turned just in time to see the airplane taking off at the far end of the lake. It flew straight toward them, over their heads, and then disappeared over a hilltop.

"Thank God he left," Lynn said

"Let's make sure everything is okay back at the cabin," Matt replied.

They hiked quickly back toward the cabin. When they arrived, they looked around outside and then went in. They took a gaze around the room and inspected all their things. Lynn looked at Matt, breathed a sigh of relief and said, "I guess we're getting paranoid."

"It looks that way," Matt laughed. "Let's just forget this happened and start the day over, okay?"

"Good idea," Lynn said and opened the door to go outside. "Ahhhh!" She screamed as she nearly ran into a dark-skinned man standing in the doorway."

"Excuse me, Ma'am."

Matt rushed over and jumped between Lynn and the big Indian.

"Who are you?" Matt asked.

"I'm Tali Aku, I live here on the lake with my family. Sorry if I startled you."

"Oh, you're the caretaker," Lynn said.

"Yes."

"Did you know a man was looking in the window of our cabin this morning?" Lynn asked.

"Yes, I heard the plane land. I've been searching for it since dawn. When I finally found it, I told the two men who were camping that this was a private lake and they must leave."

"Oh, so that's why the plane left?"

"Yes."

"Was one of the men bald headed?"

"Yes, his name was Hans or something. I heard him talking to his friend."

"Hans?" Lynn said. "Hmmm."

"Anyway, I just wanted to make sure they hadn't disturbed you."

"No, not really," Matt said. "They just startled us. We weren't expecting company."

"I don't think they will be back, but I'll keep a close watch just in case."

"Thank you," Lynn replied. "We really appreciate it."

Matt wasn't too concerned about the unexpected visitors. He figured they had nothing to do with him or Lynn and was anxious to resume their quiet holiday. Lynn, however, was troubled by it all and couldn't sleep that night. She didn't want to upset Matt and spoil his vacation, but she didn't buy the idea that the plane had just accidentally landed on Paradise Lake. She had an ominous feeling about Hans. She wondered who had sent him and what they want.

# 6

It was several days after Matt and Lynn had left on their vacation. I had just gotten home from work and crashed on the sofa. It had been a hectic week with all the extra bankruptcy business Matt's office had been referring. After Erica and I watched TV for a while, the ten o'clock news came on. I was tired and was having trouble staying awake. Then I heard the reporter mention the name Coleman, which got my attention.

"The State Bar of Texas today was granted an ex-parte temporary restraining order by the 111th District Court against the Debt Relief Centers of Texas, Inc., a company owned and operated by Dallas attorney Matt Coleman. The TRO prohibits the company from airing any more of its TV advertising spots for ten days until a temporary injunction hearing is held to determine if the company has violated the State Bar of Texas' rules on advertising.

"The controversial TV spots accuse banks, mortgage companies, and other financial institutions of conspiring to financially enslave the American people. According to Coleman, these institutions lure consumers into frivolous and irresponsible credit card spending, so they will be forced to pay an endless stream of interest."

"Since the advertising campaign began," the reporter continued, "bankruptcy filings are up 77 percent in the Northern District of Texas, sparking concern that the continuation of the ad campaign could trigger a banking crisis in Texas which could possibly spread to other states. Although the ad campaign is only being aired in the Dallas-Fort Worth area, it is anticipated that other attorneys around the nation will start copying Mr. Coleman's advertising tactics since they have been so successful. According to the State Bar, the advertising is misleading and deceptive and could have a devastating effect on the U.S. economy as well as the lives of those persons persuaded to file bankruptcy under allegedly false pretenses."

"Mr. Coleman was unavailable for comment. Reportedly he is on vacation this week," the reporter concluded.

"Did you hear that, Erica?"

"Yes, what does it mean?"

"It means Matt's in big trouble. I warned him this marketing plan wasn't a good idea."

"But everything he said was true, wasn't it?"

"Probably. That's why the bankers are getting nervous."

"What should we do?"

"I don't know. There aren't any phones where he went. I doubt if we can communicate with him. I'll have to call his office manager, Tom Hartsfield, and tell him to cut the advertising until Matt gets back."

"What do you think Matt will do when he finds out?"

"I don't know. I warned him his ad campaign was too aggressive. He just doesn't listen."

"Didn't he say he checked out the ad campaign with another attorney?"

"Oh, you're right. Maybe I can find out who it was and call him."

I went into my study, opened my briefcase, and pulled out an address book. Flipping through it, I found the number I was looking for, and I dialed it.

"This is Rich Coleman, Matt's father."

"Oh, hi. How are you?" Tom replied.

"Not so good. Did you see the news?"

"No, I was watching the Ranger game."

"There's been a restraining order issued against Matt running any more advertisements."

"What?"

"The State Bar went to court today and got a TRO. You've got to pull all your advertising for ten days, or you'll be in contempt of court."

"But I can't do that without Matt's consent."

"You don't have any choice. You're under a court order."

"I can't believe this. We haven't even been notified of a complaint?"

"Didn't Matt have an attorney who was an expert in this area of the law?"

"Right, Bradley Davis."

"Do you have his number?"

"Not here at the house, but I'm sure directory assistance can give it to you."

"Okay, thanks. I'll have Mr. Davis call you tomorrow with instructions what to do, okay?"

"Fine."

I tried to contact Bradley Davis at his home, but he was not in. I left a message on his voice mail and waited anxiously for a return telephone call. While I was waiting, I contacted Matt's travel agent to see if there was any way to contact him. The agent said he would look into it and get back with me in the morning. Finally, the telephone rang. It was Bradley Davis.

"Yes, did you see the news?"

"Yes, I was trying to get in contact with Matt."

"He's on vacation."

"Oh, great."

"Can you do anything about the TRO?"

"Maybe. I'll file a motion to dissolve it in the morning. The judge shouldn't have granted it without a hearing anyway. It must have been a visiting judge who signed it."

"If I can help in any way let me know."

"Have Matt call me if you hear from him."

"I will. Thanks."

I went back to the family room where Erica was watching TV. I noticed the evening news was just coming on, so I sat down to watch it.

"What did you find out?" Erica asked.

"Matt's attorney's going to file a motion to dissolve the TRO in the morning."

"Will that work?"

"He thinks so."

"Good. Matt would be so upset if he knew what was going on."

"It's a good thing he lined up an attorney to represent him. He's a pretty smart kid."

"Takes after his dad."

"I don't know. I was never as brash as he is."

As they were talking, the news began. The first story was about a tornado that had swept through Ada, Oklahoma, leveling two square miles. Then the reporter started talking about State Bar of Texas restraining order.

"In the past month, bankruptcy filings have been up 77 percent in the Northern District of Texas. This tremendous increase in filings is attributed to one attorney's efforts. Matt Coleman, a young man just out of law school, has convinced record numbers in North Texas that there's a conspiracy amongst banks and mortgage companies to lure consumers into a life of financial slavery. He says they intentionally give consumers too much credit and charge obscene interest rates to get from them every dime possible."

"The State Bar of Texas got a temporary restraining order against Matthew Coleman prohibiting him from doing any more advertising until a hearing can be held on a State Bar complaint alleging his advertising is misleading, deceptive, and irresponsible."

I pushed the mute button on the TV and turned to Erica. "Can you believe that?" I said. "Wait until Matt finds out he's been the main subject of the evening news."

The next morning, I got a barrage of calls about the news report. What did he think of it? Did Matt see it? Is Matt going to respond to his critics? I told everyone I didn't want to comment on it since it was Matt's ad campaign and not mine. Later that morning I got a call from Bradley Davis.

"I've got good news."

"You do?"

"Yes, I got a hearing set for tomorrow morning on my motion to dissolve."

"Good. Do you think you'll be successful?"

"We have a pretty good shot at it, I think. The judge is back from vacation, and he's usually fair-minded. He doesn't normally grant ex-parte requests for relief, so he'll take a close look at what the visiting judge did. Since we've got a temporary injunction hearing next week to fully address the issues, I don't see any justification for the TRO."

"Well, Matt will be back in town next week, so I'll have him call you immediately when he arrives. What do you think our chances are at the temporary injunction hearing?"

"Very good actually. Freedom of speech is a pretty fundamental right. I can't see any court telling him he can't speak his mind."

"Well, I hope you're right, but I'm sure the State Bar will come up with a persuasive argument nevertheless."

"Oh, you can bet on that. It will be up to the judge. He could go either way."

"Well, thanks for your help. I'll have Matt call you just as soon as I talk to him."

After hanging up the phone, I told the staff the good news. When I was done, I called Erica to let her know. Then I called Matt's travel agent to see if he had been able to contact Matt.

"We've been trying to contact the company that runs the camp, but no one is answering their phones."

"That's sure strange."

"Well, it's a small company, and, if somebody is sick, the dispatcher has to help fuel the plane and get it ready for the next flight."

"Really?"

"Yeah, do you want me to try again?"

"No, the crisis is over. Matt will be home in a few days. Let's not spoil his vacation. Just forget about it."

"You sure?"

"Yes, I'm sure. Thanks for your help."

"No problem."

When I woke up the next morning, I went outside as I did every morning to walk around the neighborhood. It was a beautiful day with puffy white clouds dancing across the sky and a light wind from the south. When I returned, I picked up the newspaper and went inside. Erica was making breakfast. The smell of fresh coffee lured me into the kitchen. I sat down and began reading the paper. Erica walked over and put a cup of coffee in front of me.

"Thank you, honey," I said. After reading the front section, I pulled out the Metropolitan section and raised my eyebrows at what I saw.

"Oh no," I said.

"What?" Erica asked.

"There's a big article on Matt and the State Bar injunction in here. . . . They say Wall Street will be watching the State Bar action against Matt very closely. They're concerned that if he isn't stopped, financial institutions will face massive losses from the stampede of bankruptcies that will likely occur."

"How can what Matt's doing have such an impact on the whole country?"

"I don't know. I guess he's just charismatic. He's got your charm and my good looks."

"Oh! Thanks a lot. You can sleep on the sofa tonight."

"Seriously, he's just hit a nerve. There's a lot of truth to what he's been preaching."

"Well, I'm worried about him. He's up there in Alaska and doesn't have any idea what a mess is waiting for him."

"Luckily his attorney has everything under control, I think. He seems very confident."

"Call me just as soon as you hear something today, okay?"

"Sure."

At nine the judge of the 111th District Court invited Peter Robertson, the State Bar of Texas attorney, and Bradley Davis into his chambers. The numerous members of the press who were seated in the courtroom tried to follow but were stopped by the bailiff. The judge sat down behind his big oak desk covered with a dozen or so volumes of the *Southwestern Reporter*. The two lawyers each sat in plush leather side chairs across from the judge.

"Gentlemen, what do we have today?"

"Your Honor," Bradley said. "As you may know, Judge Hawthorne, sitting in for you while you were on vacation, granted the State Bar of Texas a Temporary Restraining Order against my client, Matthew Coleman. The order prohibits him from running his very popular TV spots on the credit conspiracy that has allegedly enslaved millions of Americans."

Peter sat up in his chair and said, "Your Honor, it's an unapproved advertising campaign and nothing more."

"Your Honor, if I can finish."

"Let him finish, counselor, you'll get your turn."

"Thank you, Your Honor. . . . Our first complaint, Your Honor, is that this action was done ex-parte. Mr. Coleman retained me some time ago to advise him on the propriety of his TV spots. Had he been advised of this complaint, we would have advised the bar of this arrangement. It was totally inappropriate for a TRO hearing to take place without my client being represented."

Robertson sat back in his chair and shook his head. Bradley continued, "Secondly, Your Honor, the court is quite aware that a TRO is an extraordinary remedy and the applicant must show irreparable injury and no adequate remedy at law. The applicant falls short on both grounds. Your Honor, these ads have been airing for several months, so I can't see why it is so critical that they are stopped immediately.

"My client shouldn't be denied his First Amendment right of free speech without at least having a full evidentiary hearing. Ten more days of these ads couldn't possibly cause irreparable injury to the State Bar."

"Thank you, Mr. Davis. . . . Mr. Robertson."

"Yes, Your Honor. It's well settled that the State Bar has the right to regulate lawyer advertising. These TV spots being aired by Mr. Coleman are nothing but TV ads. They are calculated to bring in bankruptcy business to the Debt Relief Centers and nothing more. The damage that is being inflicted on the public by these false and misleading ads will cause irreparable damage as hundreds, maybe thousands, of people will be induced into filing bankruptcies in bad faith. There is no adequate remedy at law, Your Honor, as the damages that will be inflicted on the public would be incalculable and there is no way Mr. Coleman could respond to a damage award if the court were to grant it."

"What about the lack of notice to Mr. Coleman or his counsel?" the Judge said.

"Your honor, we called Mr. Coleman's office, and they said he was on vacation and could not be reached."

"Did you ask who was in charge and communicate what you were planning to do?"

"Well . . . no."

"There are an office manager and three or four other attorneys in the office," Bradley advised.

"Okay, I'm ready to make my ruling. . . . I'm going to dissolve the TRO. I don't think there's been a showing of irreparable harm if the TV spots are allowed to run until the temporary injunction hearing. There are important First Amendment considerations here that should be addressed. It's only fair that both sides have notice and an opportunity to present their evidence to the court before any injunctive relief is granted."

"Thank you, Your Honor," Davis said.

Robertson nodded at the Court's decision and then stood up. "Very well, Your Honor. We'll see you in a few days."

When Bradley stepped out into the hallway, he was met with a half dozen reporters. He didn't stop to talk to them but headed for the elevators.

"What happened in there, Mr. Davis?" a reporter asked.

"The TRO was dissolved," Davis replied.

"So does that mean your client is free to advertise?"

"It means he is free to continue to run his TV spots until the temporary injunction hearing next week."

"Are you pleased with the outcome?"

"Yes, of course. My client has a right to speak his mind. His TV spots are simply his opinions on important issues facing American consumers. No one, not even the State Bar, has the right to interfere with his exercise of his First Amendment right of free speech."

***

When Bradley got back to his office, he called me and told me what happened at the hearing. That night on the way home I turned on the six o'clock news.

"This is Ralph Fuentes with the Six O'clock Evening News. In the 111th District Court today the temporary restraining order issued yesterday against Dallas attorney Matt Coleman was dissolved. The effect of today's ruling is that the ads or TV spots will be allowed to continue at least until next week's temporary injunction hearing. Banks and stocks in the financial sector were generally down today. Investors reportedly are concerned with the action taken today in the 111th District Court."

"A three-alarm fire hit downtown Fort Worth today—"

I shut off the radio and got on my mobile phone. I dialed a number and waited.

"Hello."

"Hi, honey. Have you been listening to the news?"

"No, I've been cooking dinner."

"You better turn on the TV. I guess Matt's got Wall Street worried."

"What?! I can't believe this. I wish he were home. I'm so worried."

# 7

When they heard the sound of the airplane landing, they gave each other a sorrowful look. Matt continued to pack his suitcase and Lynn went to the front door to watch the plane land. Soon the plane taxied up to the dock, and the pilot disembarked. He secured the plane and then walked briskly to the cabin.

"Hi," Lynn said.

"Good morning," he replied. "So did you have a good time?"

"Oh yes, this was the happiest week of my life."

"What did you like best?"

"Solitude. No telephone, no TV, and no problems. You know Matt and I actually talked for hours on end. It was wonderful."

As they were talking, Matt stepped out carrying two suitcases. He set them down, smiled and said, "Hello, how was your flight?"

"A little bumpy, there's a cold front approaching from the north, so we best not linger."

"Oh, well we're all ready to go, I suppose, although I think Lynn would like to stay another week."

"Could we?" Lynn said.

Matt smiled and replied, "I'd love to, but we might be pushing our luck if we stayed any longer."

"Oh come on, what can happen in a week?"

Matt shrugged, picked up the bags and headed for the dock. The pilot went inside and grabbed a couple of bags and followed Matt. In fifteen minutes the plane was loaded, and they took off for Juneau. After they were airborne, the pilot pulled something from his pocket.

"Oh, I almost forgot. This message came in for you a day or two ago, Matt."

Matt took the message and said, "Oh, thanks." He opened it up and started reading it. Lynn watched as his face dropped and he became pale.

"What's wrong?"

"The State Bar's trying to shut me down!"

"What?"

"I have a temporary injunction hearing in four days. Jesus! I can't believe this!"

"But why?"

"They don't buy our position that we're not advertising."

"Oh, shit. I thought you got a legal opinion."

"I did, but it was just an opinion. It doesn't mean jack."

The pilot asked, "Are you the Matt Coleman everyone's been talking about?" the pilot asked.

"Huh?"

"There's some guy in Texas named Matt Coleman who's leading some kind of debtor's revolution—telling everyone to file bankruptcy."

"You've got to be kidding," Lynn said. "He's talking about you, Matt."

Matt didn't respond but just slumped back in his seat. Lynn looked at him for a second and then turned to the pilot. "So how are people reacting to all of this?"

"A lot of people think your husband is right on, but most of the commentators are against him. They say it's irresponsible to advocate that everyone should file bankruptcy."

"Hmm," Lynn said, and then turned to Matt. "You're a celebrity, honey. Isn't that wonderful?"

"I don't know, is it?"

***

On the day of the hearing, Matt was very anxious about how it would turn out. He arrived early and parked in his usual lot west of the Earl Cabell Federal Building. Leon Cash, the attendant, greeted him as he always did when Matt attended court. Leon was a great guy, always upbeat, and invariably would lift Matt's spirits if he were down or nervous about a court appearance. Leon was a tall black man—an ex-SMU tackle who missed going pro due to a knee injury his senior year. Today Matt really needed a little friendly banter to calm his nerves. He drove up and rolled down his window to a smiling Leon.

"Hey, Matt. What's happening bros?"

"Hi, Leon. Just the usual shit."

"Yeah, I heard 'bout it on TV. You can't let them shut you down now. That ad you've been runnin' just tells it like it is."

"Thank you, Leon. I appreciate the vote of confidence."

"You're doin' a fine thing here, Matt. It's 'bout time someone stood up to them bankers."

"That's what I was thinking."

"So, give 'em hell, okay?"

"You got it, bros," Matt said smiling broadly. "Let's kick some butt."

"Hey, now you're talkin'. You're my man."

Matt parked in his usual spot and walked over to the courthouse. When he arrived, the courtroom was filled with spectators and the press. Bradley Davis was standing at one of the counsel tables pulling books and files from his briefcase. Peter Robertson was seated at the opposite counsel table conferring with an associate. As Matt entered the courtroom, several reporters swarmed around him attempting to get a statement. He declined and went straight to Bradley and sat down beside him.

"You ready?" Bradley said.

"I guess so."

"Did you ever expect your little ads to cause such a ruckus?"

"No, this is ridiculous."

The door opened, and the court reporter entered the room and sat down. Then the bailiff stood up and said, "All rise," as the judge entered the courtroom and took the bench. He rummaged around with the files on his desk, then looked up and said, "Are we ready to proceed?"

Robertson and Davis stood up. Robertson replied, "The plaintiff is ready, Your Honor."

"The defendant is ready, Your Honor."

"You may proceed, Mr. Robertson," the judge said.

"Thank you, Your Honor. The matter before the Court is the application brought by the State Bar of Texas for a temporary injunction against Matt Coleman and the Debt Relief Centers, Inc. from continuing to use misleading and deceptive advertising in violation of the State Bar rules governing legal advertising. As the court is aware, Mr. Coleman and his organization have been airing spots on local television claiming that many creditors are engaged in a conspiracy to impoverish them by giving out too much credit and charging obscene interest rates. Although at first blush this seems like a noble cause, in reality, it's nothing but an advertising campaign to get bankruptcy business for Mr. Coleman and his bankruptcy mill.

"We will show the court through the testimony of the chairman of the State Bar Advertising Committee that these TV spots violate several sections of the State Bar's advertising regulations and accordingly should be stopped. Thank you, Your Honor."

"All right, Mr. Bradley."

"Your Honor, may it please the court. What we have here is not advertising but merely one man exercising his right of free speech. If the court views the TV spots, it will see that they are nothing more than Mr. Coleman's opinions and theories about why a large segment of our population is insolvent. At no time does he solicit bankruptcy business for the firm. These are just public interest broadcasts, and any business generated by them is simply incidental.

"Your Honor, I would liken what Mr. Coleman is doing to running for political office. Lawyers do that every year, and as part of the process they buy TV time and express their position on a variety of public issues over the airways. Now it's no secret that sometimes these lawyers receive legal business from these TV ads due to this added exposure to the public. If the State Bar has jurisdiction over Mr. Coleman's public interest spots, then it would follow that they would have jurisdiction over lawyers campaigning for political office as well. Surely that couldn't be the case, Your Honor. I would reaffirm Mr. Coleman's right of free speech and deny the plaintiff's application for a temporary injunction. The State Bar of Texas simply lacks jurisdiction over what Mr. Coleman is doing. Thank you."

"All right, Mr. Robertson. Call your first witness," the judge said.

"Thank you, Your Honor. The Plaintiff calls Mr. Howard Ross."

A tall dark-headed man stood up in the front row of the gallery and began walking to the front of the courtroom. Mr. Robertson looked at him and pointed to the witness stand. The man nodded and walked up next to the court reporter and sat down in the wooden witness chair. The bailiff swore him in.

"State your name please?"

"Howard Ross."

"Mr. Ross, how are you employed?"

"I'm an attorney with Goggan, Walls & Ross here in Dallas."

"What is your relationship to the State Bar of Texas?"

"I'm the chairman of the Advertising Enforcement Committee."

"I see. . . . What is the purpose of the Advertising Enforcement Committee?"

"To monitor lawyer advertising around the state to be sure the members of the bar comply with the advertising guidelines that have been established."

"In the performance of these duties did you have an occasion to monitor the advertising of Matthew Coleman?"

"Yes, we did."

"How did that come about?"

"We got several complaints that his TV advertising was misleading, deceptive, and highly inflammatory."

"Really? What did you do as the result of those complaints?"

"We obtained tapes of the advertisements and began to study them."

"Did your committee reach any conclusions after viewing the tapes?"

"Yes, first it was the consensus of the committee that the TV spots were advertising despite Mr. Coleman's contention that they were not. Secondly, it was determined that the advertising was in clear violation of several of the State Bar advertising rules."

"In your opinion how do the TV spots violate the advertising guidelines?"

"First of all, they disparage the financial institutions of this country unfairly to engender hatred and contempt for these institutions. The purpose of fostering consumer hatred and contempt is to help them to overcome their natural shame and embarrassment in filing bankruptcy. Many people think a lot about bankruptcy when times get tough, but most don't do it because it is an admission of failure and they fear public ridicule."

"So the TV spots are simply an attempt to shift the blame for the financial failure to financial institutions and away from the individuals themselves?"

"Objection. Counsel is leading the witness," Bradley said.

"Sustained."

"I'll rephrase. In your opinion, how are these TV spots misleading?"

"They advocate bankruptcy not as a legitimate right of every citizen in financial distress, but as a way to get revenge against financial institutions for allegedly making consumers spend money and hooking them into a lifetime of debt repayment."

"Thank you. Pass the witness."

Robertson sat down and whispered something to his assistant. Bradley stood up and began to question the witness.

"Mr. Ross. Who was it exactly who complained about Mr. Coleman's TV spots?"

"Several persons complained."

"Who were they?"

"Several law firms."

"Would it be fair to say they were some of Mr. Coleman's competitors?"

"Yes, they felt if they had to follow the rules so should Mr. Coleman."

"Who else complained?"

"The American Creditors' Alliance."

"Is that an organization made up of financial institutions around the country?"

"I believe so."

"So they were obviously upset with the conspiracy theory espoused in the TV spots."

"Yes."

"And the increased bankruptcy filings were hurting them of course?"

"Yes."

"So they would stop at nothing to put an end to these highly effective TV spots, wouldn't they?"

"I don't know what you're talking about."

"Never mind. . . . Let me ask you this. Did you receive any complaints from consumers?"

"Consumers?"

"Right."

"Well . . . no, not specifically."

"So the people these advertising regulations were designed to protect didn't have a problem with the TV spots?"

"No, they just typically don't complain."

"So your committee takes it upon itself to play God and determine what's good and bad for the consumer?"

"Objection. Argumentative."

"Sustained."

"No further questions."

The State Bar called several other witnesses and when they all had finished testifying the judge looked at Bradley and said, "You may call your first witness, Mr. Davis."

"Thank you, sir. I'd like to call Matthew Coleman."

Matt looked at Lynn; she smiled as he got up and approached the witness stand. Once seated the bailiff swore him in as the gallery watched with great anticipation. After some preliminary background questions, Bradley asked, "Mr. Coleman, what exactly did you intend when you started airing these TV spots?"

"My wife had been a student of Professor Swensen at SMU. She was very interested in his economic conspiracy theory. She told me about it, and it made a lot of sense. I wanted to learn more, so I met with Professor Swensen, and he was kind enough to share his knowledge and research into the topic."

"Okay, but the TV spots. Why did you launch them?"

"Well, the professor had been preaching his theories for years, but nobody listened. It was a real shame. Every day in my bankruptcy practice I saw the victims of this conspiracy. Families tore apart by economic calamity. People robbed of not only their physical possessions but their dignity and self-respect. I wanted to do something to right this terrible wrong."

"I see, so the TV spots were purely a public service?"

"Exactly. They were a way to wake up the American people to what was happening to them."

"Now it's no secret your bankruptcy practice prospered as a result of these advertisements, right?"

"Yes, people were grateful that we woke them up and showed them what was happening to them."

"In your advertising do you ask the audience to file bankruptcy?"

"No, we simply explain to them that there is no shame in bankruptcy, especially in light of the fact they have been manipulated all these years by their creditors. We never tell them to file bankruptcy, nor do we ask them to bring their business to us."

"So what do you think about the State Bar's position that your TV spots are nothing but cold, calculated advertisements?"

"It's simply not true. My wife and I only wanted to express our opinion and promote the theories of Professor Swensen as a public service. Nothing more."

"Thank you. Pass the witness."

Bradley sat down, and Robertson stood up. The judge nodded for Robertson to begin his cross examination.

"Mr. Coleman. Do you expect this court to believe that your TV ads were never intended to increase your bankruptcy business?"

"Yes, I do."

"Have you ever been active in politics?"

"No."

"Do you belong to a political party?"

"No, I'm an independent."

"How much do these advertisements cost you?"

"The TV spots cost about three thousand a week."

"So you suddenly decided to spend $3,000 per week or $156,000 a year as a public service with no expectation of recovering that money?"

"It was the most effective way we could think of getting our message to the people."

"A message that was sure to increase your business."

"Sure, we realized our business might profit by it, but that doesn't change the fact that we were voicing our opinion as we have a right to do as citizens of this great nation."

"So you admit this whole thing was profit motivated."

"No, it was motivated by an outrage at what the financial institutions of this nation have done to the American people."

"You state that there has been a conspiracy to enslave the American people. What evidence do you have of that conspiracy?"

"Look around you, Mr. Robertson. Do you watch television? Do you get a dozen credit card applications in the mail every month? Have you looked at the growth of the consumer debt in this nation? Have you checked the divorce rate lately?"

"That's not proof of anything, Mr. Coleman."

"You're right, it's not, and I'm not saying I have proof, but I have an opinion as to what is causing the destruction of the family and a decline of morality in America, and I have a right to espouse that opinion."

"Not when it—"

"Objection. Argumentative," Bradley said. "Mr. Robertson is testifying."

The judge said, "Sustained. Do you have any more questions of this witness?"

Robertson gave the judge a frustrated look and then shook his head and said, "No, Your Honor."

The judge sat up in his chair, looked at his watch and said, "We'll break for lunch and take your next witness then. Be back here at 1:30 p.m."

# 8

Tom Hartsfield took a seat at a table in the corner of the Easy Street Bar and Grill. He had a clear shot to the front door so he could see everyone who came through it. He lit up a cigarette and opened the menu, pretending to be undecided as to what he should order.

Tom was the office manager for the Debt Relief Centers. He was a short, stout man of about forty-five, with dark brown hair and a husky voice. He majored in business administration at Austin College but never graduated. His wife was a nurse for an orthopedic surgeon in Plano. They had five children and as one would expect, had difficulty making ends meet. Tom had been one of Rich's paralegals and had always performed well. When he found out Matt was looking for an office manager, he begged Rich to let him apply because the job paid more. Rich acquiesced, and since he had referred him, Matt trusted him implicitly.

Tom gave everyone who entered a once over. He had no idea what the man who had summoned him looked like, but he figured he'd know him when he saw him. Finally, a tall, bald man entered the bar. He said something to the hostess, and she pointed toward Tom. He squirmed in his chair as the bald man approached.

"Tom Hartsfield?" he said as he stood over the table.

"Yes, you must be Hans."

"That's right," he said and then took a seat.

"So, I'm here. What do you want?"

85

"How is your son these days?"

"My son? He's fine. What's he got to do with this?"

"Nothing, if you do as you're told."

"Do as I'm told? What are you talking about? I don't have to do anything for you!" Tom said as he stood up.

"Sit down, Mr. Hartsfield," Hans ordered.

Tom remained standing. "I came here out of curiosity, but if you think—"

"Your son Ronnie is a sophomore at Baylor University. He lives at 442 Ridgeway, Apartment 222, in Waco. Every morning he jogs 2.6 miles from his apartment to the Student Union and back. His girlfriend drives a red Chrysler Le Baron. She has a tattoo of a rosebud just to the right of her belly button."

Tom sat down and said, "Okay, okay. I'm listening."

"Your boss is messing with something that's none of his business. He's pissed a lot of people off. You need to talk some sense into him. Get him to agree to a permanent injunction. Get him to back off this crusade of his. He's already made lots of money. It doesn't pay to get greedy."

"He won't back off. He's a very stubborn man, and even if he wanted to quit, Lynn wouldn't let him. She's more driven than he is."

"If you care about him, you'll convince him. You won't like the alternative."

"What alternative?"

"Jail."

"Jail? Matt would never commit a crime."

"Not knowingly . . . but that's where you come in."

"I don't know what you're talking about."

"It's really very simple. You're going to set up another bank account for the firm, but you're not going to tell Mr. Coleman about it. Approximately 10 percent of the firm's deposits will go into that account."

"Are you going to steal his money?"

"No, just leave it in that account but under no circumstances should the account ever be disclosed to Mr. Coleman."

"How am I supposed to keep this account secret? All client payments are reconciled each month."

"You'll figure out a way. Your son's life depends on it. Of course, if you can get Mr. Coleman to quit using his TV ads and drop his campaign then all this becomes moot."

"How do you know I won't go to the FBI?"

"Because the moment I smell an FBI agent, you'll be a dead man. And when I'm done with you, I'll still track down your son and kill him too."

"You've got the wrong man. I'm not a good liar. I'll never be able to pull it off."

"Maybe so, but it's too late to worry about that now. Either you do it, or we kill you. It's your decision."

Tom took a deep breath and rubbed his temples. Finally, he raised his eyebrow and said, "Okay, but how do I know you'll leave my son and me alone once this is all over? It would be a lot safer for you just to kill us. If I'm going to die anyway, why should I set Matt up?"

He grimaced. "You're starting to irritate me, Tom. I gave you my word. That's the best I can do, okay?"

Tom chuckled. "Your word? I'm supposed to trust a hoodlum."

Hans stood up, walked around the table, and grabbed Tom by the collar. Some customers nearby stopped what they were doing and watched. Hans whispered, "Okay, come on outside so I can kill you right now!"

Tom raised his hand. "No! No! I'm sorry. Your word is fine."

Hans let go. Tom dropped back in his chair, and Hans sat down. Hans glared at the customers staring at them, and they turned away. He said, "That's better. Just do your job, and nobody will mess with you."

After Hans had left, Tom went to the telephone and dialed a number. The phone rang several times before someone picked it up.

"Hello."

"Is Ronnie there?"

"No, who's this."

"His father."

"Oh, no. He just left for class."

"You saw him?"

"Yes, he just left here a minute ago. Is everything okay?"

"Yes, just tell him I called to say hello. It wasn't anything important."

"Okay, I'll tell him."

Tom hung up the receiver and stood there, staring at the telephone. Finally, he picked up the receiver and dialed 1411.

"This is Bob, what city please?" an electronic voice said.

"Dallas."

"What number please?"

"The FBI."

"Thank you."

Tom dialed the number and waited.

"Federal Bureau of Investigation. May I help you?"

Tom didn't respond.

"Hello. May I help you?"

Tom started to talk and then slammed down the phone. "Shit!" he muttered under his breath. "No matter what I do, someone is going to get hurt. Oh, God, what am I going to do?"

***

When the injunction hearing continued, Bradley called Professor Swensen. His testimony took nearly three hours. He savored this rare opportunity to discuss his conspiracy theory before the court and the national media. When he finally stepped down, it was nearly five o'clock. The judge thanked both sides and said he'd have to take the matter under advisement. He promised to make a decision in the next few days and notify the parties immediately when a decision was reached. After the hearing, Matt was accosted by several reporters.

"Mr. Coleman. How do you think the hearing went today?"

"Very well, if there is anything that came out of the hearing it is the fact that my TV spots are simply the communication of my point of view, which I have the perfect right to state as a citizen in a free society."

"Mr. Coleman, what do you think about the bill introduced today in Congress requiring all bankrupt individuals gainfully employed or with a regular income to file Chapter 13."

"That bill is introduced every year. It's ridiculous. The problem we have today isn't with the bankruptcy system. It's with the financial institutions of this country who are looting the American people and forcing unprecedented numbers of citizens into bankruptcy."

"What do you think will happen to the U.S. economy if this trend continues?"

"Eventually there's going to be a crisis. A crisis, no doubt, worse than the savings and loan crisis of the mid-eighties. Congress needs to take a look at interest rate regulation now before it's too late. Usury laws should be reinstated and given teeth. It's time that loan sharking is once again made a crime in this country."

"What do you think will happen if you're successful in defending yourself against the State Bar of Texas?"

"Nothing earth-shattering. This whole thing has been blown out of proportion. I'll just go back to helping desperate consumers get a clean slate and reclaim their lives."

"What about all the attorneys who are reportedly gearing up to adopt your advertising strategy, if you come out unscathed?"

"It's not an advertising strategy, it's simply one man trying to show the American people how they've been tricked into economic slavery so they can see their way to freedom. If other attorneys want to help that's fine with me," Matt said and then started to move forward. "That's all folks. I've got to get going."

Matt and Lynn pushed their way through the crowd and finally made it out of the courthouse and into the parking garage. When they got back to the office, Tom greeted them with a barrage of questions.

"So, how did it go?" Tom asked.

"Very well, actually," Matt replied.

"So the judge didn't issue a temporary injunction?"

"No, not yet. He took it under advisement."

"So, you still might lose?"

"Yes, that's quite possible, but we might win too."

"Have you tried to negotiate with the State Bar?"

"What do you mean?"

"Well, maybe if you talked to them you could tone down the ads a little so they would be more palatable."

"But why? They're so good. I don't want to do anything to diminish their effectiveness."

"We've got more business now than we can handle. It wouldn't hurt to back off a little until the dust settles."

"Maybe so, but I can't let the State Bar tell me what to say or not say. That's un-American."

"You know there are other people out there besides the State Bar who want you stopped."

"Who? The banks? Sure, I bet they'd love to shut me up, but that makes all of this more fun. I hate those sleazy bankers almost as much as the IRS."

"You're not taking this seriously enough, Matt," Tom said, with a slight strain in his voice.

Matt looked at Tom and frowned. "Are you all right, Tom? This whole thing is really bothering you, huh?"

"Well, I'm concerned for you. You're getting too much attention. You should back off."

"No way. That was the whole point of the ad campaign—to get people's attention. We've got to take advantage of the situation now while we can. How long do you think bankruptcy is going to be a matter of national debate? I give this thing another week or two, and I won't be able to buy an interview."

"I'm not so sure," Tom said, with a hint of resignation in his voice.

"I just hope when this is all over that I've gained enough notoriety to keep a steady flow of debtors coming through the door."

As they were talking, Lynn walked in looking rather concerned.

"Matt, my sister just called. John's left her again. She's very upset."

"Oh, no. That's too bad. What happened?"

"They got into another fight over her going to college. John doesn't want her to quit work. He says they need the money worse than she needs an education."

"He just can't stand the fact that she's smarter than he is. I knew that marriage would never work."

"Anyway, I need to fly up to Oklahoma City and be with her a few days. She needs help with the twins."

"Oh crap! Do you have to?"

"Yes."

"Damn. I wanted to go out and celebrate tonight."

"We haven't won yet."

"I wanted to celebrate that we haven't lost yet."

Lynn laughed, "Any excuse to party, right?"

"Exactly."

"Call Jason and go to a Rangers game or something."

"All right. . . . When's your flight?"

"There's one at six-thirty, so I'm going to go home, grab a few things, and head off to Love Field."

"Do you want me to take you?"

"No, you've got work to do. I'll be fine."

"Okay, Honey. I'll miss you."

"I'll miss you too," Lynn said and then gave Matt a long kiss goodbye. She smiled and then left.

"You're a lucky man," Tom said.

"Boy, you don't know the half of it. She's a doll. I can't believe she's mine."

"You know, for her sake, you ought to settle this State Bar thing. Something like this could destroy your marriage."

Matt frowned, "Tom, where have you been hiding? She's responsible for the ad campaign, remember? If I suggested abandoning it after it has been such a success—well, *that* would jeopardize our marriage."

Tom shrugged and went back to his office. Matt worked the rest of the day trying to catch up on his work. That night on the way home he stopped and got some Chinese food for dinner. As he sat in the kitchen eating an egg roll, he longed for Lynn. The apartment was so quiet

and lonely without her. When he was done eating, he went
to turn on the TV when the phone rang.

"Matt, what's happening?"

"Jason, not much. What are you doing?"

"Watching you on the Six O'clock News."

"Oh really? What did they say about me?"

"That you're going to get sanctioned by the State Bar
if the court finds in the State Board's favor."

"So they fine me a few bucks. No big deal."

"They were talking suspension."

"What? That's bullshit."

"I think so, but the news commentator said it was a
real possibility."

"Well, I'm not going to worry about it. I've got the
best attorney in Texas defending me. You know it's so nice
to have money so you can afford the best."

"So, what are you up to tonight?"

"I was just going to turn on the TV. Lynn had to go
to Oklahoma City to console her sister."

"You're alone?"

"Yes."

"Hey, let's go out. It'll be like old times."

"I don't know. I'm a married man now. I shouldn't be
out bar hopping."

"Ah, come on. It'll be fun."

"Well, maybe a couple of drinks at Louie's wouldn't
hurt. A little cool jazz would be appropriate tonight."

"Good, I'll pick you up in thirty minutes."

"All right. See you then."

Matt got up and went into the bedroom to change
into something more appropriate for the evening. He felt a
little guilty going out. If Lynn called and he wasn't home,
she'd be worried. He decided to call and tell her he was
going out. He dialed the number, but no one answered. He

figured she hadn't arrived yet and her sister had gone to pick her up at the airport. He left a message on the recorder. As he hung up the doorbell rang, so he went to the door and opened it.

"Hey, ready to go?" Jason said.

"Un huh. Let's go."

Jason turned and walked toward the car. Matt closed the door, locked it, and followed Jason to his white Toyota Camry. After a ten-minute drive, they parked across the street from Louie's and went inside. The nightclub was crowded with a middle-age crowd. Matt coughed a few times from the thick stench of smoke. Jason lit up a cigarette as Matt scanned the room for a table.

"Over here," Matt said pointing to an empty table in the corner of the club. They walked over to it and sat down. A bar maid spotted them and walked over. They flirted with her a minute before giving her their order. The band was playing *Grooving High* which was one of Matt's favorites. He immediately began to respond to the music. Jason, who preferred rock to jazz, smiled, amused at Matt's sudden transformation.

"This is great, huh?" Matt said.

"Not bad. . . . Kind of an old crowd though," Jason observed.

"Good, maybe you'll be able to keep your mind on the music instead of every piece of ass in the joint."

"Don't count on it," Jason laughed and then nearly fell out of his chair when a tall blonde walked by brushing him with her large breasts.

"Hey, I'm a married man so don't get any ideas."

"You may be married, but I'm not."

"Oh, you're going to pick up some blonde and leave me here without wheels."

"I'll pay your cab fare home."

"Great. I thought you were going to keep me company tonight."

"Well, if I strike out, I'll be back. Otherwise, don't call me before eleven tomorrow."

"Oh, God. You're hopeless."

The bar maid came with the drinks as Jason was getting up to give chase to the blonde. He took his drink and headed in her direction. Matt watched him as he eased his way in and sat down beside her. He knew it would only take a second to reject him. If he lasted two minutes, he would likely never return. Matt picked up his drink and watched the two strangers talk. He looked at his watch and after the big second hand had swept around two times, turned his attention back to the band and the sweet sounds that were drifting his way.

After thirty minutes Jason and the blond left. The bar maid saw that Matt's glass was empty and brought him another round. He thanked her and then noticed a well-dressed woman at the bar staring at him. Their eyes made contact. She was quite attractive in her black cocktail dress and diamond necklace. She seemed overdressed, too elegant for a casual jazz club. Matt turned away feeling guilty about how the woman excited him. He decided he'd better leave.

He got up, dropped a twenty on the table, and turned to leave when the lady suddenly got up and walked toward him. He froze as he watched her approach. She walked up so close he could smell a strong scent of perfume. He took a deep breath enjoying the pleasant aroma.

"You're not leaving are you?" she said.

"Huh?" he blurted out, startled that she had addressed him. "Well, actually I do have to leave. It's getting late."

"You sure you wouldn't want to buy a girl a drink?"

It was a tempting thought, but he knew he shouldn't even consider it. "Well, maybe another time. I've really got to go."

"How are you going to get home? Your friend took your wheels."

Matt frowned. "How did you know that?"

"You're an attractive man, and I've had my eye on you. I know you came in with a friend and I saw the friend leave. So, if you came in the same car and he left, that leaves you here without wheels."

"Wow," Matt said. "You should be a detective." He smiled and gazed into her alluring eyes for a long moment.

She said, "So, you gonna buy me a drink or what?"

He shook his head and motioned for her to sit down. She did and he sat across from her.

"What are you drinking?"

"Gin and tonic."

"Okay, I'll buy you one drink but then I've got to go— seriously."

"If you must."

Matt motioned for the bar maid to come over. She finished what she was doing and then walked over to the table.

"Gin and tonic for the lady and bourbon and Seven for me."

"All right," she said and left.

"What's your name?" Matt said.

"Monica. . . . Monica Sommers."

"Nice to meet you, Monica. I'm Matt Coleman."

"I know. I saw you on the news tonight."

"Oh . . . you did?"

"Yes, I think it's wonderful how you're helping so many people free themselves from financial troubles."

"You do? That's good to hear. Sometimes I wonder if I'm doing the right thing. A lot of people think I should back off and leave the system alone. They say what I'm doing might raise havoc with the economy."

"No, they're wrong. I love what you're doing. You're a brave man fighting the big banks and finance companies. It's time somebody had the guts to do that."

Matt smiled. The barmaid returned with two drinks and set them on the table. Monica reached for her drink and knocked her purse on the ground. Matt jumped off the stool and bent down to retrieve it. While he was looking down, Monica deposited a white powdery substance into his drink. When Matt got back up, he handed Monica her purse.

"Jesus, I'm so clumsy sometimes," she said.

"No problem, I'm the same way."

Monica opened her purse and said, "I hope I didn't break anything. . . . No, everything looks intact."

"So, what do you do for a living?" Matt asked.

"Oh me, well . . . I'm a social worker."

"Really, then you probably see a lot of the same people I deal with every day— the victims of our cruel society."

"Probably so. Don't you find it rewarding helping people in trouble?" Monica asked.

"Yes, that's really the point of what I'm doing."

"Is it?"

"Well, I'll admit at first it was the money, but you know in the past few months I feel like I've accomplished more than I did in the first twenty-seven years of my life."

"That must be a good feeling."

"It is. It really is."

"So where is your partner tonight?"

"My partner? Oh, you mean Lynn?"

"Right."

"She's with her sister in Oklahoma City."

"Umm. Too bad for her."

Matt looked at Monica who was giving him a seductive look. He tried to fight off the sexual feelings that were welling inside him. Suddenly he felt weak and dizzy. Everything turned white. He blinked and shook his head, trying to clear his vision.

"Let me give you a ride home?" she said.

"Oh, no. That would be too much trouble."

"Don't be silly. Where do you live?"

"In an apartment near Prestonwood Mall."

"Oh, that's on my way home. It won't be out of my way at all."

"Well, if you're sure."

"Come on."

Matt stood feeling very wobbly. He was glad he wasn't going to be driving. Monica grabbed his hand and led him out of the bar. As they walked across the street to the parking garage, there was a sudden flash of light.

"What was that?"

"Some Japanese tourist taking pictures."

"He didn't take our picture, did he?"

"No, he was just getting a shot of the club."

Matt looked back at the club trying to get a good look at the man who took the picture. He wondered why he felt so drunk after only a few bourbons.

"Come on; my car's over here."

Matt followed her to a red Mazda Miata. She opened the door and motioned for Matt to get in. He stumbled over to the passenger side of the car and opened it.

"Nice car," he said and then got in.

"Thanks, it's a lot of fun to drive."

"I bet."

Monica took off, and Matt sat back and closed his eyes. The cool night air felt good. His vision began to improve. Monica looked at him causing him to smile. *What was he doing driving around with a beautiful woman? God, how did this happen?*

"I live in the apartments overlooking the golf course behind Prestonwood. Just get on Beltline, and I'll show you the way."

Monica got off the Dallas North Tollway at Beltline and headed east. Matt directed her to the apartments, and she pulled up into his parking space.

"Thanks for the ride," Matt said.

"You're not even going to invite me in?"

"No, I'm sorry. You know I'm married."

"I also know your wife isn't home."

"I guess I'm old fashioned, but I believe in monogamy."

"Well, let me help you to the door anyway. I'd hate you to fall and get hurt. I'd never forgive myself."

Matt opened the door and stood up rather unsteadily. "I don't know why I'm so wobbly. I guess I can't hold my liquor anymore." He extended his arms like he was taking a sobriety test and tried to walk a straight line. "See, I'm fine," he said and then stumbled.

Monica got out and came around and took his arm. When they got to the door, Matt unlocked it. Monica tried to slip inside but Matt stopped her.

"I'm sorry Monica, I may be drunk but I know enough not to let you in. We'd both regret it in the morning. Thanks for the ride."

Monica backed off and gave Matt a scathing look. "All right, it doesn't make any difference to me. I've already been paid, and I don't give refunds."

"Paid?" Matt said.

"Yeah. Didn't you know I was a gift?"

Matt stared at Monica as she walked off—his mind too muddled to comprehend what she had said. Finally, he closed the door and as he turned to walk into the living room everything went white, and he collapsed, unconscious.

# 9

A dense fog engulfed Matt as he walked toward the sound of ocean waves crashing onto the shore. The familiar salty odor of the sea filled his lungs. He was a child walking alone along the beach he loved so much. There was laughter ahead which made him quicken his pace. He stopped and looked at his grandmother and grandfather sitting in front of a raging fire. His grandmother saw him.

"Matt, where have you been? I made a hot dog for you. It's in the picnic basket."

"Thanks. . . . Hey grandpa, I think I saw some grunion coming in down the beach a ways."

"Oh, really?" he said and looked down at his watch. "They're not due until seven forty-five."

"Maybe they're going to come early."

"Well, get your hot dog and then go back to the beach and keep a lookout. Take your brother with you. Yell when you see them."

"Okay."

Matt got his brother, Ryan, who was building a sand castle and took him down to the water's edge. Matt watched as the sun dipped beneath the sea and it began to get dark. Soon the beach was lit only by the full moon and a sky full of radiant stars. Suddenly the sand began to sparkle as thousands of shiny grunions flooded the beach.

"Grandpa! Come quick! They're here." Matt said as he began to jump with joy.

Grandpa and Grandma hurried down to the shore with several gunny-sacks in hand.

"Quick! Grab a gunnysack and fill it up!"

Matt and Ryan reached down and tried to pick up the grunion, but they were so slippery they couldn't catch them. Suddenly a wave crashed in front of them and knocked them over.

"Be careful kids," Grandma said as she helped Matt and Ryan back up on their feet.

Grandpa had his gunny sack half full of fish which made Matt mad since he hadn't been able to catch any.

"Ryan, hold the bag for Matt so he can use two hands."

Working as a team, the two children began to fill their sack more effectively. Then just as quickly as the silvery fish had come, they were gone.

"Wow, that was the best catch I think we've ever had," Grandpa said.

"God, what are we going to do with all those fish?" Grandma said.

The scene faded and Matt found himself alone in the darkness. It was quiet except for the faint sound of a TV in the distance. Suddenly he was jolted from his unconsciousness. He picked up his head and looked around. The room was spinning. He struggled to his knees and crawled over to the end table. Placing his hand on the table, he pushed himself to his feet. The objects in the room began to come into focus. After taking a deep breath, he walked over to the window and opened the drapes. The bright sunlight stung his eyes. Quickly closing the drapes, he looked down at his watch and saw it was 11:13.

"Jesus! I've been out for over twelve hours."

The phone rang. Matt looked at it but didn't move. It rang again, so he struggled to his feet and slowly made his way over to it and picked up the receiver.

"Hello," he whispered.

"Matt, where in the hell have you been," Lynn said.

He rubbed his aching forehead, struggling to think. "Unconscious, I think."

"Unconscious?"

"Yeah, Jason and I went to Louie's last night, and some broad insisted on having a drink. I told her no, but she wouldn't take no for an answer. I think she slipped me something. . . . Oh, God! I bet she robbed me."

Matt reached into his back pocket and pulled out his wallet. He quickly searched it.

"Huh. Everything's here. I don't know what's going on."

"You didn't sleep with her, did you?"

"No! Of course not. I tried to get away from her but whatever she gave me knocked the shit out of me."

"Ohhh! You better be telling me the truth."

"I wouldn't lie to you. You know me better than that. I could kill Jason for deserting me."

"Why did he desert?"

"He saw some blond and got a hard-on. They hit it off, and he was gone. . . . I didn't have a ride home, so I was going to take a cab. This broad seemed to know who I was and insisted on taking me home. I was so out of it I had no choice but to go with her."

"You better go see the doctor. I'm coming home on the first flight. Can you pick me up?"

"I think so. Everything seems to be coming into focus now."

"Take a hot shower. That should help. I'll call you back after I call Southwest and get an arrival time."

"Okay, I'll be here."

"You better be. . . . God, I go away one day and look what happens. Jesus!"

Matt got in the shower. He suddenly felt hungry. After he was done, he went into the kitchen and made himself some toast and coffee. Then he went outside and got the newspaper. The bright sunlight nearly blinded him, so he quickly went back inside. After putting some butter and jam on his toast, he sat down to eat and read the newspaper. He picked up his coffee and took a sip as he unfolded the newspaper. The picture on the front page jolted him. Hot coffee splattered on his hand.

"Ouch! Shit!" he said as he starred incredulously at the photo. It was he and Monica in front of Louie's Place. The caption read: "Bankruptcy attorney Matt Coleman, photographed with a prostitute, Monica Sommers, outside Louie's Place in Addison. Was he helping her file bankruptcy? Mr. Coleman has been unavailable for comment."

Matt dropped the paper just as the phone rang again. He went to the wall phone and picked it up.

"Hello."

"Mr. Coleman, this is Randy Bealle from the *Dallas Morning News*. We wanted to ask you what you were doing with a hooker last night?"

"I didn't know she was a hooker. She just drove me home. That's all. Nothing happened."

"Do you really expect anyone to believe that?"

"Yes, it's the truth. . . . Goodbye," he said and hung up the phone. It immediately rang again. He looked at it a moment and then answered it.

"What do you want?"

"Hey, don't bite my head off. I didn't take that picture."

"You might as well have, you son of a bitch! Why did you have to desert me last night?"

"I'm sorry. I had no idea something like this would happen. What *did* happen, anyway?"

"I got set up! Some sleazy bastard hired a hooker to drug me so I could be led in front of a photographer."

"Damn. Is there anything I can do?"

"Yeah, see if you can find her. I want to know who put her up to this."

"How am I going to do that?"

"Her picture's in the paper. Her name is Monica Sommers. Find her for me. It's important."

"Okay, I'll try, but I'm no detective."

"Just do your best."

"Okay, what are you going to do?"

"I'm going to the doctor. Maybe he could do some tests to prove I was drugged."

"Good idea."

"I'll see you later."

"Bye."

Matt checked in with the admissions clerk at the Medical City Hospital Emergency Room. His doctor had told him to meet him there as his office was closed on Saturdays. As he waited, he began to worry about Lynn's reaction to the newspaper photograph. He hoped she wouldn't see it before he picked her up.

The nurse called his name, so he got up and walked over to her.

"Yes, I'm Matt Coleman."

The nurse gave him a hard look and then said, "Dr. Monroe is here. He told me to put you in an examining room."

"Good, thanks."

Matt followed the nurse into a treatment room. She told him to sit on the examination table and wait for the doctor. Matt read the chart on the wall depicting the upper respiratory system. Then he scanned the contamination warning on the trash can. He tapped his foot against the table leg for a while and then read a brochure about the latest in antibiotics. Finally, the door flew open and Dr. Monroe appeared.

"Matt."

"Hi, Doc."

"What's this about being drugged?"

"Did you see the newspaper this morning?"

"Yeah, what were you doing with a hooker?"

"She came on to me at Louie's and slipped me some kind of drug. You've got to do some tests or something to prove what I'm saying is right. If you don't, I'm screwed."

"Okay, I'll get a urine sample and do a blood test. If you were drugged, there should be traces of it."

"Good. How long will it take?"

"The test results should be back in a day or two."

"That long?"

"Yeah, the lab has a big backlog. It will be a while before they can get to it."

"All right, I guess I can fend off the press for two days. Call me as soon as you get the results."

"I will. I'll have the nurse come in and get some blood," the doctor said and then handed Matt a paper cup. "In the meantime, give me a urine sample."

"Sure. Thanks for your help, Doc."

"No problem. I just hope the test proves your theory."

"Huh. Tell me about it."

Matt barely arrived at the airport before the flight from Oklahoma City landed. He waited nervously as the passengers began to disembark. When he saw Lynn, he smiled and waved. She hurried over to him and they embraced.

"God, am I glad to see you," Matt said.

"Are you all right?"

"Yeah, the doctor said I was fine. He's doing some tests to see what drug the bitch gave me."

"Huh. How did it make you feel?"

"Like I was completely drunk but not sick drunk, you know. It felt kind of good actually. I don't know how I kept her out of our apartment, but I do remember shutting the door in her face."

"You better not be lying to me."

"Honey. I swear to God."

Lynn took a deep breath as she looked at Matt warily.

"I've got some more bad news."

"What?"

"This whole thing was a setup to embarrass me."

"What do you mean?"

"Somebody hired this hooker to drug me so she could drag me in front of Louie's to be photographed."

"Photographed? What are you talking about?!"

Matt handed Lynn the newspaper. She quickly opened it and let out a gasp.

"Oh God, no! Matt, look at this. What will people think?"

"After the test results come back, we'll have a news conference and explain how I was set up. Everything will be all right."

Lynn began to cry. "Why is this happening? Our life was so perfect."

"I know. But we'll get through this."

"Who would do something like this?"

"I don't know. I doubt if it's the State Bar."

"I hope not."

"Tom told me I was making a lot of enemies. I guess he knew what he was talking about."

"We can't let them beat us," Lynn said. "This really pisses me off. You know it?"

"You and me both."

"They think they can scare us into backing off. They must be really worried about what we're doing. The bastards."

"Who are *they*?" Matt asked.

"I don't know—bankers, finance people."

Matt said, "Yes, but there are a lot of people who fit into that category, but I don't think they are linked together in any manner."

"True, it's probably some officers or directors at a bank or finance company who has or will soon be hurt by our campaign."

"Maybe Tom is right; we should back off awhile and let things die down," Matt said.

"No, we can't give in. Let's go on the offensive."

"Huh?"

"It's time to open offices in Houston and San Antonio," Lynn said.

"Are you serious?"

"Yes, if they think they can intimidate us they're in for a rude awakening."

Matt laughed. "Where did I get you? You've got more balls than a Marine drill sergeant."

"Thank you. I love you too."

# 10

The crowd of reporters began to assemble in the Canary room at the Marriott Hotel. It had just been announced that the judge had denied the temporary injunction sought by the State Bar of Texas and Matt was ecstatic. Now with test results back proving he had been drugged, he was elated. Lynn went up to the microphone and tapped it with her finger. The tapping sound could be heard quite well, so she motioned for Matt to begin the news conference. He grabbed Dr. Monroe's arm, and they both walked up to the microphone.

"Ladies and gentlemen," Matt said. "Thank you for coming out on such short notice but, as you know, today the State Bar's Application for a temporary injunction was denied. This is a tremendous victory for freedom of speech, and I wanted to tell you all how pleased I am with the court's decision.

"Now you may be wondering who I have up here with me today," Matt continued. "This is my doctor, Dr. Frank Monroe. Dr. Monroe has had some tests done after the little incident you all covered so well a day or two ago. As I told many of you, I was drugged that night by a prostitute named Monica Sommers. She was hired to drug me and then do whatever she could to embarrass and humiliate me so I would lose credibility with the public."

Matt turned to the doctor and said, "Dr. Monroe, would you explain the test results?"

"Yes, Matt. The urine, taken the day after the incident, showed traces of a drug called Meddelin. This is a popular drug used by teenage boys at parties to liven things up and make the girls lose their sexual inhibitions. A small dose makes the user feel very relaxed, calm and light-headed. A larger dose can cause dizziness, slurred speech, difficulty walking, and even unconsciousness.

"I feel confident the prostitute photographed with Matt gave him this drug."

"Dr. Monroe, how is this medication dispensed?"

"It comes in a white powder, and when dropped in any liquid, dissolves almost instantaneously."

"Wouldn't Mr. Coleman have seen it?" another reporter asked.

"No. When it is dissolved, it's a clear liquid."

"Do you have any idea who would want to embarrass Mr. Coleman?"

"No, but I think Matt can speak on that topic."

"Yes, as a matter of fact. We managed to find Monica Sommers, and she has told us a man with a German accent paid her $500 to drug me."

"Mr. Coleman," a reporter said. "Are you going to press charges against her?"

"No, I've promised not to press charges, as long as she continues to cooperate in finding out who hired her."

"Mr. Coleman," a third reporter asked, "what are your plans now that the court has denied the State Bar's temporary injunction application?"

"I'm glad you asked that. We've decided to open offices in Houston and San Antonio this month. And if everything goes well, we'll open offices in El Paso, Corpus Christi, and Amarillo by the end of the year."

"Mr. Coleman," the first reporter said. "Do you know if the State Bar of Texas will appeal the court's decision today?"

"I wouldn't know. You'll have to ask them. . . . Okay, that's all for today. Thanks again for coming out."

After the news conference, Matt and Lynn decided to drive back to the office. On the way, they decided to stop at Campisi's for lunch. The noon news was just coming on.

"In Dallas just a few minutes ago Matt Coleman held a news conference with his doctor to explain how he had been drugged by a prostitute who had been hired to embarrass and humiliate him in hopes of putting a stop to his crusade against banks and financial institutions, this on the heels of the 111th District Court's decision today not to grant a temporary injunction against the Debt Relief Centers, Inc.

"On Wall Street, financial stocks took a nosedive on fears that today's action will result in thousands of attorneys adopting Matt Coleman's evangelistic approach to marketing bankruptcies. If they are as successful as Matt Coleman has been, many financial institutions will suffer catastrophic losses as hundreds of thousands of Americans flock to the bankruptcy court to rid themselves of their debts."

"God, I can't believe what's happening," Matt said. "I never expected your little ad campaign to have such a profound effect on the country."

"It's not the ad campaign itself, Matt. It's you. You've taken this thing to heart. You believe in it now, and so you've become very convincing."

"You think so?"

"Yes."

"Well, we'll see how convincing I am tomorrow when I address the Dallas Bar Association luncheon."

"Hmm. That should be interesting. I'm surprised you accepted their invitation."

"How could I refuse an opportunity to explain my position to my colleagues?"

"I'm sure they invited you just to ridicule you."

"I don't think so. There are a lot of attorneys who don't like their advertising censored. I'll have some friends in the audience. I'm sure."

That night Matt prepared for his luncheon speech. He wasn't preaching to his usual flock so he knew he'd have to take a different approach to win over his audience. There wouldn't be the hatred and distrust of financial institutions for him to tap into with this audience. He'd have to be more logical, more precise with his facts and concentrate on his constitutional right of free speech.

***

The Belo Mansion was packed with members of the bar and local media. Matt suddenly felt sick as he sat at the head table looking out at hundreds of his colleagues. He questioned his decision to speak before them. Why was he here? He didn't need this.

"Ladies and gentlemen," the president said, "Today we have with us a man who has turned the legal profession upside down these last few months. Matt Coleman has single-handedly built the largest bankruptcy practice in the state of Texas almost overnight, sent financial stocks crashing, defeated the State Bar of Texas on its own turf, and successfully torpedoed a bizarre attempt, just two days ago, to smear and discredit him. We're very grateful that Matt has agreed to address us today. Ladies and gentlemen, Matt Coleman."

Matt got up and bowed to the polite applause from the audience. As he moved to the microphone, he had a sinking feeling, panic overcame him, and he couldn't remember what he had planned to say. He looked out over the sea of faces and almost fainted. He shook his head and took a drink from a glass of water that someone handed him. The room was deadly silent.

He swallowed, tried to smile and finally said, "Thank you for that very generous introduction. I'm afraid it's somewhat exaggerated, but I have enjoyed some measure of success of late in spreading an important message to the people of Dallas and the great state of Texas.

"My wife was telling me yesterday that the reason I've been so successful is that I truly believe in what I'm telling people. That's when it hit me. The reason I feel so strongly about what I've been preaching is my own experience as a child. You see. I personally felt the debilitating effect of excessive credit on the family.

"When I was young, my brother and I used to spend a month each summer with my grandparents out in California. We loved them dearly and always looked forward to the visit. My grandparents had been married thirty years and were still deeply in love. Their love spilled over to everyone they knew and especially to my brother and me. My grandparents weren't rich, but they had all the essentials of life. Unfortunately, I remember now quite vividly. One night I was awakened by screaming. You don't know how upset I was as my grandparents never argued. Each scream was like a knife piercing my heart. I got violently ill. It was as if they had suddenly become each other's worst enemy the way they were carrying on. And do you know what they were arguing about? Credit cards.

"My grandmother had been hooked by the slick Madison Avenue advertisers into thinking she needed a lot of things that they could have done without. She believed all *her* family and friends who told her she had to have credit cards in this modern age to be happy. Likewise, my grandfather believed all *his* family and friends who insisted that good credit was an essential element of success. It's not that family and friends lied. They were just repeating what their family and friends had told them and what Madison Avenue reinforced in its billion-dollar advertising campaign to dupe the American people."

"My life changed after that night. I had trouble sleeping. My grandparents went for days without talking to each other. The love that once flowed between them turned to bare tolerance. Life became a day-to-day chore rather than a joyful experience. My parents would have helped them out financially, but my grandparents were too proud to accept financial assistance. In time my grandparent's marriage failed, and now I visit each of them in different cities. They are both sadly alone, their love severed by greed and cold hard plastic.

"Unfortunately, their situation is not unique. It's an everyday experience for most middle-class families. That's why today most marriages fail. Big business has sucked the life out of the American family."

"From a legal standpoint, this is all very good, right? As bankruptcies rise to record levels, families disintegrate. The divorce business has never been better. As families break up crime rises and the criminal courts are filled to the brim. The future is bright for those of us who make a living out of human misery.

"Everybody who is thrilled about this situation, stand up and cheer!

A dead silence prevailed over the luncheon crowd.

"What's the matter? . . . Aren't you happy that business is so good? Or do you have the same empty feeling inside that I'm feeling? What's wrong with our legal profession? I'll tell you what's wrong. We've become the coroners of our wretched society. When one of our citizens gives out, we're called to sanitize the scene of the crime.

We're paid quite handsomely to make each citizen's social demise nice and legal, so our reputation for having a free and democratic society is not soiled.

"When I first started to do bankruptcies, it was so depressing I could hardly stand it. But then when my wife and Professor Swensen explained how the American people have been the victims of the credit conspiracy, I realized that bankruptcy was not so bad. It was good in fact. It was the only way the average American could ever again be free. This is the message I bring the American people. Bankruptcy is the ultimate loophole that will liberate you from a lifetime of oppression.

"Some people say what I preach is irresponsible. Well, as an attorney I must be my clients' advocate. I must advise them to do what's best for them. If they're in bondage and I know how to set them free, I'm duty bound to point out the way. My duty is not to Wall Street, not to Madison Avenue nor is it to Washington. To them, I may be irresponsible, but in reality, I'm simply true to my oath as an attorney.

"So, now you know. That's what Matt Coleman is all about. He's just another attorney, like each and every one of you, looking out for his clients the best way he knows how. Thank you."

There was a moment of silence, and then a few people in the audience began to clap. Matt smiled and bowed slightly to them. Then more and more people joined in until the audience was giving Matt a rousing round of applause. Matt smiled and waved at the crowd. Finally, several people stood up, and before long Matt was the proud recipient of a standing ovation.

That evening Matt took Lynn out to celebrate. He never expected to get such a warm reaction from his colleagues, and it felt good. He was on top of the world, and he wanted to savor every minute of it.

"That part about your dream was wonderful, Matt," Lynn said. "Where in the hell did you come up with that?"

"It was true. I did have that dream the night after I was drugged."

"You never told me your grandparents had financial troubles."

"I had forgotten about it. But the dream brought it all back quite vividly. Now I can appreciate what kids are going through today. No wonder we have such a problem with gangs, runaways, and suicides. There is so much stress and negative emotion in the home today kids don't want to stay there. They must feel they have to escape to keep their sanity. Unfortunately, they usually end up some place worse."

"It's pretty sad, but at least you've started people thinking," Lynn said. "I was really proud of you up there."

"Don't tell me you're starting to become a believer too," He asked.

"Well, I must confess the money doesn't seem as important anymore. Maybe we should cut back on our fees so more people can afford to file."

"That's a wonderful idea. We're doing such a big volume we'll still make plenty of money."

The next day, a press release was sent out from the Debt Relief Centers, Inc. as follows: "To make it possible for more Texans to regain their economic freedom the Debt Relief Centers are cutting their fees in half. Now for only seven hundred-fifty dollars and a filing fee, anyone can file bankruptcy through our offices. The staffs of the Debt Relief Centers are looking forward to helping more and more Texans improve the quality of their lives by freeing themselves from the shackles of economic tyranny."

# 11

It was nearly two o'clock when Doug Barnes drove up in front of the Men's Club. The parking attendant gave him a valet parking ticket and drove off. After paying the cover charge, Barnes strolled into the club and scanned the room until he spotted Hans Schultz at the bar with a dancer hovering over him. He went over and sat down beside him. The dancer got down on her knees and dangled her breasts in front of them erotically. Barnes ignored her.

"So, what's up?" Hans said. "You sounded upset over the phone."

"I *am* upset! What in the hell happened with Monica Sommers?"

"I don't know. Monica's a pro. I've used her before, but this guy is a tough son of a bitch."

"Well she not only failed you miserably, she told them you hired her to seduce Matt," Barnes complained.

"I know. I'm going to take care of that bitch, don't worry."

"You better because if she identifies you, you'll have to disappear."

"I know. Don't worry. I've got it covered."

"I think we've seriously underestimated Mr. Coleman," Barnes said. "He's totally out of control, and we've got to put a lid on him soon. Do you have anything on him yet?"

"Yes, I've got his office manager on board."

"Good, how long will it take for him to do his job?"

"Thirty to sixty days, I would imagine."

"That's too long. This guy is moving fast. There's no telling what kind of damage he'll do in sixty days."

"What about the FBI?"

"I got a man who's going to see them today. In a couple of weeks, we'll have his ex-wife spill the beans to the U.S. Trustee. It should be downhill from there."

"That's good, but FBI investigations take forever. It might be six months before anything happens."

"Well, I've checked his background, and he's squeaky clean. His wife's clean too. I'm not sure there is anything legally we can do to stop him."

"Well you've got to stop him, whatever it takes to do it," Barnes reiterated.

Hans raised his eyebrows and said, "Whatever it takes?"

"That's what I said. Whatever it takes."

He smiled. "Fine. Consider it done."

"Good."

Barnes left, and Hans resumed his flirtations with the topless dancer. She sat down on the bar directly in front of him, dangling her legs on both sides of him. Then she leaned over and brushed her nipples across his cheeks. He smiled and then flashed a fifty-dollar bill in front of her. She leaned down and grabbed it with her teeth, then slid off the table and stood beside him.

"Thanks, honey," she said. "Your friend is an asshole."

"I know," Hans replied. "He doesn't appreciate the finer things in life."

She sat down in his lap, put an arm around him and asked, "So why do you work for a jerk like that?"

"He pays me a lot of money."

"To do what?"

"You ask too many questions."

"I'm just curious."

"I'm kind of like a private investigator. I follow people around, check out what they're doing . . . you know . . . intelligence work. Everything's highly confidential. That's why I can't discuss it with you."

"Oh."

Hans gently pushed the dancer off his lap and stood up. He smiled and said, "Gotta go. I'll see you when you get off work."

She gave him a seductive wink and said, "Bye, honey. Be careful."

Hans left the club and headed downtown. He parked in a lot next to McDonald's across from the Federal Building. A long-haired man dressed in military fatigues immediately approached him.

"Sir, I haven't eaten today. Could you spare a dollar?"

"Sure," he said as he pulled an envelope from his coat pocket and handed it to the man.

"You're so kind, sir. God bless you," he said.

***

Hans got in his car and watched the man walk to the corner and join a group of street people engaged in conversation. He glanced at the south end of the courthouse and then back at the men. He looked at his watch and waited. About ten minutes later Hans spotted Matt coming out of the courthouse. He sat up in his seat as Matt waited for the light. When it changed, Matt started to cross the street. The man in the military fatigues moved toward Matt. Matt altered his path to avoid running into him.

"Sir, I haven't eaten all day. Could you spare a dollar?"

119

Matt frowned and tried to ignore the man. Then the man grabbed Matt's arm and jerked him around.

"What the hell!" Matt said as he tried to pull away. Suddenly Matt was surrounded by street people.

"You can't spare a lousy dollar, you rich bitch!" one of them said.

"Get a damn job, leave me alone," Matt replied. He tried to push his way through the crowd but was repulsed.

"Okay, take my money. What the hell!" Matt said and then pulled out his wallet and threw his money at them. The money fell to the ground, but no one picked it up. There was dead silence broken only by a *click*. Matt saw the big blade sparkle in the sunlight. He looked around for an avenue of escape, but they had him surrounded. The men started to close in on him. He spun around desperately searching for help. The man lunged at him, and he felt the blade graze his stomach. Blood oozed from the wound, saturating the front of his shirt.

"You cut me, you bastard!" Matt shrieked. "Oh God! I'm bleeding." The man lunged for him again, but Matt managed to pull one of his assailants in front of him to act as a shield. The poor bastard screamed as the knife sliced through his hand, nearly severing his thumb. In the ruckus Matt again tried to run but was tackled and wrestled to the ground. The street people held Matt down while the man with the knife moved in for the kill. Suddenly a tall, muscular black man came running out of the parking lot tossing the street people out of his way. The man with the knife looked up just in time to see the black man's fist coming down on him hard. He fell back onto the street dazed, then he got up quickly and ran off.

Hans slammed his fist on the dashboard, muttered some obscenities and then started the car. He backed up quickly, came to a stop, and shifted into drive. As he took off, his tires squealed, and he left a trail of burnt rubber. Matt watched the car disappear down Commerce Street. The black man came over and helped Matt up.

"Thank you so much, Leon," Matt said. "You saved my life."

"Are you okay? You're bleeding."

Matt looked down at his blood-soaked shirt. He pulled up his shirt and examined the wound. "It's just a flesh wound. Nothing to worry about. Boy, am I glad you showed up. How did you know I was in trouble?"

"I just happened to look your way, and I saw those guys crowding around you."

"Boy, I never heard of street people running in packs before."

"Those weren't street people. No way."

"That's what they looked like."

"I've never seen any of those guys before. I know all the street people around here."

"Hmm. I wonder who they were?"

"I don't know, but somebody's doesn't like your ass."

"I guess not."

"I can't believe you risked your life to save me. I'm so grateful."

"Hey, you're one of my best customers. I can't let anybody mess with you. Besides, you helped me out of that jam last Christmas. I'm glad I had an opportunity to pay you back."

"Well I'd like to say we're even but I think saving my life puts you way ahead."

"Don't worry about it. I may need you to file bankruptcy for me. My wife lost her job."

"Oh, no. . . . Well, call my office if you're serious. Tell them you have a free bankruptcy coming."

"Really?"

"Yeah, I think you've earned it."

"Thanks. I'll call your office. You better go get someone to look at that cut."

"I will. Thanks again."

Matt got in his car. He called Lynn on his mobile phone and asked her to meet him at home. He didn't explain why so she wouldn't be upset. The bleeding had stopped, but Matt was feeling a bit weak and light-headed. When he pulled into his spot in front of the apartment, she ran out to see him.

"What's wrong?" she said and then saw his blood-soaked shirt. "Oh my God! What happened to you?"

"A pack of street people tried to kill me."

"What?" she said and then began to inspect the wound.

"Down in front of the courthouse. They came at me with knives. Thank God Leon saw them."

"Leon?"

"Yeah, Leon Cash, you remember. The parking lot attendant at the Federal Building."

"Right. You should go to the hospital."

"No, it's not that bad."

"I don't know. You've lost a lot of blood."

"It looks worse than it is."

"Hmm. . . . Come on inside so I can clean it."

"Okay," Matt said. They went inside the apartment and into the bathroom. Matt took off his shirt, and Lynn began to clean the wound.

"How did he stop them?"

"You've never seen him, I guess."

"No, I don't think I have."

"He's about 6' 5" and weighs 275."

"Hmm. You're lucky he bothered to help you. Not many people would get involved in a street fight."

"He and I are friends. I see him every day."

"Even so—"

"He's married and has three kids."

"Really?"

"Yeah, and last year he bought them all a bunch of nice presents. He spent every extra cent he had for them. He was so excited about it. He couldn't wait to see their faces when they opened all of them. Then two days before Christmas he was robbed and all the gifts were stolen."

"Oh my God, no. That's terrible."

"He was devastated, so I gave him four hundred bucks to buy new presents."

"You did? That was sure nice. . . . I'm kind of surprised he accepted it though."

"I told him I had taken up a collection from the attorneys in the courthouse. It wasn't true, but I thought he would be more likely to take the money if told him that."

"Well, that turned out to be a good investment."

"I guess so."

Lynn put a bandage over the wound and then carefully taped it so it wouldn't fall off.

"Okay, all done."

"Thank you. I can't believe my luck lately."

"You should call the police and report this."

"What are they going to do?"

"Find the bastards and put them behind bars."

"I just hate to get any more publicity right now. . . . You know the press is just looking for some way to smear me."

"You were the victim here."

"I know, but somehow they'll twist it into something entirely different. Let's just forget it happened."

"I don't know if that's wise."

"It's the best thing. I'm sure."

"Okay."

"What time is it?"

"Three o'clock."

"I've got to go back to the office."

"Why?"

"Tom booked an appointment for me at four."

"You're kidding. Why can't someone else handle it? You should stay home and rest."

"He said it was a complicated case and he thought I had better handle it. I'm fine, really. I'll go do this one appointment and then come right home."

"I'll come with you. You shouldn't be driving."

"Okay, let's go."

When they walked into the office, a middle-aged man was seated in the reception area. Matt went into his office to clear off his desk. Lynn went to her office to do paperwork while Matt was in a conference. When his desk was clean, he came out and greeted the new client.

"Hi, Mr. Green. I'm Matt Coleman."

The man stood up and said, "Hello, I'm Wallace Green."

"Come on in and we'll get started."

Mr. Green followed Matt into his office and sat down in a maroon side chair in front of Matt's desk. He scanned the room noting the pictures of Lynn on Matt's credenza. Matt sat down and smiled.

"So, what can I do for you?'

"I'm interested in filing bankruptcy. I saw one of your ads on TV."

"Good. . . . Are you married?"

"No."

"Do you have your own business?"

"Yes, I'm a landscape contractor."

"Residential or commercial?"

"Residential primarily. I've been doing the irrigation and landscaping for Bruce Westerfield Homes out in Arlington."

"So what does the problem seem to be?"

"I lost my contract. Bruce merged with another builder, and his landscape guy underbid me."

"Really? That's too bad. Do you have any other customers?"

"No, I'm out looking, but by the time I find another contract and then wait sixty to ninety days to start getting paid my credit will be ruined."

"What kind of debt do you have?"

"A home loan, credit cards, and a few medical bills."

"So, do you have any cash, stocks, bonds, or other investment assets?"

"No, just the cash in my checking account."

"How much is that?"

"About six hundred dollars."

"Well, cash is not exempt so be sure you don't have more than $1,000 on the day you file. Otherwise, the trustee might want it."

"What's a trustee?"

"He's a person the court appoints to oversee your bankruptcy. His job is to collect as much as possible for your creditors, so if you have a significant amount of cash, he may want you to give it to him."

"I'll make sure I don't have more than $500 in my account on the day I file."

"You can't have cash in your personal possession either. All your property must be disclosed including cash on hand."

"How would they know whether I had any cash or not?"

"You're going to have to swear that your bankruptcy schedules are true and correct. You don't want to commit perjury and end up going to jail. There's no reason not to disclose everything. The exemption laws are very generous. Your home, cars, household furnishings, IRAs, pension plans, clothing, and jewelry are all exempt up to $30,000."

"Oh . . . okay."

"About how much credit card debt do you have?"

"A hundred thousand or so."

"What about trade debt?"

"Thirty thousand."

"Do you have any income at all right now?"

"No. Not yet."

"Then you'll probably have to file a chapter 7 since you have to have a regular income to file chapter 13."

"Whatever you recommend."

"Do you have any business assets?"

"Not to speak of. I just have my tools."

"We'll take a look at those. We may be able to claim them exempt as tools of the trade."

"Good, I don't want to lose them."

Matt continued to question Mr. Green about his assets and liabilities, and then they did a budget. When the bankruptcy schedules were completed, Matt explained what would happen next.

"In about ten days you'll get a bankruptcy notice. It will have the date and time for your creditor's meeting. Be sure and put that on your calendar because you'll need to be there. Somebody from our office will also be there to go through it with you."

"Do I have to go before a judge?"

"No, just the trustee. It should only take ten or fifteen minutes. In the meantime, if any creditors call, don't talk to them. Just have them call us."

"Good. I'm sick of those bastards calling and harassing me."

"Well, once you file there's an automatic stay—a court order that goes into effect that prohibits them from calling you anymore. So you should get some immediate relief from the harassment."

"Great. I feel so much better already."

"All right then, thanks for coming in. If you have any questions, please feel free to call us."

Mr. Green and Matt stood up. They shook hands and then Matt saw him to the door. After he had left, Matt went directly to Lynn's office.

"I'm done, honey. Let's get out of here."

Lynn looked up and smiled. "Okay, just give me a minute to finish this report. Start shutting down the computers and I'll be right there."

"Okay, hurry up. I'm really tired."

"I'll be just a minute."

Matt left and walked around shutting off all the computers and printers. Lynn walked in as he was shutting off the copier.

"Let's go," she said.

Matt shut the lights as they left each room and then locked the front door. On the way home, they stopped at the Black-Eyed Pea for dinner. They had the waitress bring them a couple of strawberry margaritas and then sat back and relaxed.

"What a day," Matt said.

"I know. You must be exhausted. I'll give you a nice massage when we get home."

"That would be nice."

"Tom gave me the month-end reports while you were with Mr. Green."

"Oh really, how did they look?"

"Unbelievable. Filings are up 30 percent since the Bar Association luncheon."

"Jesus, are we getting backlogged?"

"No, the staff is doing very well at keeping up. Tom's been letting them work overtime."

"That's expensive."

"I know, but we don't want to increase overhead until we're sure the volume increase is permanent."

"That makes sense. You and Tom are doing a great job managing the business."

"Thanks, but sometimes I wonder how it all gets done."

"Don't you wish we could go back to Alaska?"

"Oh God, do I. We had a wonderful time, didn't we?"

"The best," Matt said.

"I'll talk to Tom. Maybe we can get away for a few days next month."

"You think so?"

"Sure, remember we promised ourselves we'd enjoy our money."

"That's right. Don't ever let me forget that."

"I won't. Trust me."

They laughed, and Lynn picked up her drink and began sipping it. Matt stared into her eyes. She put the drink down and said, "What are you staring at?"

"You're so beautiful. . . . I love you."

"Don't get any ideas. You're not in any condition to be fooling around tonight. You're a wounded man."

"This little flesh wound isn't going to stop me."

"It's not? Hmm," She said as she flipped off her shoe and began caressing Matt's thigh with her foot.

"Don't do that unless you want me to make love to you right here."

"You wouldn't dare."

Matt slid out of the booth and slipped over to Lynn's side. He put his arm around her and began kissing her passionately. She broke away laughing, "Matt, not here! Are you crazy?"

Matt laughed. He was embarrassed as he looked around and saw half a dozen people watching them. He let Lynn go and sat up straight.

"Get on your side!" Lynn said. "God, you're a maniac. I can't take you anywhere."

"It's your fault. You provoked me," Matt replied and then returned to the other side of the booth. A second later the waitress showed up with some bread and took their orders. After dinner, they went home.

Matt took a shower and then Lynn gave him the massage he had been promised. By the time she finished, Matt was sound asleep. She sat and listened to him breathe for a while, then covered him up, got undressed, and put on a nightgown. She looked at the clock radio and saw it was 9:55. After taking one last look at her sleeping husband she went into the living room and turned on the TV. The ten o'clock news was just coming on.

"Good evening, ladies and gentlemen. I'm Marsha Smith here with Donald Seidman with the Channel 4 News. Donald."

"Yes, Marsha. Financial stocks continued to take it on the chin today on Wall Street as bankruptcy filings in North Texas soar. Quarterly reports for many Texas banks came out today, and earnings are down from a year ago. Some banks even reported losses for the quarter. An analyst with Merrill Lynch told Channel 4 News today that the situation is likely to get worse unless Congress takes measures to stop the flood of bankruptcy filings in Texas started by Dallas attorney, Matt Coleman. . . . Back to you, Marsha.

Marsha continued, "Senate Banking Committee hearings on the subject are scheduled for next week, and on the witness list is Dallas' own Matt Coleman and Professor Swensen from SMU. The fear on the Hill is that the bankruptcy crisis in Texas will spread to other parts of the country. Hopefully, Congress will develop a strategy to avoid that catastrophe."

"Fires continued to rage out of control in Southern California's Angeles National Forest. The fires have already destroyed five homes and charred twenty thousand acres of precious watershed. Today fire fighters built a fire break between the southern perimeter of the fires and the Silver Creek Resort and Hotel. When the blaze reached the fire break, helicopters dropped thousands of gallons of water on it and, fortunately, the Silver Creek Resort is still standing. Firefighters hope to have the fire contained sometime tomorrow. . . . Donald."

"Well Marsha, we have another story tonight involving attorney Matt Coleman. In Dallas today police found the body of a young prostitute drifting down the Trinity River. The coroner has identified the woman as Monica Sommers. Ms. Sommers, a known prostitute, was recently in the news for allegedly drugging Dallas attorney Matt Coleman, in an apparent blackmail scheme. Police have commenced a homicide investigation but have refused to speculate as to who might be a suspect in that killing."

"Oh my God!" Lynn said. She ran into the bedroom and turned on the light.

"Matt! Matt!"

Matt sat up, shaded the glare from his eyes and looked at Lynn curiously.

"Huh. . . . What's wrong?"

"Monica Sommers is dead."

"Who?"

"Monica Sommers."

"She's dead? What happened to her?"

"She was murdered and dumped in the Trinity River."

"Oh shit! ... I wonder who did it."

"The same person who wants you out of business. Oh, Matt! I'm so scared. What are we going to do?"

"Don't panic, honey. It may not be as bad as it looks."

"Matt! Those street people were probably hired to kill you! And now Monica has been murdered. Somebody wants you dead!"

"I know, I know. I guess we better call the police."

Matt went to the telephone and picked it up.

Lynn said, "Did you know you've got to testify before the Senate next week?"

"What?!"

"It was on the news. They've subpoenaed you for next week. You haven't got served yet?"

Matt hung up the phone. "No. Shit. That's all I need."

Lynn gave Matt a sympathetic look. "You won't be alone. They've subpoenaed Professor Swensen too."

"Thank God for small favors."

"It will be okay. This will give you an opportunity to tell your side of the story."

Matt sighed. "Yeah, if I live that long."

# 12

Matt was nervous as he got off the big jet after landing at Baltimore Washington International Airport. He had never even visited Capitol Hill before, yet in just a few hours he was scheduled to testify before the Senate Banking Committee. Fortunately, Professor Swensen was also going to testify, so he'd be there to help him answer the senators' questions. Lynn stayed home to help Tom as the volume of bankruptcies was still climbing. As they got off the plane, they saw a man holding up a sign with their names on it. They went over to him.

"Hi. I'm Matt Coleman."

"Welcome. My name is Arthur. I'll be your driver while you're in town."

"Good," Matt said. "This is Professor Swensen."

"Nice to meet you. I've been instructed to drive you to Capitol Hill at once."

"All right. We'll need to go get our luggage."

"Of course."

After getting their luggage, Arthur drove them to Capitol Hill. An aide showed them to a small conference room where they would wait. She told them it would be thirty minutes to an hour before they would be called.

"So why do you think they subpoenaed me, Professor?"

"Oh, they just wanted to see you in person to size you up. You started this flood of bankruptcies so they figured they'd better study you to see if you'd give them some insight into how to stop it."

"So they're trying to figure out my weaknesses?"

"Exactly. If they can discredit you in any way, it will help to get everybody back in line."

"Great . . . and I have to put up with this shit."

"They have the tanks, remember."

"Umm."

"You might have a friend or two on the committee, though."

"Really?"

"Yes, Senator Goss from New Jersey is a big consumer advocate. He's never had any support from the financial sector. He might stick up for you. In fact, he said he was going to try to stop by and say hello before the hearings began."

"Who should I be worrying about?"

"Senator Bennington. He's the senator from Delaware."

"That makes sense. Delaware's the credit card capital of the world."

"Exactly. So he'll be out to eat you alive."

The two men turned as they heard the door open.

A short grey-haired gentlemen and a pretty young lady walked in. Matt and the professor stood up.

"Hello, gentlemen. I'm Senator Goss and this is my aide, Sandy."

"Hi, nice to meet you," Matt said.

"I just wanted to personally thank you for what you've done these past few months. It's about time somebody stood up for the consumer. I just hope you can keep your momentum going so finally Congress will do something to protect the American people from the banking and finance industries.

"They control the American people today like a cocaine dealer controls an addict," Senator Goss continued. "They brainwash us with their media campaigns and then pick our pockets without us even realizing it. At least with the cocaine dealers, there are no hidden charges or fees. You know exactly what you are buying and what it costs. These people are greedy bastards who will stop at nothing to pillage the American people."

"Are there others in the Senate who feel like you do?"

"Yes, but most are afraid to speak out. They know what will happen to them if they join a movement against the people who control the purse strings and then fail. The people who control the finance industry are an invisible government. What you've launched, Mr. Coleman, whether you know it or not, is the beginning of a coup. If you fail, you and everyone associated with you could be killed."

Matt stood silently for a moment and then replied, "So what can I do to be sure I don't fail?"

"Evidence. You've got to provide evidence that there is an illegal conspiracy against you. Evidence that the invisible government is at work trying to silence you. Then the Senate will have no other choice but to investigate."

The door opened again, and a member of the committee staff entered the room.

"Are you ready, gentlemen?"

Matt looked at Senator Goss and replied, "Yes, I suppose so."

"Good, follow me."

The two men followed the staff member into another conference room where the hearings would take place. One of them directed Matt to a table, and he and the professor took a seat. The chairman banged his gavel, and the hearing came to order. The clerk administered the oath to the witness.

"All right. If everyone will come to order, we'll commence our questioning of Mr. Coleman." The room became quiet, and the chairman continued, "Thank you, Mr. Coleman for appearing before this committee today," the chairman said.

"It's my distinct honor, sir."

"I'll start off by asking you a few questions that have been bothering me ever since you started your highly successful advertising campaign."

"I don't consider it an advertising campaign, sir. I'm just speaking out on issues that are important to me."

"You may have convinced the Dallas court of that, Mr. Coleman, but I'm not that naive. It's obvious you're speaking out for one reason and one reason only . . . and that is to enhance your business."

"You know, to be honest with you it might have started out that way. But early on I abandoned the original profit motive. You see, I've come to realize that what's more important here is to set the American consumer free."

"You sound very sincere, Mr. Coleman, but forgive me if I don't believe that you're not motivated by profit. You've admitted it was a scam in the beginning. Now you expect us to believe everything's changed."

"I didn't say it was a scam. I said in the beginning profit was an important element of what I was doing. Now profit is the least important aspect of what's going on at the Debt Relief Centers. What is important is that every day we help dozens of Americans regain their freedom and I'm proud of that."

"It sounds good, Mr. Coleman. But I still don't believe that profit is your last priority."

"You don't have to believe anything I say. I'm here because you asked me to come. I'll try to answer any question you might have for me, but I'm not here to try to convince you of anything."

"Very well. I'll yield the floor to the senator from Delaware since he has informed me he has quite a number of questions for you."

The gallery erupted in conversation as everyone's attention turned to Senator Bennington. The chairman banged his gavel, and the talking stopped.

"Thank you, Senator. Mr. Coleman, so you'd like this committee to believe that profit isn't your primary motive in what you've been doing these past few months?"

"That's the truth."

"I'm curious. Just how many bankruptcies have you filed this year so far?"

"The last count I saw was 4,201."

"That's amazing! How do you keep up with all of them?"

"Well, before we started our practice, we hired a consultant to help us set up a very efficient bankruptcy plant to process a large volume of business. The system has worked very well."

"The committee has viewed several of your TV spots, as you call them, and I find your conspiracy theory quite imaginative but bearing little resemblance to reality."

"You're entitled to your opinion, and I'm sure you'll agree I'm entitled to mine."

"Of course, but that doesn't give you the right to slander the fine financial institutions of this nation and brainwash the American people."

"No, sir. It's not slander if it's the truth. Professor Swensen has very carefully documented the conspiracy over the past forty years. All this time people have believed that good credit is the most important thing in their life, next to good health. But this is fallacy. People would be much better off without credit. We've done calculations to show that more than one-third of the average American citizen's income goes to paying interest. Interest that often is totally unnecessary if the consumer had the self-discipline to save rather than borrow."

"Have you ever studied economics, Mr. Coleman?"

"Yes, in college."

"Then you should know that spending is what fuels our economy and credit greatly enhances the amount consumers spend."

"Maybe so, but I don't think people should be forced into economic servitude just to provide giant corporations big profits."

"Okay, Mr. Coleman. If there's a conspiracy, could you identify for the committee all those involved in this conspiracy?"

"That would be impossible. There are too many of them."

"Then tell us who the leaders are so we can subpoena them and get to the bottom of your accusations."

Matt leaned over and whispered to Professor Swensen. He shook his head affirmatively. Matt stood up straight, looked Senator Bennington in the eye and said, "Do you really want to know?"

"Mr. Coleman, if you think this is all some kind of joke, please let me assure it is not. Now if you have information about a conspiracy to enslave the American people, this committee demands that you give it to them."

"Very well. Then all you have to do to see the conspiracy is to open your eyes and look around. It's open and obvious. Just turn on the radio, watch television for a few minutes, open your mail, or surf the internet. Every day the American people are barraged with a relentless campaign to entice them into buying things they don't need with money they don't have."

"Good God! Mr. Coleman," Senator Bennington exclaimed. "That's no conspiracy, that's capitalism!"

"Exactly. And just as the conspirators have the right to try to enslave the American people, so do I have the right to try to set them free."

"That is nonsense, sir. There are no conspirators, and there is no conspiracy. I am outraged by your frivolous accusations."

Matt smiled. "I'm not surprised by your outrage since you are part of the very conspiracy that I've been warning people about."

"Mr. Chairman, Mr. Coleman's behavior is contemptuous. He has slandered this committee, and I demand he be sanctioned."

"Mr. Chairman," Senator Goss said. "If I could have the floor, I believe I can help Mr. Coleman clarify his position."

"Mr. Bennington, will you yield?" the chairman asked.

"Yes, I should like to hear this explanation."

"Very well, Senator Goss. You have the floor."

"Thank you. Mr. Coleman, let me see if I can help you clarify your position."

"Certainly."

"Do you really think that the members of this committee are consciously a part of this so-called conspiracy of yours?"

"I'm sure many of them don't realize it. This conspiracy is very subtle. They influence Congress with their lobbyists, big campaign contributions, and with the help of Madison Avenue, through their manipulation of public opinion."

"So you're saying over a period of time through the use of television, motion pictures, advertising, and the print media the American people have been convinced that they should live above their means and finance the deficit on credit cards."

"Yeah, kind of the way Congress operates this country."

Several members of the gallery burst out in laughter. The chairman gave them a dirty look.

"Exactly, but do you think bankruptcy is the only way out for these people?"

"Not for everyone, but there are a lot of people out there who could never pay off their credit card debt in a million years. For these people bankruptcy is their only hope."

"I understand you blame a lot of the social ills of this country on excessive credit. Is that true?"

"Most definitely. The high divorce rate in the country can be directly tied to the increased stress level in the home due to inadequate income or the excessive use of credit. And we all know the consequences of the breakup of the family unit; a decline in moral values, increased use of illegal drugs, gang activity, promiscuity, and a decline in religious affiliation."

"Aren't you oversimplifying it?"

"Obviously, but excessive credit has been a very important element in producing all of these social ills."

"So this isn't an active conspiracy, right? It's just something that has evolved. Am I correct?"

"Yes, but it *is* active, and it's spiraling out of control. The finance industry has gotten so greedy its leaders will do anything to lure innocent consumers into a lifetime of bondage. They start with high school and college students extending credit to them before they even have jobs. Many of these poor kids are candidates for bankruptcy before they are old enough to drink."

"Thank you, Mr. Coleman. I yield to Mr. Bennington."

Mr. Bennington continued, "If it is an active conspiracy, who is its leader?"

"I don't know how it's organized. I'm not sure if there is a single leader, a committee, or what."

"So you can't give us a name?"

"I can't give you a name, but there is someone directing the operation. I know that for a fact."

"How is that?"

"As you know there have already been several carefully conceived attempts to compromise me. Luckily none of them has worked."

"So you think we should get the FBI to investigate this conspiracy against you," he said facetiously.

"Actually, that wouldn't be a bad idea."

"I understand much of your theory has come from Professor Swensen at SMU?"

"Yes, he explained the conspiracy to me, but it doesn't matter how it evolved or who controls it. The mere fact that it exists is the reason it must be destroyed."

"If he is right, then why is he the only person in academic circles who holds this view? My research indicates he has been unable to get any support from his colleagues around the country. Isn't it true that the only reason you support him is that his theories help you sell bankruptcies?"

"No, none of his colleagues support him because they're afraid."

"Afraid of what?"

"Afraid of the conspirators coming down on them and ruining their lives."

"If this cartel exists why hasn't it come down on Professor Swensen already?"

"Because he has been so vocal about it, if something happened to him people would suspect he had been right. Their strategy has been to label him a paranoid eccentric. As long as no one believed him, he wouldn't be dangerous."

"But now you've brought him into the limelight. Millions of people believe his theory because you've convinced them it's true. If they are so powerful, why are you still alive?"

"Only by the grace of God. They tried to kill me last week."

The gallery erupted in excited conversation. The chairman smacked his gavel on the podium and demanded order.

"Someone tried to kill you?" the senator laughed.

"Yes, a group of street people tried to murder me in downtown Dallas."

"My word! And you can prove the banking industry was behind it."

"Obviously, Senator, I cannot."

"I believe your time is up, Senator," the chairman said.

"If you'll indulge me, Mr. Chairman, I have one last question."

"Very well, go ahead."

"Mr. Coleman, are you familiar with Professor Swensen's academic background?"

"Not intimately."

"Well, perhaps Professor Swensen hasn't told you why he never received his doctorate."

"No, he hasn't."

"Well, correct me if I'm wrong, Professor, but I believe his doctorate thesis was on this very topic. The control of the nation by a handful of wealthy businessmen and it was soundly rejected by the institution as rubbish!"

Matt looked over at Professor Swensen. He shrugged and took a deep breath. Matt turned back to the committee members.

"That doesn't surprise me, Senator. What educational institution would risk going against those who control their money? It would be financial suicide."

"Thank you, Mr. Coleman, for coming here today," the chairman said. "We'll be in touch if we need anything further from you."

As Professor Swensen and Matt left the hearing room, they were swamped by reporters. As they made their way through the crowd, the reporters threw many questions at them.

"Who do you think tried to kill you?" a reporter asked.

"I don't know, but I'm going to find out," Matt said.

"Professor Swensen, have there been threats on your life?" a third reporter asked.

"Yes, many times," the professor replied.

The committee aide finally got them out of the public area and escorted them back to the garage where a limousine was waiting. A tall man with short black hair was standing by the limo. The aide introduced them.

"This is Agent Paul Radcliff from the FBI," he said.

"Hello," Matt said as the two shook hands.

"If you don't mind, I'll ride with you to the airport."

"Sure," Matt said.

They all got in, and the limo drove off.

"So, are the Dallas police investigating the attempt on your life?"

"Yes, they said they would."

"Do they have any leads?"

"Not really. All but one witness has disappeared."

"Who's the witness?"

"A parking lot attendant. Luckily I knew him and he intervened when he saw me in trouble."

"Can I get his name? I'd like to talk to him."

"Sure, but why? It's not your jurisdiction."

"I've been instructed to verify the attack on your life. If someone is trying to kill you, the committee wants to find out who's behind it."

"Good. I'll sleep a lot better once they are behind bars."

Matt gave Agent Radcliff a long look, wondering if the FBI really would try to find his assailant. As the limousine pulled into the airport, the three men were silent. Finally, the big limousine pulled up in front of the terminal and came to a stop.

"Have a good flight home, gentlemen," Agent Radcliff said as he fumbled to find a card. He handed each of them one and said, "If you find out anything about your assailant give me a call, okay?"

# 13

In the weeks that followed there were many stories about Matt and the invisible government that the media was calling the Wall Street Cartel. Did it exist? If so, were the leaders of the cartel really trying to kill Matthew Coleman? Had he actually uncovered a sinister plot against the American people? Had they already lost our most precious treasure—liberty—without even realizing it? Many commentators acknowledged that much of what Matt said was true and commended him for awakening the American people. Others condemned him as just another opportunist with a get-rich scheme.

It didn't help when Professor Swensen signed a seven-figure deal for a new book, "Go Broke, Die Rich." It was to be a self-help book for the middle classes—a step by step manual on how to go from rags to riches. In the book, Swensen outlined his formula for success. Since the average middle-class American was paying more than a thousand dollars a month on interest payments to credit card companies with no hope of ever paying off the principal, he advocated filing bankruptcy and then investing that same thousand dollars each month. The net effect would be a dramatic shift of wealth from big business back to the middle classes where, he said, it belonged.

The problem with the theory was it failed to take human nature into consideration. Few people after filing bankruptcy and getting their fresh start would have the discipline to invest this sudden surplus of money. The temptation to spend it would be overwhelming, and most would miss this incredible opportunity to shift from being an interest payer to an interest earner.

Matt was annoyed by Professor Swensen's book deal and his short-sighted philosophy and tried to distance himself from it. He was beginning to envision something much grander and more important for the American people. He wanted no less than a rebirth of economic freedom and financial independence for all Americans. He believed that by freeing the middle classes from this economic straitjacket, there could be a rebirth of morality, a strengthening of the family, and a drastic decrease in crime and drug dealing. But he wasn't naive like Professor Swensen. He knew it would take a monumental effort to educate the American people and turn them away from materialism. He had no idea how to accomplish this, and at the moment had more pressing problems.

Early one morning, several weeks after the Senate hearing, Matt arrived at work and found Tom frantic.

"We just got a call from Wallace Green down at the courthouse. Joe didn't show up for the meeting."

"Is there anybody else around who can go?"

"No."

"Okay, just tell him I'm on my way. Do you have the file?"

"No, Joe has it."

"Shit! How am I supposed to do a 341 meeting without a file?"

"I can run a copy of the bankruptcy on the computer."

"No, that would take too much time. I'll just have to wing it."

"I'm sorry, Matt. Joe is usually very reliable."

Matt raced to the courthouse and was surprised to see a representative from the U.S. Trustee's office in the audience. He took his client aside.

"I'm sorry I'm late. Joe from our office was supposed to be here. I don't know what happened to him."

"It's okay. I'm just glad you got here. My ex-wife showed up."

"Really? Why would she be interested in this hearing?"

"She probably just wants to watch me hit bottom. She's a vindictive bitch."

"Well, don't worry about it. If she's not a creditor, I'll object to her asking any questions."

"Good."

The trustee finished up with the meeting that was in progress and the parties involved left. He flipped through his files, pulled one out and said, "Green."

Matt and Mr. Green went over to the table and sat down. Mr. Green's ex-wife joined them at the table. The trustee looked through the file and then said, "Mr. Green, do you swear to tell the truth?"

"Yes," he said.

"Mr. Coleman, you may proceed."

"Thank you. . . . Please state your name for the record."

"Wallace Peter Green."

"Mr. Green, I'm showing you the schedules and statement of affairs you filed in this case, and I ask you: Are you familiar with these documents?"

"Yes."

"Is everything stated therein true and correct to the best of your knowledge?"

"Yes."

"What kind of business are you in?"

"I'm a landscape contractor."

"What were the circumstances that caused you to file this bankruptcy?"

"I lost my only contract."

"Have you been able to replace it?"

"No, I've tried, but it may take months to find a new contract."

"So, you have no income now?"

"None."

"You own a home, correct?"

"Yes."

"And you're claiming it exempt along with your car, household furniture, clothing, jewelry, and an IRA, correct?"

"That's right."

"Pass the witness."

The trustee looked over at the ex-wife and said, "Ms. Green, do you have any questions?"

"I'm going to have to object to Ms. Green asking questions," Matt said. "I don't believe she's a creditor in this estate."

"He was a month behind in his child support when he filed. I sure am a creditor."

Matt looked at Mr. Green and said, "Is that true?"

Mr. Green shook his head and said, "I was only ten days late, not a month."

"Then that qualifies her as a creditor, Mr. Coleman," the Trustee replied. "You may proceed, Ms. Green."

"Thank you. . . . Okay, what Wally didn't tell you about was the insurance money."

"Objection, I don't think it's appropriate for Ms. Green to testify. If she has a question, that's fine, but . . ."

"Please just ask questions," the trustee said.

"Where is the insurance money?"

The trustee and Matt looked at Mr. Green intently. He squirmed in his seat and then looked at Matt and said, "I told you this wouldn't work."

"Huh?" Matt said.

"She's had a private detective following me around. She must have seen me stash the money."

"What money?"

"The insurance money I got when the last construction project burned down."

"You never told me about that."

"I sure did. You said as long as it was in cash nobody could ever trace it."

Matt looked at the trustee and said, "This is ridiculous. I would have never said anything like that!"

The trustee glared at Matt and then asked Mr. Green, "How much money did you collect on the insurance?"

"A hundred and fifty thousand dollars."

Matt turned white and nearly fainted. The representative from the U.S. Trustee's office stood up. Matt looked at her in disbelief at what was happening. She shook her head and said, "You'll be hearing from the FBI, Mr. Coleman!"

Matt sat back in his chair as all eyes were on him. The trustee cleared his throat and said, "I'm going to continue this meeting to a later date after I've had a chance to discuss it with the United States Trustee's office. Thank you."

By the time Matt recovered enough to stand up, Mr. Green was gone, and everyone had left the room. As he sat there, his mind raced to remember his first interview with

Mr. Green. He hadn't mentioned anything about insurance money. What was going on? Why would he lie like that? Matt left the room and went to the phone to call Lynn.

"Matt, you had to do a 341 meeting, huh?"

"Yes, and it will probably be my last."

"What's wrong?"

"I'm screwed!"

"What happened?"

"Mr. Green was concealing a hundred and fifty thousand dollars, and he claims I knew all about it."

"What! But that's a lie."

"I know it's a lie, but it's his word against mine. I'm screwed."

"Why would he lie like that? . . . Oh God!"

"What?"

"It's the cartel. They weren't able to kill you, so they set you up. Oh, Matt! I'm so scared! What are we going to do?"

"I don't know. I'm going to see Dad. Maybe he'll have some ideas."

Lynn broke out into tears and sobbed, "We should have listened to your father."

"It's too late to worry about that now. I'll call you after I've talked to him."

***

I was about to go to lunch when I received a frantic phone call from Matt. I canceled my luncheon appointment and instead told Matt to meet me at Carelli's. I arrived there before Matt and went inside to wait. As Matt was entering the restaurant, I noticed a car pull up. The two male occupants of the car got out and walked toward the entrance to the restaurant.

150

Matt walked over and sat across from me in the booth. The two men came in and took seats at the counter. An ill feeling came over me.

"Let's go somewhere else, son. I think you've been followed."

Matt nodded. We got up to leave. The two men looked over at us. We walked casually out of the restaurant and got in my car. Then we bolted out of the parking lot as fast as we could. The two men rushed out of the restaurant, but Matt and I were several blocks away before they could get to their cars. I knew the neighborhood pretty well so I made a few strategic turns and lost them.

"I didn't feel like Italian anyway," I said.

"I'm so sick; I doubt I could eat."

"So what happened?"

"I've been set up by a client."

"Set up? How?"

"This guy Wallace Green claims he told me about a hundred and fifty thousand dollars that he had stashed away from an insurance claim. It's total bullshit but how can I prove it?"

"Well, this guy could go to jail too. I can't believe he would admit to bankruptcy fraud."

"Unless he was confident he'd be granted immunity."

"Oh, God. You think the cartel is behind this?"

"Dad, you talk like you're a believer."

"Well, I've always been a believer. I've just been afraid to challenge it. I mean, until you proved me wrong, I didn't think one man could do anything against such a powerful force."

"No, you were right. I was naive to think I could just throw grenades into their playground with impunity. You know, I was under this delusion that as an American I could say anything about anyone and not have to fear retaliation. Now I realize how stupid I was to think that."

"So what are you going to do?"

"That's what I was hoping you could help me with."

"Obviously you should get an attorney."

"I'll call Bradley Davis. One of his partners is a criminal attorney, Bruce Pierson, I think is his name."

"Good. In the meantime, you better stay out of bankruptcy court and don't do any client interviews. It's going to get pretty ugly over the next few months with the U.S. Trustee's office watching you like a hawk."

"I wasn't supposed to have done Mr. Green. Normally someone else in the office handles these cases. I can't believe my luck."

"Here's Dickey's Barbecue. You want to eat here?"

"No, I'm not hungry. Just take me back to my car."

"Okay," I said and then did a U-turn and headed back toward Carelli's. As Matt was getting out, he said, "I'll call you after I talk to Brad."

"Good. I think I'll call a friend over at the U.S. Trustee's office and see if I can learn anything. It would probably be a good idea to hire someone to do a background check on Green. Maybe he's got a criminal history."

"Good idea. I'll get someone on that."

"Keep me posted."

"All right, I'll talk to you soon."

***

Matt got in his car and took off. It wasn't long before he noticed his tail was back on him. Feeling a bit like the situation was hopeless, he didn't try to shake them this time. When he got home, Lynn was waiting at the door.

"Matt! Oh, honey. Are you all right?"

"Yes, physically I'm fine. Mentally I'm a wreck."

"I can't believe this. How could something like this happen?"

"It's the Cartel. I'm sure. They want to destroy me any way they can, obviously."

"Can't you just claim you were set up?"

"What evidence do I have?"

"Maybe Mr. Green will have second thoughts?"

"I hope he does, but I'm not going to count on it."

# 14

Professor Swensen got in his white Lexus and headed for Stonebriar Centre. He had received a phone call from a woman who claimed she had information about the people who wanted Matthew Coleman dead. He desperately hoped this wasn't a hoax, as he needed specific evidence of the cartel so that the Senate could be persuaded to launch an investigation. He knew this was his one and only chance to be vindicated. He had devoted his life to proving the Cartel's existence and how he had the Senate listening to him. He had to give them something meaningful, something startling, something they couldn't ignore.

He parked and went in the northeast entrance of the mall to a bench overlooking the ice rink. He sat down and watched a dozen skaters practicing their ice dancing while he waited for his contact. He looked at his watch and saw that it was 11:27. Precisely at eleven-thirty an older man sat next to him and began reading a book. After reading a few moments, he set the book down and then got up to leave. Professor Swensen looked at his watch again and saw it was 11:45. He squirmed in his chair and took a deep breath. Where could she be, he wondered?

A little before noon he realized the old man had left his book. He picked it up and read the title, *The Richest Man in Babylon*. Then he flipped to the bookmark and opened the book. There was a small piece of paper inside. Suddenly he realized the note might be for him. Not wanting to let anyone know they'd contacted him, he didn't dare read the note in public. He moved quickly to the restroom, went inside and found a stall where he could read it in private.

He unfolded the paper and read the note:

*Professor,*
*You're probably being followed so if you want to see me you'll have to lose your tail. Go to the main southwest entrance to the mall precisely at 1:00 p.m. Immediately upon your arrival a black Jeep Cherokee will pull up. Get in quickly, and the driver will take you to me. Good luck.*

The professor folded the note back up and stuck it in his back pocket. He then proceeded to the southwest entrance of the mall. As he walked up to the curb, a black Jeep Cherokee screeched to a halt. He opened the door, jumped in and they took off. Two men rushed to the curb and watched the jeep disappear across the big parking lot.

The professor looked over at the young driver, smiled and said, "This is exciting. I feel like I'm in a James Bond movie."

"Are they following us?" he asked.

Professor Swensen turned and looked back at the mall entrance. "I don't think so."

"Good. It's very important that my mother's identity is never compromised. They'll kill her if they know she has talked to you."

"Your mother?" Professor Swensen said.

"Yes, I'm Michael, her son. I'm the only one she could trust. You've got to realize these people don't tolerate disloyalty."

"Why is your mother doing this then?"

"Because Matt Coleman is right. It's time to wake up the American people."

Professor Swensen nodded. "How much farther is it?"

"Just a few blocks now."

"If I can get some concrete evidence of the cartel's existence from your mother, I can take it to the Senate Banking Committee. I think they'll commission an investigation. They'll have to."

"But, can they protect my mother? That's what I'm worried about."

"Sure they can, once they realize that the cartel exists and your mother is a key witness they'll protect her."

"You're going to have trouble convincing her of that. She doesn't trust anyone."

"I don't blame her."

Michael pulled the Jeep into the parking garage of the Hotel Continental and stopped in front of the main entrance. He checked his rear view mirror, looked around nervously and then said, "She's in room 424. Knock twice and say it's Uncle Joe."

"Okay, thanks for the ride."

The Jeep took off, and Professor Swensen went inside and walked over to the elevators. When the door opened, he got in, punched four, and the big elevator quickly began its ascent to the fourth floor. He followed the corridor until he found room 424. He knocked twice and said, "It's Uncle Joe." The door opened.

"Professor, come in."

The professor walked in and looked around the small room. He smiled at the middle-aged woman and said, "Well, I hope our meeting is as exciting as the ride over here."

"I'm sorry about that, but—"

"No, don't be. Your son told me how risky this meeting is for you. I'm just glad to be here."

"Good. I've wanted to talk to you or Matt ever since you testified before the Senate Banking Committee."

"I'm glad you called me. What did you want to talk about?"

"I'm Martha Simonton, the secretary to the chairman of MidSouth Bank, Frank Hill. MidSouth is a subprime lender operating primarily in Oklahoma, Texas, and Louisiana. The main bank is in Houston, and there are branches in Dallas, Oklahoma City, and New Orleans. Our primary business, however, is credit cards."

"I see."

"All the things that Matthew Coleman has been preaching are true. Our bank spends millions of dollars on advertising and marketing to induce people to obtain and use their credit cards. It's such a lucrative business that the board has made it their top priority to increase our market share. To accomplish this, they have eliminated almost all the usual requirements for obtaining a credit card like having good credit or a job. Anybody with a social security number pretty much can get a credit card."

"If you issue a credit card to anyone," Professor Swensen asked, "isn't your default rate pretty high?"

"It's been running about 10 or 11% but that is quite acceptable compared to the profit we make from the other 89%. . . . At least it was before Matthew Coleman stepped into the picture."

"Oh, I see. So the default rate is up?"

"Yes, it's running nearly 18% right now and climbing. Needless to say, the board is very concerned about Mr. Coleman's activities."

"I should think so," Professor Swensen said. "I wouldn't have thought Matt could have caused that much of an increase in the default rate."

"As I said, we market credit cards very aggressively. Consequently, we have a lot of marginal accounts. They have proven to be very susceptible to Matt Coleman's movement."

"Movement?"

"Yes, his market strategy is being copied more and more throughout the south. If the trend continues, the bank's future could be severely impaired."

"So, are you saying MidSouth Bank is behind the attempts to compromise and silence Matt? Not the cartel?"

"I'm afraid so. That's why I called you. I know Mr. Hill hired someone to take care of Matt."

"Take care of him?"

"Yes, I don't know exactly what is planned, but I overheard Frank tell someone to 'take care of him.'"

"You're sure they were talking about Matt Colemen?"

"Oh, yes. Matt has been almost the exclusive topic of conversation these days. Frank hates him."

"I see. So why didn't you go to the police?"

"And tell them what? I don't have any specific knowledge of anything. I called you just to warn you and Matt. I think he's doing a very brave thing and I don't want him to get hurt."

"Well, I appreciate you calling me. Do you think you could snoop around and get us some hard evidence? We need to know who the board hired to "take care" of Matt and what exactly they have planned."

"I don't know. It's all done verbally. There's no written record of it. But I'll keep my eyes and ears open, and if anything comes up, I'll call you."

"Good."

The Professor got up, said goodbye, and left. He was glad he found out who was behind the attacks on Matt but was disappointed that it was just one banker. When he got into the lobby, he realized he didn't have a car, so he hailed a cab. As he took off in the direction of Stonebriar Centre, the two men who had followed him took up a watch at the elevators of the hotel.

It wasn't until six that evening that Martha Simonton finally stepped out of the elevator. The two men perked up as they saw her walk toward the parking garage with her son at her side. They followed at a safe distance. As mother and son approached the Jeep Cherokee, the two men rushed them and opened fire. Michael dropped to one knee as a bullet pierced his right thigh. He pulled out a revolver and returned the fire. Ms. Simonton screamed and ran for cover, but it was too late. A bullet hit her in the back, and she immediately collapsed.

Michael held off the two men for a minute, but he was a sitting duck lying in the middle of the parking garage. Soon he was hit again and again until he lay motionless on the cold concrete. The two men rushed Ms. Simonton, finished her off with a bullet to the head and then ran off.

Professor Swensen immediately called Matt when he got back to the SMU campus. Matt was at home when he took the call.

"Hey, how did it go?"

"Better than I could have ever dreamed."

He told Matt everything he had learned.

"So it's not the cartel."

"No, it's just one pissed-off banker, but if he fails, I'm sure there will be others."

"Damn. Now, what do we do?"

"I don't know. We don't have enough to go to the FBI."

"What if Ms. Simonton testified?"

"I don't think she would. She just wanted to warn you and let you know that you're on the right track."

"I do feel relieved to know that we're not fighting windmills."

"You mean you didn't believe what I've been telling you?"

"Yes, I believed you in theory, but it's nice to have a witness who actually has personal knowledge of the conspiracy."

"True. I just wish she would testify so people would take us more seriously."

"Yes, it would definitely help our credibility."

"So, what now?" Professor Swensen asked.

"I'll update Lynn on what we've found out, and we'll decide what our next step will be. I appreciate your help."

"No problem. Take care."

Matt hung up the phone and looked at Lynn with a solemn face. "It's MidSouth Bank that's after me."

"You're kidding?"

He shook his head back and forth. "No, I'm afraid not."

Lynn took a deep breath and slowly exhaled. She looked at the TV and noticed the news was coming on. "Turn the TV back on. I want to catch the news."

Matt hit the mute button, and the TV sound came blaring out of twin speakers.

"In financial news, the Eagle National Bank of Dallas, Texas is reportedly in trouble. The bank is asking stockholders to come up with the $2.1 million infusion of capital that has been demanded by bank examiners. Last month the small bank reported a $1.1 million loss on forty-seven bankruptcy filings. Eagle Bank, a subprime lender, has specialized in high-risk credit cards and up until this last quarter was doing quite well."

"Okay, we have a late breaking story. Let's go to Brian Harper at the Hotel Continental where a woman and her son were gunned down tonight in the parking garage of this popular north Dallas hotel. Brian."

"Thank you, Nancy. It was a pretty grizzly sight on the second floor of the hotel parking garage tonight. An unidentified lady and her teenage son were gunned down execution style not ten yards from their Jeep Cherokee. No one seems to know the motive for the murders as apparently nothing was stolen from the victims."

The phone rang again, so Matt hit the mute button and picked it up. "Did you see the story that was just on the news?"

"Yes, about the murders."

"Un huh. That was Martha and her son Michael."

"Oh, my God! I never dreamed—"

"I feel so terrible, Matt. Somehow we must have been followed. God, I can't believe I led them to her."

"It's not your fault," Matt said. "You did exactly as you were told. These people have no conscience. They'll do whatever it takes to protect themselves."

"I can't believe they're dead. Michael was just a teenager. God, what is this world coming to?"

"I don't know. Now, what are we going to do?"

"Don't ask me," Professor Swensen said, "I have no idea."

The following day the two bodies were identified as a Lois Small and her son Michael. The press speculated that the murders were related to a feud between two local gangs. Although Matt and Professor Swensen knew differently, they had no way of disproving the report.

At Professor Swensen's insistence, Matt started looking for a bodyguard. When I heard about it, I suggested he call Bill Ross, an old client of mine who worked for the Mesquite police department. Bill had a propensity for getting in trouble, and I was called on often to help extricate him from it. He was excited about working for Matt, so he immediately took a 90-day leave of absence from the force. Fortunately, they didn't take away his badge since he was still on call in case of an emergency.

***

It was a cold winter day in early January. The barren trees swayed in the brisk wind that swept through the cemetery. Professor Swensen, Matt, Lynn, and Bill Ross were the sole mourners at Martha and Michael's funeral. Professor Swensen's pastor agreed to conduct the ceremony although he had never known Martha or her son. After a brief grave-site ceremony, Matt and Lynn began the short walk to their car, with Bill Ross leading the way.

Hans knelt down before a grave site a few hundred yards away and watched them. As they approached their car, Agent Radcliff appeared with another man. Bill motioned for them to stay back as he continued toward Agent Radcliff.

"Please get away from this car," Bill demanded.

Agent Radcliff pulled out his badge and flashed it in front of Ross' face.

"FBI?"

"That's what it says."

Matt and Lynn walked up next to Bill who looked confused.

"Good morning, Mr. Coleman," Radcliff said.

"Hello, Agent Radcliff."

Radcliff looked over at his partner and said, "This is my partner, Agent Shane."

"Hello."

"I'm sorry to bother you on such a sad occasion, but I'm curious as to why you and the professor attended this funeral. You're not family, are you?"

"You've been watching me?" Matt said.

"You know we've been investigating your claim that someone was trying to kill you."

"Well, you found your first witness. . . . Too bad she won't be able to talk to you."

"What do you mean?"

Matt told Agent Radcliff and Shane all he knew.

"What a shame. The committee will be very disappointed that we weren't able to talk to Ms. Simonton. But we will take a look at MidSouth Bank. Maybe there are some other employees who would be willing to talk."

"Hopefully," Matt said.

Agent Radcliff and Shane didn't move. Matt suddenly felt uneasy.

"Is there something else?"

"Yes, we wanted to give you some bad news."

"What's that?"

"Agent Shane and I have been assigned to question you about Wallace Green."

Matt's heart sank. He regretted telling them about Ms. Simonton. They were there to get evidence to put him behind bars. "Jesus. It figures. ... Well, I'm sorry to disappoint you, but I can't talk to you about that now."

"And why is that?"

"My attorney advised me not to discuss the case without him being present."

"Well, why don't you call him so we can all get together and discuss how you missed a hundred and fifty thousand dollars of cash on Mr. Green's Schedule B?"

"No problem," Matt said sarcastically. "When would be a good time for you?"

"How about right now?"

"I don't think so. Let's go with Monday morning at my attorney's office. ... Ten o'clock?"

"Who's your attorney?"

"Bruce Pierson," I replied. "If you call my office, my secretary will give you his address and telephone number."

"Fine. We'll see you Monday."

"Good. Now, will you excuse us?"

"Sure, have a nice day."

Bill opened the back door, and Lynn and Matt got inside. Bill gave the two agents a nasty look and then got in and drove off.

"What an asshole," Lynn said.

"You noticed."

"Why would they send him to Dallas to investigate you? I'm sure they must have local agents."

"MidSouth probably isn't alone in this. A lot of financial institutions are in trouble. I saw something on the news just tonight about Eagle National Bank. Agent Radcliff obviously is doing somebody's dirty work. Somebody who has connections in the FBI."

"What if they indict you?" Lynn asked with a hint of fear in her voice.

"There's no *what if*. They are going to indict me. You can bet on it."

"Oh Matt! ... Do you think you'll be convicted?"

"I don't know. It's going to be Mr. Green's word against mine. It depends on who the jury believes."

"They have to believe you. I couldn't stand for you to go to jail."

"At least it would be a federal prison. . . . I'd have a lot of time to work on my tennis game," Matt laughed.

"It's not funny," Lynn moaned. "What are we going to do?"

"Bruce Pierson is an excellent criminal attorney. He worked for years in the District Attorney's office. I'm sure he'll get me off."

"I'm so worried," Lynn said.

"Don't worry; it won't do any good. You just need to assume everything will work out okay."

"I wish I could."

"It's too bad we don't know who Frank Hill hired to kill me."

"Well, we might be able to figure it out," Bill interjected.

"You got some ideas?"

"Not yet. Give me a little time."

"I didn't know you were a detective?" Lynn said.

"I'm not officially, but I've had a lot of experience and training in criminal investigation. Don't worry, Lynn, I'll find out who they've hired to kill Matt. And when I do, I'll make him wish he was never born."

Matt and Lynn looked at each other and smiled. They liked Ross' enthusiasm.

# 15

A strong southerly wind provided unusually warm weather for February. Bill pulled off his sweater and threw it into the back seat of his '97 Nissan 300ZX. He took a deep breath as he looked over the SMU campus and then pulled out a small note pad. After finding Professor Swensen's room and building number, he began walking toward where he thought it would be.

As he walked toward his destination, he wondered if he'd been a little rash in accepting this assignment. Although he felt like he knew what he was doing, he was worried about failing. Matt was depending on him, and as the minutes began to tick, the pressure began to build inside him. When he got to Professor Swensen's office, he knocked on the door and waited. When the door opened, Professor Swensen was there smiling. They exchanged greetings, and then Bill sat in a big overstuffed chair.

The room was cluttered with books, magazines, papers and used Styrofoam cups. He had adorned the walls with diplomas, photographs of family and friends, and an original G. Harvey depicting downtown Dallas in the 30s. Professor Swensen poured them each a cup of coffee.

"Well, how is Matt doing?"

"Not too bad. Actually, I'm more worried about Lynn. She's not taking this well."

"I can understand. One moment she and Matt are on the top of the world and the next they're fighting for their lives."

Professor Swensen shook his head and gave Bill a somber look. "This is all my fault. I shouldn't have tried to sell my conspiracy theory to Lynn. I'll die if something happens to Matt."

"Don't worry about him. Nobody's going to touch him."

Professor Swensen smiled. "I'm glad they hired you as a bodyguard. I'll sleep better now. . . . So, how can I help you?"

"I need to figure out who was following you at the Stonebriar Centre. Can you describe the two men?"

"Well, one of them was short, maybe five foot two. He had dark brown hair and a pot belly. . . . Let me see. . . . He was wearing a badly wrinkled gray suit with a red tie."

"And the other guy?"

"Much taller. He was maybe six feet, muscular with blond hair and one earring. He looked European—German, Austrian maybe."

"Okay. They may still be lurking about, so I'll keep an eye out for them. If *you* see them, call me."

"I will. Good luck."

Bill went back to his car and drove to the Addison police station. He went inside and asked the receptionist for Sergeant Showalter. After a minute a robust man with gray hair appeared. "Bill, how the hell are you?" The two shook hands and then embraced.

"I'm fine."

"What are you doing in this part of the woods?"

"I need your help on something."

"What's that?"

"You know that lady and her son who were executed over at the Hotel Continental the other day?"

"Yes, what about it?"

"I'd like to know if anyone has contacted you about them."

"Why?"

"It's a long story, but the bottom line is they've been misidentified. Somebody is trying to cover up their identity, and I'd like to find out who it is."

"Okay, we can take a look at the case file. Maybe there will be some notes in there."

"Thanks, I really appreciate it."

Sergeant Showalter turned and headed down a hallway with Bill at his heels. They turned left at the end of the hall and then down a flight of stairs. Finally, they came to a chain link cage manned by a young police officer.

"Morning, Jake. I need to go inside a minute."

"Who's that with you?" Jake asked.

"This is Bill Ross from the Mesquite PD. He needs to look at a file."

"Okay, sign in, please."

Showalter and Bill signed in and then made their way to the cabinet where the file was supposed to be. Once they located it, they pulled it out and set it on a work desk.

"Let's see," Showalter said. "There is a note that two FBI agents, Shane and Radliff, reviewed the file."

"That figures."

"Anything else?"

"Yes, the bodies were identified by Raymond Small, Lois Small's brother."

"That's interesting. She told Professor Swensen she didn't have any relatives," Bill said.

Bill left the Addison Police Station and went directly to the address in the file for Raymond Small, D.D.S. He called ahead on his mobile phone to see if he could have five minutes of the Doctor's time. He lied and said he was working for the Mesquite Police department to be sure he got the appointment. When he checked-in with the receptionist, he was escorted to Dr. Small's office. After a moment, Dr. Small entered the room.

"Detective Ross?"

"Hi, Dr. Small. Thanks for seeing me."

"No problem. What can I help you with?"

"I was just over at the Addison Police Department, and they said you identified the bodies of Martha and Michael Small and I was wondering what your relationship was to them?"

Dr. Small swallowed hard. "Martha Small was my ex-wife, and Michael was her son by a former marriage. I hadn't seen them in ten years."

"Hmm. Did she ever go by another name?"

"Well, her maiden name was Clayburn. She was from the Midwest—Indianapolis."

Bill pulled a photograph of Martha out of his pocket and showed it to the doctor. "Is this your ex-wife?"

He took the photograph and studied it a moment as if he were in deep thought. Then he blinked, twisted his head slightly and said, "Right. That's her."

"Why do you suppose she was gunned down like that?"

He shook his head. "As I said, I hadn't seen her in years. I don't know what she got involved in."

"Did she ever live in Houston?"

"Not to my knowledge. But, as I said, I didn't keep tabs on her."

"Does the name Simonton mean anything to you?"

"No. Sorry."

"How did the Addison police know to contact you?"

"Ah, well . . . I think they found one of my cards in her wallet."

"Oh. Have you been at this office ten years?"

"Listen, I'd love to chat with you, but I've got another appointment."

"Sure, you've been very helpful. Thanks for your time."

Bill wasn't convinced of Dr. Small's veracity. He seemed uncomfortable and tentative with his answers. Either he or Martha Simonton had been lying. He didn't think it was Martha, however, since she had been killed for giving information to Matt. But how would he prove that Martha Small was Martha Simonton? He suspected if he called down to Midwest Bank they'd deny ever knowing her. He decided to call a friend at the Texas Workforce Commission.

"Yes, Martha Simonton. She works for Midwest Bank."

"Good. I didn't see how they could erase her from all the government databases, but for a minute—"

"You say she's dead?"

"Right. She died two weeks ago."

"Well, according to the last payroll report she got a paycheck last Friday."

"You're kidding? Do you have an address on her?"

"Of course."

Bill went back to his car and began flipping through his notebook, his mind racing, trying to analyze the new information he had obtained. Finally, he put the key in the ignition and started the car. He decided a trip to Houston would be wise. He called Matt to be sure he wasn't needed in the next twenty-four hours and then headed toward I-45.

The Villa Capri apartments, located off Westheimer near the Galleria, were old but well maintained. Bill suspected the land was worth much more than the apartments themselves due to their prime location. He walked up to Martha's second-floor apartment and peered inside the window. It didn't look like anyone had disturbed the place yet, so Bill picked the lock and went inside.

The large two-bedroom apartment was clean and neat. The pantry and refrigerator were well stocked although the milk was rancid. A big screen TV was set up against the wall. It appeared watching videos was Michael and Martha's primary entertainment. Bill put on latex gloves and began to search the place. He dug through the cabinets, through drawers, and inside the closet. After thirty minutes he had found nothing unusual. He went over to the sofa and sat down to think. *Where would she keep something she didn't want anyone to see?*

He started looking in less obvious places; he looked for loose boards, felt for lumps in pillows, and examined the mattresses for holes or fresh stitching. He pulled up carpeting, examined under drawers, and looked inside the toilet tanks. When he was about to give up, he noticed an urn on the mantel. It appeared to contain someone's ashes. Picking it up, he wondered if something might be hidden inside. After carefully removing the seal, he examined the surface. Not wanting to disturb the ashes too much, he found a long fireplace match and dug around them. The match cut through the ashes with some difficulty. He felt a ridge at the bottom that made him feel compelled to empty it out for closer examination. A wave of guilt gripped him as he contemplated pouring the ashes into a bowl.

He held the urn in one hand and started opening cabinets looking for a bowl. Loud knocking at the door startled him. He dropped the urn, and it smashed on the floor. A cloud of dust lifted from the pile. His heart began to pound as he looked toward the front door. The intruder knocked again, louder this time. He looked down at the mess beneath his feat. There was a key scotch taped to the bottom of the urn. He picked it up and tore it from the piece of porcelain. He examined it. It was a key to a safety deposit box.

After the knocking stopped, he opened the door and peered out. He saw a young woman starting to leave on a bicycle. His curiosity got the best of him.

He yelled, "Sorry, miss. I was on the phone and couldn't get to the door quickly enough."

The young brunette nodded and smiled. "Who are you?" She asked.

"Oh, I'm . . . Martha's ex-husband. I'm supposed to meet her here. She told me about a key under the mat, so I let myself in."

"Oh, do you know where Michael is?"

"No, I haven't seen him. Maybe he'll be with his mother."

Bill stared at the young lady, thought for a moment and then said, "What's your name? I'll tell him you dropped by."

The girl frowned and replied, "Julia."

"Okay, is there a message?"

"Yes, tell him he's a son of a bitch for standing me up Saturday. He promised to go to a wedding with me, but he didn't show. He knows how much I hate to go to those things alone. Damn him!"

"I've got some bad news."

"Huh? What?"

"Michael. . . . I'm sorry, but . . . Michael is dead."

Julia's face dropped. She didn't respond. She just stared at Ross, her eyes glazed. Then she began to weep. "How did it happen?"

"He was murdered."

"Murdered?! But who—"

"Hit men. They were after his mother. She had some evidence against the people she worked for and was prepared to turn it over to . . . well, I can't tell you anymore, but anyway, they had her killed."

"I knew something weird was going on with him when he told me he had to be with his mother whenever she went out. He took her to work, picked her up. It was really bizarre. I thought maybe he was just a momma's boy but the fear in his eyes told me otherwise."

"How long have you known him?"

"Just a few months. . . . Damn it! Why did he have to die? I really liked him."

"I know. It's really terrible. Maybe you can help me nail his killers."

"How?"

"Michael's mother had some evidence on the people who murdered her. I've got to figure out where she hid it."

"You got me. I'm clueless."

"How often did you see Michael?"

"Every Monday and Thursday. We'd meet at the laundromat. Once in a while, we'd get together on the weekends if Michael could get away."

"Did you ever meet his mother?"

"No, he wouldn't let me. He said she had a bitter divorce and didn't trust anyone. She didn't want him to date until he was older."

"Did Michael tell you anything about his mother's past other than the divorce?"

"Oh, just that she was a secretary for some big shot at a bank, but that's about it."

Bill wondered how he was going to keep Julia quiet about his visit to Martha's apartment. He pulled out his Mesquite police officer's badge and showed it to Julia.

"Listen, Julia. As you can see, I'm kind of out of my jurisdiction here, so please don't tell anyone about this conversation or that you saw me today. I'm trying to find out who killed Michael, but I don't want anyone to find out about my investigation. Only the killer and I know that Michael and his mother are dead. Officially they are both still alive."

Julia nodded. "I totally understand," she said. "If I can help, please let me know."

Bill smiled and gave her a card. She stuck it in her purse and left down the stairs. Bill went inside and resumed his search. This time he looked for bank statements. He needed to know where Martha might have a safety deposit box. He found a checkbook for Bank One. After jotting down the address, he looked at the broken urn and the ashes scattered all over the carpet. He went to the kitchen and found a broom and a dust pan. After sweeping up the broken porcelain and ashes, he put them in a paper bag. He took the bag with him as he left the apartment.

On the way to Bank One, he stopped at a public park. There was a pond with a water fountain and ducks swimming around. He stopped and took the bag with him into the park. He found a trash can, carefully picked out the broken porcelain pieces, and discarded them. Then he went to the pond and scattered the ashes over the water. He gave the sign of the cross and dropped the paper bag in the trash on the way back to his car.

At Bank One he stood a moment in the lobby, wondering how he could get away with getting access to the safety deposit box. He had the key, but he didn't know who was authorized to enter the box. His only hope would be that Michael was on the signature card. Although he was ten years older than Michael, that might be overlooked. He had looked through a bank statement and knew that

Michael wrote checks on the account. Michael's signature was a series of unreadable swirls that could easily be forged. He thought he could pull it off, but wondered about the consequences if he failed. He took a deep breath and proceeded to the vault.

In front of the vault, there were a table and a sign-in book. He went up to it and signed in. Seeing him at the table, a young lady came over and said, "Do you need to get into your box?"

"Yes, ma'am," he said. He noticed her name tag read, Ms. Reed.

"All right, what's the number?"

Bill looked at the key. The number 239 was chiseled into the face of the key. He said, "239."

She nodded and went over to a desk with a file box on it. After flipping through the signature cards, she stopped and studied one of them, comparing signatures. Bill held his breath. She frowned and shook her head. Bill's heart plummeted. She closed the lid of the file and walked back to where he was standing.

She smiled. "You must be a doctor or something. I couldn't read your signature if my life depended on it."

Bill laughed. "I know. That's what everyone tells me."

Ms. Reed escorted Bill to a private cubicle, took his key and returned with a box. She left him alone. He opened the box slowly and studied the contents.

# 16

Matt was shown to the small conference room of Smith, Pierson & Davis. The receptionist indicated Mr. Pierson would be there shortly. Matt took a deep breath and closed his eyes. When he opened them, he got up and poured himself a glass of water. Then he walked out into the hall and watched a secretary banging away on a computer. Glancing at his watch, he noticed Pierson was eight minutes late. He turned, went back to the table and sat down. Finally, Pierson walked in with a thin file and yellow pad.

"Mr. Coleman, how are you?"

"I've had better days."

"For sure. Well, I'm glad you didn't talk to Agent Radcliff before I had a chance to prep you. FBI agents are highly trained interrogators."

"I can imagine."

"Since you're innocent, I think the best thing to do is answer their questions as best you can. There's a chance Mr. Green might trip up and lose credibility. If that happens, they may not recommend an indictment."

"I'm just going to tell them the truth."

"Good."

A secretary walked in and advised them Agent Radcliff had arrived. Pierson told her to show him in. A minute later he walked in the room.

"Hello, Mr. Pierson," Agent Radcliff said. "Mr. Coleman."

"Hi, Agent Radcliff," Pierson said. "Can I get you anything?"

"No, I'm fine."

"Well, then let's get this over with."

"Okay, I just have a few questions of your client. Mr. Coleman, as you know, Wallace Green claims he advised you of a hundred and fifty-thousand dollars he had received from an insurance settlement."

"It's not true. I knew nothing about it," Matt said firmly.

"He says when he told you about it you advised him he would lose it all if he filed bankruptcy."

"If he had told me about it, that's probably what I would have told him, but he didn't."

"He says you two discussed how he could hide the money so the bankruptcy trustee wouldn't find out about it."

"No way. He's having pipe dreams."

"He says he offered to split the money with you, if you two could pull it off."

"That is totally ridiculous. I wouldn't have done that. No way."

"Are you sure you never discussed the money?"

"Absolutely, positively."

"Well, then I guess it's his word against yours."

"I guess so."

"Agent Radcliff," Pierson said. "My client was doing very well. He had plenty of money. What possible reason would he have to jeopardize his career for seventy-five thousand dollars? That's not a lot of money for a successful lawyer."

"I don't know, but you've got to understand someone is lying here. Until we find out who it is we'll have to keep the investigation going."

"I wish I could help you," Matt said. "I'm innocent, so if I can do anything to aid your investigation, let me know."

"I appreciate that Mr. Coleman. I'll keep that in mind. . . . Well, I'll contact you in a couple of weeks to let you know what's going on."

Everyone got up and left the conference room. Matt said goodbye to Pierson and went outside to the elevator. He took it to the basement and walked to his car. Feeling rather depressed, he went home. Lynn had taken the day off so he figured they'd spend the day together. When he walked in the apartment, she immediately quizzed him on the interview.

"So, what happened?"

"Nothing really. He just told me what I already knew, and I told him Green was full of shit."

"Do you think he believed you?"

"No."

"Hmm. . . . Oh, Tom called and said the background check came in on Wallace Green."

"And?"

"It was negative. No criminal history."

"Shit!"

"I'm sorry, honey."

"Well, let's just forget about Wallace Green, okay?" Matt said. "I just want to do something fun with you today." He put his arms around Lynn and drew her next to him.

"Hmm," She said as she put her arms around his waist. "What did you have in mind?"

"Well, we'll shut off the phones, get a couple of beers, and climb in the hot tub."

"Oh, yes. That's sounds good. I'll take care of the phone and get some towels. You get the beer."

"Okay," Matt said as he released Lynn from his embrace. She ran off toward the bathroom. He watched her ass wiggle as she strolled down the hall and disappeared around the corner. He smiled and then went into the kitchen for the beer.

As he was coming out of the kitchen, he got a glimpse of Lynn's naked body descending into the hot tub. He put the beers down a minute, took off his clothes, and joined her, beers in hand. Lynn watched him with a seductive smile. He handed her a beer and sat down beside her.

"Maybe we should leave the country," Lynn said. "I checked the savings account, and we've got two hundred and thirty-two thousand dollars in there right now."

"You want to be a fugitive the rest of your life?"

"At least we'd be fugitives together."

"That's not a bad idea, but do you think we could get away from the FBI? They've got a tail on me everywhere I go."

"I'm sure we could figure out a way to sneak off."

"What about MidSouth Bank? Don't you think they'd love for us to run off?"

"What do you mean?"

"The only thing that's keeping us alive right now is the fact that we're in the limelight. Once we run, then we're on our own. If we disappeared off the face of the earth, who's going to care?"

"Damn it. I just thought maybe you and I could buy a little hacienda on a beach somewhere in Mexico. I heard it's really cheap to live down there. We could get a maid and live a life of leisure."

"That sounds good to me," Matt said as he slid around in front of Lynn. She closed her eyes and took a deep breath as she felt his hand caress her inner thigh. She moaned as he began to stroke her breasts while gently biting her neck. She grabbed his shoulders. He could feel her fingernails digging into his back.

He slipped one hand behind her bottom and pulled their bodies together. She opened her eyes and gave him a half-crazed look. He held her firmly as he thrust himself in and out with a power that overwhelmed them both. Suddenly they heard chimes as if the Dallas Symphony was orchestrating this sexual encounter. They stopped momentarily, and Matt said, "Damn! Somebody's at the door."

Lynn held Matt tightly and replied, "Don't answer it! Keep going!"

"But what—"

"No, keep going I'm about to climax."

Matt resumed his penetrations, and the doorbell rang again. He pushed harder and harder until Lynn let out a scream, "Ahhh! Oh God!"

Matt quickly got up and grabbed a towel. Then he went to the door and said, "Just a minute!" He looked out the peephole and then said to Lynn, "It's Bill."

"Don't open the door until I get into the bathroom."

"Okay," Matt said smiling.

While Lynn was gathering up her things and scampering into the bathroom, Matt dried off and put his pants on. Then he opened the door.

"Hey, I hope I didn't interrupt anything," Bill said.

"Yeah, you did. But it's okay. We were just sitting in the hot tub talking."

"I hope you had your clothes on."

"Why?"

"There was someone on the roof next door watching you."

"You're kidding? Who?The FBI?"

"Probably."

"Those bastards! Goddamn them!"

"You better watch what you say. The house is probably bugged."

"Great."

Bill began to search the room for bugs. After a few minutes, he found a small microphone in a flower arrangement. Then he checked the phone and found that it was tapped.

"Okay, the room's clean now. I'll check the rest of the house before I leave. Just assume now that everything you say will be recorded."

"Those little weasels! Damn it!" Matt said shaking his head. "So, what brings you by?"

"Oh, I came by to update you on my investigation."

"Good, have a seat. Can I get you a beer?"

"Sure."

The door to the bathroom opened and Lynn came out in a white terry cloth bathrobe. She smiled and said, "Hi, Bill."

"Hi, Lynn."

"Guess what, honey?"

"What?"

"The FBI was watching us make love."

"Huh?"

"Some agent was on the roof next door getting an eyeful."

Lynn went out onto the patio and looked toward the roof next door. "Those assholes! Can they get away with that?"

"I guess you could call the police and report a peeping Tom," Bill laughed.

Lynn came back in with a somber look on her face, shaking her head. Bill took a seat on the blue leather sofa. Lynn sat down in the matching love seat while Matt went and got everyone a beer. When Matt returned, he sat down next to Lynn. Bill filled them in on his activities up to the gaining access to the safety deposit box.

"It appears there is a new Ms. Simonton working for Mr. Hill at the bank."

"How do you do that?" Lynn asked. "Switch identities?"

"It's not hard," Bill replied. "You pay someone just to start pretending they are someone else. An actress maybe."

"What about family and friends? Wouldn't they find out what you were doing?"

"Why should they?" Bill said. "Martha's parents are dead. She hadn't seen her ex-husband in years. They probably transferred all the employees that knew her. The Social Security Administration or IRS will eventually figure out something is wrong, but that could take years. I only figured it out because I was specifically looking for it."

"Hmm. . . . So, did you get into the safety deposit box?"

"Yes, and that's where I found the evidence we've been looking for—a black Day-Timer with names, addresses, and notes of Hill's activities."

"So what do we do with it?" Matt asked.

"We can't give it to the FBI. I'm not sure they can be trusted. We could take it to the press," Bill thought out loud.

"Don't they have to verify everything before they go public?" Lynn said. "They might just sit on it."

"True. What about that senator, the one who tried to protect me before the committee?"

"Senator Goss?" Lynn said. "Yes, he did seem to be on our side."

"Okay, he's our man, but we have to move fast," Matt said. "We don't have a lot of time. The FBI will be giving the Justice Department a report in the next few weeks, and then I'm likely to get indicted."

"Don't worry. I'll call Senator Goss' office right away and try to set up a meeting. Hopefully, he'll see me next week."

"Keep me posted," Matt said as Bill got up to leave. They shook hands, then Bill and Lynn embraced.

"Good luck," Lynn said.

"Thanks. You two hang in there and be careful."

"We will."

Matt closed the door and followed Lynn to the patio. She sat on a lounge chair. Matt sat next to her, put his arm around her and squeezed her tightly.

"Can you believe they were watching us?" Lynn said.

"I know. It was pretty sick. I'm sorry, honey."

Lynn began to cry. "How are we going to get through this? It is so horrible."

"Come back inside. I'll turn the TV on just in case Bill missed any of the bugs."

Matt went to the TV and turned it on. Then he took Lynn's hand and sat her down on the sofa. Matt looked at the TV and saw the noon news was coming on.

"This is Hal Smith with the noon news. Another bank is in trouble in Texas—the second this month as a result of massive losses from bankruptcy filings in the state. The Valley State Bank of Brownsville announced its president had resigned due to a government investigation into staggering losses posted in the last ninety days. A spokesman for the comptroller's office, when asked if more banks were in for trouble, indicated there might be other small, thinly capitalized banks that have problems, but that in general, he had complete confidence that most institutions would weather the current storm unscathed.

"A columnist for the *Dallas Business Review* today voiced a different viewpoint, forecasting a banking crisis similar to that of the mid-1980s."

"That's just great," Matt said. "All we need is more pressure on the government to come after us."

The next day Matt and Lynn both went into the office. It was a cold, miserable day. It had rained during the night, and the streets were wet. Bridges and overpasses had patches of ice and traffic was heavy and slow. By the time they got in it was nearly 9:30. Tom greeted them as they came in the door.

"Good morning. Tough day out there?"

Lynn shook her head and replied, "God, it's terrible. I'm so cold."

"Matt, Pierson's in your office."

"What?"

"He came by at nine and said he had to talk to you."

"Oh, shit. He couldn't have good news."

Matt and Lynn went directly to Matt's office. Pierson was standing at the window watching the cars slipping and sliding below.

"Bruce."

Pierson turned, smiled and said, "You made it in one piece, huh?"

"Yeah, what's up?"

"I'm afraid I've got bad news for you."

"What?"

"I've been told an indictment will come down today against you."

"Oh no, they're going to indict me with only Wallace Green's word against mine?"

"No, I'm afraid they have more."

"What could they possibly have?"

"They've traced $75,000 from Wallace Green to one of your bank accounts."

"What? That's crazy!"

"An account at Bank of America."

"I don't even have an account at Bank of America."

"Yes, you do. I verified it with Tom a minute ago."

"Huh? Lynn, we don't have an account at Bank of America, do we?"

"Not that I know anything about."

"Tom!" Matt yelled.

Tom came running in and said, "What?"

"What's this account at Bank of America?"

Tom took a deep breath and replied, "Ah. You remember I set that up last fall to accumulate some funds for a new location in El Paso."

"I don't remember that."

"You signed the signature cards."

"I did?"

"Uh huh."

"What have you been putting in there?"

"Ten percent of our gross, just like you said."

"That's bullshit! I never told you to do that!"

Tom jumped back as he feared Matt was about to strike him.

"Okay, okay, calm down," Pierson said. "We can sort this out later. Right now I've got to take you to the U.S. Marshall's office."

"No!" Lynn said. "This can't be happening!"

Lynn gave Tom a scathing look, "You son of a bitch! You're the asshole who set Matt up!" Lynn charged at Tom and began beating him wildly. Matt grabbed her and tried to pull her away, but she was out of control. Finally, Matt and Pierson managed to separate the two. Matt glared at Tom and said, "Tom, you're fired! Get the hell out of my office!"

Lynn began crying hysterically. Matt took her in his arms and held her tightly. Tom closed his eyes, took a deep breath, then turned and left the room. He went back to his office, closed the door and then slumped in his chair. Tears began to flood from his eyes. He picked up a picture of his son on his desk, looked at it a moment and then slipped it in his briefcase. Ten minutes later he was gone.

"We're going to get through this, Honey. You've got to be strong," Matt said to Lynn, who was beginning to calm down.

Matt looked at Pierson and said, "Let me take her over to my parents' house. My mom can take care of her. She needs someone with her right now. Then we'll go to the Federal Building."

"Sure, Matt. That will be fine," Pierson said.

# 17

The Deputy U.S. Marshall led Matt into the magistrate's courtroom and told him to sit at the counsel table. The room began to fill up with the media that had flooded the Federal Building upon the news of Matt's arrest. Matt watched them as they walked in. When he saw Lynn and her friend Lori Keyes, he choked up and nearly burst into tears. Lynn smiled and blew him a kiss. Matt spotted his mother, smiled at her, and then turned back toward the bench. Finally, Pierson showed up with an associate and joined him at the counsel table.

"Hi, Matt. You hanging in there?"

"Yeah, I guess."

"This shouldn't be too bad. I don't think the magistrate will set the bond too high."

"I sure hope not. I don't want to spend any time in the Dallas County Jail."

Matt looked over at the opposite counsel table and saw a middle-aged man and a woman sit down.

"Who's the prosecutor?" Matt whispered to Pierson.

Pierson looked over and said, "Russell Lewis."

"Is he any good?"

"Yeah, the best they have."

"Figures."

Suddenly the door to the magistrate's chamber opened, and a young law clerk walked out and sat down.

Then the court reporter came in through another door. The bailiff stood up and said, "All rise!"

The magistrate took the bench and began shuffling through some papers. He looked up and scanned the packed courtroom. "Well, let's see, Mr. Lewis, what do we have here today?"

"Matthew Coleman, Your Honor. As you know, Mr. Coleman is an attorney licensed to practice before the federal courts of this district. Mr. Coleman has been charged with participating in a scheme to conceal assets belonging to the estate of a Wallace Green."

"I see. What's your bail request?"

"We believe there is a substantial flight risk, Your Honor, and would request bail be set at five hundred thousand dollars."

"Mr. Pierson, what do you say about that?"

"Your Honor, Mr. Coleman is a member of the bar, he has strong roots in the community, no priors, and we intend to prove that someone framed him. Five hundred thousand dollars is ridiculous."

"You have some testimony, Mr. Lewis?"

"Yes, Your Honor. Agent Carl Rigsbee of the Federal Bureau of Investigation."

"Very well, bring him up."

The bailiff swore the witness in, and Lewis began to interrogate him.

"Mr. Rigsbee, where are you employed, sir?"

"The Federal Bureau of Investigation."

"And what do you do for them?"

"I'm a special agent."

"And what is your current assignment?"

"To keep an eye on Mathew Coleman and gather evidence to aid in his criminal prosecution."

"And were you observing him two nights ago, February 21st?"

"Yes, we had a court order allowing us to tap his phones and place wires in his home. We also had him under visual and audio surveillance."

"Where were you situated?"

"In a van parked down the street from his house."

"What were you doing in the van?"

"Listening to a conversation he was having with his wife."

"And you were authorized to do that?"

"Yes, we had a court order."

"And where were they when you were listening?"

"In their hot tub."

"Did they talk about anything relating to the subject matter of your investigation?"

"Yes, they were planning to escape the country and hide in Mexico."

"Do you have the recording of that conversation?"

"Yes."

"Would you play it for us?"

Agent Lewis slipped a cassette out of his coat and put it in a tape recorder that had been set up next to him. He played the tape.

'Maybe we should leave the country. I checked the savings account, and we've got two hundred and thirty-two thousand dollars in there right now.'

'You want to be a fugitive the rest of your life?'

'At least we'd be fugitives together.'

'That's not a bad idea, but do you think we could get away from the FBI? They've got a tail on me everywhere I go.'

'I'm sure we could figure out a way to sneak off.'

Agent Lewis shut off the tape.

"No further questions, Your Honor."

"Mr. Pierson, your witness."

Pierson stood up and glared at the witness. "So you're saying because in a private, intimate conversation between a husband and a wife the idea of fleeing the country came up Mr. Coleman is a flight risk?"

"Exactly."

"Didn't he reject the idea in the tape?"

"Objection, Your Honor. The tape speaks for itself."

"Your Honor, we haven't heard the entire tape. I think it's a fair question."

"Overruled. Answer the question," the magistrate ruled.

"Yes, ultimately he did."

"In your observation of Mr. Coleman, has he bought any airline tickets?"

"No."

"Have you observed him packing bags?"

"No."

"Has he withdrawn large sums of money from his checking or savings account?"

"No."

"What did Mr. and Mrs. Coleman do directly after the conversation you just played for us?"

"What do you mean?"

"Did you continue to monitor their activity?"

"Yes."

"What did they do?"

"They made love."

"Did you hear them? Did you watch them make love?"

"I heard them, but I didn't watch them. Agent Covey watched them."

"Did Mrs. Coleman scream when she climaxed?"

"Objection! Your Honor!" Lewis yelled.

"Did you get a hard-on?"

"Objection!"

"Pass the witness."

"No further questions," Lewis replied.

"Is there any more testimony?" the magistrate asked.

"Not from the prosecution, Your Honor."

"Mr. Pierson?"

Pierson called several witnesses, the last one being Lynn. Lynn walked slowly to the witness stand and took a seat.

"Mrs. Coleman, you're married to the defendant, correct?"

"Yes."

"Are you aware that you and your husband were tape recorded in the hot tub the other night?"

"Yes, I heard later that an FBI agent was on the roof watching us."

"What else were you doing in the hot tub beside talking?"

"Making love."

"So you and your husband were having an intimate moment in your hot tub and the FBI was listening in? Do I have that right?"

"Exactly."

"Now you brought up the question of fleeing the country, right?"

"Yes, but I was just dreaming. I knew we couldn't do it. Why should we do it? Matt is innocent."

"Did your husband ever say he wanted to flee to Mexico or anywhere else?"

"No, he basically said it would never work."

"At the end of the tape, he seemed to agree to leave the country with you."

"He was just playing along with my dream. It was part of our foreplay."

"Thank you, Mrs. Coleman, and I apologize for the legal system that allows the violation of your right to privacy. Pass the witness."

"Mr. Lewis?"

"No questions, Your Honor."

"All right, then I don't really think deep down we have a flight risk here but the very fact that fleeing the country came up is a problem. I'm afraid in this case it would be prudent to err on the side of caution rather than take a chance that the defendant would run off with his pretty young wife. Accordingly, I'm setting bond at $500,000 as requested."

"Your Honor! Pierson exclaimed. "That's ridiculous!"

"You may not like the ruling counselor," the magistrate said, "and that is your right. But you better show a little respect for this court, or I'll cite you for contempt."

Pierson glared at the magistrate as he got up and left the bench. Pierson turned to Matt and shook his head. "I don't believe this! Jesus, what is going on here?"

Matt put his hand on Pierson's shoulder and said, "It's not your fault, Bruce. We are fighting powerful forces here. I'll be all right. Just watch out for Lynn, okay?"

Pierson looked at Matt and shook his head. Then he shrugged and started packing up to leave. The deputy U.S. Marshall came over and took Matt away. Lynn stood at the back of the courtroom and watched Matt disappear through a side door. Tears ran down her cheeks. Lori handed her a tissue and put her arm around her to console her.

Matt was transported to the Dallas County Jail to be held until trial or the posting of a bond. He was processed and put in a cell by himself. That night he was transported by chain gang to the mess hall for supper. After he had been released from his chains, he got in line for dinner. The line was slow, but in time he was served, and he sat down. He wasn't in a very talkative mood, so he ate silently until someone addressed him.

"Aren't you that legal evangelist?"

Matt looked up and frowned at the man. "I don't know who you're talking about."

"That bankruptcy dude. Yeah, you look just like him."

"So?"

"So, what happened?"

"I don't really want to discuss it."

"What, are you too good for us working class?"

"No, I'm just depressed. I don't want to talk about it."

"Get used to it, man. Depression is the norm around here. Huh, guys?"

The guys around them laughed.

"Oh, just a tip. You better go to the john before you go back to your cell, cause this will be the last opportunity until you get back to your cell at eight."

"Really? What are we going to do after supper?"

"They're taking us to the yard, and there's no place to take a piss out there."

"Huh, okay, thanks," Matt said. Matt looked at the man a minute and then got up and went to the bathroom. As he walked in, a tall, dark inmate was in front of a urinal. He could see that several men were in the bank of stalls to his left. He proceeded cautiously, starting to unbutton his fly when several men suddenly rushed him and pushed him up against the wall.

He struggled, but there was no resisting as he was greatly outnumbered. Finally, he quit fighting and glared at his assailants.

"Okay, you got me. What do you want?"

"I've got some advice for you from a friend," the tall, dark one said.

"Oh really?"

"Yes, listen carefully, you scumbag, because I'm not going to give it to you twice."

"I'm listening."

"Tomorrow, you're gonna call your attorney and tell him that you've given this whole thing some thought and you've decided to plead guilty and take your chances."

"Oh, sure. You can tell them to piss off!"

One of the inmates kneed Matt in the groin. Matt let out a groan and doubled over. The intense pain brought tears to his eyes. Two of the inmates jerked him upright again.

"I know you don't really want me to tell them that because, if I did, your sexy little wife would end up in a watery grave at the bottom of the Trinity River."

Matt squirmed frantically trying to get loose, but it was no use as the men had him pinned tightly to the wall.

"In fact, if you don't call your attorney tomorrow just like I said, your wife will be catfish bait by the weekend."

"You bastard!" Matt screamed as he pulled one arm loose and punched one of his assailants in the eye. The angry inmate grabbed his arm and twisted it sharply. Matt let out a painful scream as he was pinned back against the wall again. He looked up at his assailants and said sternly, "If anybody touches my wife I'll kill them!"

"Yeah, like we're scared of you."

"I've got lots of money. I'll put a nice big contract out on your life, and you'll be hunted like a rabid dog."

The man laughed. "You're going to be broke by the time the people we work for get through with you."

A bell sounded, and the men quickly dispersed leaving Matt lying on the restroom floor. A guard came in to check the facility and saw him. He ran over and helped him up. The guard took him to the infirmary, where he was patched up and then taken back to his cell. In the solitude of his cell, he contemplated the chilling message that had been so painfully delivered.

Lynn was the greatest thing that ever happened to him. All his life he had been scared to death he would never find his soul mate. When he finally found her, he was the happiest man alive, and he savored every minute they spent together. He thought back to their honeymoon and the time they spent alone in Alaska. Now he was about to lose everything he cared about. Tears flowed down his cheeks. He cried into the night as he mourned the imminent loss of his true love.

After breakfast, he asked to use the phone. The guard showed him to a telephone room and locked him inside. Matt picked up the phone and called Pierson.

"Hello."

"Bruce, this is Matt."

"Oh, I'm glad you called. I've just about raised your bond."

"Don't bother."

"Huh?"

"Forget the bond. I'm pleading guilty."

"What!"

"I've been instructed to plead guilty, or they're going to kill Lynn."

"They contacted you in the jail?"

"Yes."

"I'm going to call Lewis. This is ridiculous."

"Forget it! Don't you get it? I've lost! They're too big. They control this whole damn country. There is no way I can win now. God, was I stupid starting this thing. I should have listened to Dad. . . . Oh Jesus! Bruce, what am I going to do?"

"Listen, let me come over. We need to talk about this. There's got to be some way we can protect you and Lynn."

"How? The FBI? That's a joke."

"Let me talk to some people."

"Forget it. If I plead guilty, how much time will I get?"

"Oh God, one to five years and a fine of up to $500,000."

"How about probation?"

"As I recall the sentencing guidelines, you could be out in eighteen months."

"I can live with that. Make a deal."

"Are you sure?"

"Yes, I'm not taking a chance on them killing Lynn. I couldn't face that. I love her too much."

# 18

The night following Matt's incarceration, a terrible ice storm hit Dallas, preventing Lynn from going to visit him. For two days the streets were too treacherous to be traveled. Lynn couldn't sleep without Matt in her bed, and being unable to visit him for several days was unbearable. Lori had volunteered to stay with her until Matt was released, but even with her best friend nearby, Lynn was a lost soul.

Matt missed Lynn terribly, but in a way, the ice storm was a blessing. He needed time to figure out how to tell her that he was pleading guilty. He wondered if he should tell her the truth, that he was pleading guilty for her sake, or if he should make up some other rationalization for his decision. If he told her the truth, he figured she wouldn't allow him to plead guilty and that could ultimately be her death warrant.

When the streets finally thawed out, Lynn was one of the first visitors at the jail. She was escorted to a visiting room and told to wait. Momentarily she heard a buzzer go off and a steel door open. Matt came through the door, smiled, and sat down across from her.

"Hi, honey," he said.

"Oh, Matt. Are you okay?"

"Yes."

"I'm sorry I didn't come sooner, but—"

"It's all right. I heard about the ice storm."

"You're not mad at me?"

"No, of course not. I can't believe you're here now. I heard it was still bad out there."

"It wasn't too bad. . . . Are they treating you okay?"

"Yeah, they're not very friendly, but nobody's abusing me."

"How come you're still in here? Brad said he had your bail just about arranged."

"Well, that's something I need to talk to you about."

"What do you mean?"

"Well, I could get out on bail, but it would take every dollar we have to post bond. Then what money would you have to live on?"

"I can live off the profits from the practice."

"How long do you think we'll be able to keep the Debt Relief Centers open with me in jail for bankruptcy fraud? The U.S. Trustee's office I'm sure will try to get the firm and me suspended from practicing before the bankruptcy court until the case is settled."

"You think so?"

"Yes, I'm the sole owner of the practice so they would have no other choice."

"I don't care. Even if we don't have a penny, I'd rather have you on the outside with me."

"I know, and that's where I want to be too, but we've got to be realistic. What are the chances that I can beat this rap anyway?"

"You have to beat it! You can't go to prison."

"Bruce says if I plead guilty I could be out in eighteen months. If I go to trial, no telling what will happen."

"Matt, I can't believe you're even thinking about a plea bargain. You were set up for godsakes! You've got to fight this thing. I won't let you just throw away your life to save money."

"Come on, honey. Face it. We're beaten. The bank is too powerful. If they played by the rules, we might have a chance to win, but they are ruthless. Those guys would gut their own mothers if it helped the bottom line. If I give up now and let things cool off, they might leave us alone. When I get out of prison, we'll move away from Dallas and start an advertising agency or something."

"Matt, what's going on? This isn't you talking."

"Yes, it is, damn it! You've got to face reality. There are more important factors to consider here."

"They've threatened you, haven't they? They told you if you win, you lose, right? Did they threaten to kill you?"

"No, honey. They said they'd kill *you* if I didn't give up the battle."

Lynn began to cry. "This isn't fair," she said. "They can't do this! Isn't there anything we can do?"

"I wish there were, honey, but there isn't."

"What about the Senate Banking Committee? What if I went to them and told them what's going on?"

"They want me to disappear too. I hardly think you'd get a receptive ear."

"What about the Day-Timer?"

He sighed. "That's a long shot. Senator Goss probably won't even see Bill. "

"Yes, he will, and Senator Goss will start an investigation. You'll eventually be vindicated."

"Lynn. . . . Come on, honey. You've got to give it up. Eighteen months won't be that long. I'll survive, and then we'll have the rest of our lives together."

"Oh, Matt. How could I live without you for eighteen months?"

"You can visit me every week, and in between, we can communicate over the internet."

"Will they let you do that?"

"Sure, if Charles Manson can have a website, I sure as hell can communicate with you on AOL."

"Have you talked this over with Bruce?"

"Yes, he says it makes a lot of sense."

"I still don't like it."

"I know. Listen, honey; there is something you need to do ASAP."

"What."

"Before I started law practice I did some defensive estate planning, you know, just in case a calamity struck us."

"Oh, really? You didn't tell me."

"Well, it was something best kept a secret. Anyway, I have an offshore trust. It doesn't have much in it right now, so I need you to wire transfer some money to it. I left you wiring instructions on my desk at home. While I'm in prison, the trustee will pay you an income. We need to get the money out of our account before the feds freeze it."

"Is that legal?"

"It's our money, and right at this moment, we can do whatever we want. We just can't afford to wait to do the transfer. Once I plead guilty, the court will assess a fine and then they'll take everything we have."

"Can they go after the trust?"

"No, not where I've got it. It's safe."

"Okay, honey. I'll take care of it today."

"Good," he said, holding back his tears. "I'm really sorry it turned out this way. I never realized I was putting our lives in danger. I would have never—"

Lynn shook her head. "No. It's my fault. All I could think about was bringing the masses into the bankruptcy courts so we could get rich. I never considered who would be affected by what we were doing."

"We were just too good, babe. I'm just glad we're both still alive."

"Me too. Let's keep it that way."

***

Several weeks later Matt was taken to the Federal Building to announce his plea. The courtroom was packed with the press and curious spectators. Matt came up to the U.S. Marshall's office to confer one last time with him before hearing. He briefed him on the details of the agreement and advised him that the judge didn't have to accept it. Finally, the time came to go to the courtroom. Russell Lewis was seated at the prosecution table when they entered. Matt and Pierson took their seats and waited.

The bailiff stood up and said, "All rise. The United States District Court for the Northern District of Texas is now in session, the Honorable Houston T. Cotton presiding."

The judge came in and took the bench. He smiled, rummaged around the bench for a moment and then said, "All right, I'll take announcements."

Russell Lewis stood up and said, "The prosecution is ready, Your Honor."

Bruce Pierson stood up and said, "The defense is ready, Your Honor."

"All right then," the Judge said. "Will the bailiff read the charges?"

As the bailiff read the charges, Matt scanned the room to see who had come to gloat over his demise. He didn't recognize most of those who were present, but he did see several familiar faces, Wallace Green, Agent Radcliff, Peter Robertson, Tom, his mother, and a tough-looking, bald-headed man that gave him a chill. He stared at him a moment trying to place him. He had seen him before.

He gave up and turned his eyes back to the judge. He felt angry and frustrated at what was happening to him but was relieved that it was about over. All he cared about now was serving his time and starting over with Lynn. He felt that, by the grace of God, he hadn't been killed and would still have a long life with her. It was just a matter of time before his ordeal would be over.

"How do you plead?" the judge demanded.

Matt hesitated. He didn't realize how hard it would be to say the words that would send him to prison and subject him to the public ridicule. Suddenly the anger that he had so far kept in check, swelled up inside him. He gave a scathing look to his adversaries who were gloating in the gallery. He wanted to spit in their face, but they were too far away. How could he confess to a crime he would never have dreamed of committing? His face turned red. Tears began to well in his eyes.

"How do you plead?" the Judge demanded.

Matt took a deep breath, swallowed hard, and replied, "Guilty."

"Mr. Coleman, has your attorney fully briefed you on the effect of this plea?"

"Yes, Your Honor."

"Do you realize you cannot change the plea after it has been entered by the court?"

"Yes, Your Honor."

"Are you making this plea without coercion and of your own free will and volition?"

Matt couldn't speak. He searched the room for Lynn. He wanted to run to her, to tell her he was doing this for her. He wanted to scream out that he was innocent—that he was being coerced into making this ridiculous plea. Then he spotted the baldheaded man again. Now he remembered. He had seen him around, following Lynn and he. He realized for the first time that he was working for MidSouth Bank—an enforcer, a hit man perhaps. He promised himself that someday he would hold a gun to this asshole's head and make him experience the fear and pain that he and Lynn had been feeling these past few months.

"Are you making this plea without coercion and of your own free will and volition?" the Judge repeated with a hint of irritation.

*No, Your Honor, that bald-headed asshole over there made it known to me if I didn't plead guilty here today he'd kill my wife. Is that coercion enough for you?*

Matt looked at the judge, took a deep breath and replied, "Yes, Your Honor."

"Very well, I've looked at the recommendation of the prosecution and the probation report, and I'm prepared to accept the recommendation. Mr. Coleman, it is the judgment of this court that you be remanded to the custody of the United States Department of Corrections for a term of eighteen months, with probation for an additional forty-two months and that you should be fined the sum of $200,000."

The courtroom erupted in excited chatter. Matt hung his head, too humiliated to look at anyone. Much to his relief, the bailiff came over and escorted him away. As he was leaving, he looked at Lynn and gave her a faint smile. She broke into tears as he disappeared from sight.

Lori held Lynn up as they left the courtroom. Rich and Erica wanted Lynn to come home with them, but she declined. Lori assured them she would be okay. As they were leaving, they passed Hans, who had been listening to their conversation. Hans followed them at a distance. Lynn had parked her car across the street on the south side of the building. They jaywalked to the parking lot and found it. As they drove off Hans held up his hand. Suddenly a black Mercedes came barreling around the corner. Just as this was happening, the transport vehicle taking Matt back to the Dallas County Jail rolled out of the underground parking garage under the Federal Building.

Matt saw Hans being picked up by the Mercedes. He squinted, wondering what he was doing. Then he saw Lynn's car a block down the road. Fear shot through him like a lightning bolt. He turned around and watched Hans chase after Lynn's car. "No, stop!" he screamed. "You've got to stop him! He's going to kill my wife."

"What?" the deputy said.

"That guy. The bald-headed one in the courtroom. I know he's going to kill my wife! You've got to do something. Turn around! We've got to go after them!"

Matt was frantic. He began pounding on the window.

"Are you crazy? The only place you're going is a nice comfy jail cell."

"Call the police, tell them my wife is in danger! That guy is going to kill my wife. He got into a black Mercedes. Turn around. They're following her right now."

"Get a grip, Coleman. You're getting paranoid. Nobody is going to hurt your wife."

"Please! I beg of you! Stop!"

"Just sit down. I'll call the police station. Keep your pants on," the deputy said, looking at Matt through his rear view mirror. "What kind of car does she drive?"

"A red Mazda Miata convertible, license number L-U-V-M-A-T."

The deputy got on his radio and said, "Dispatch. This is Unit 29 transporting prisoner Matt Coleman to the county jail, copy?"

"Yes, Unit 29, go ahead."

"Our prisoner has some concern for his wife's safety. He seems to think someone is following her home with malicious intentions. She's traveling east on Commerce in a red Mazda Miata, license number L-U-V-M-A-T. That's Lincoln-Uncle-Viper-Mary-Alpha-Terry. The possible suspect is driving a black Mercedes, unknown license number. Could you check it out?"

"Copy, Unit 29. I'll report it to the Dallas Police Department."

"Thank you. Unit twenty-nine out."

Matt said, "You've got to follow-up on this. I'm serious. These people have threatened to kill Lynn."

"Don't worry. I'll check up on it."

Matt sat back in his seat wondering if anyone would actually check on Lynn. Somehow he didn't think the police would give much credence to his concerns, and even if they did what was the likelihood they'd be able to do anything to stop the bank's enforcer? He regretted having pled guilty. He was helpless now to protect Lynn.

"What an idiot!" he screamed.

The deputy turned and looked at Matt. "You calling me an idiot?"

"No, damn it. I'm the idiot. I trusted those bastards. . . . Oh, God! What have I done?"

The deputy shook his head and turned back around.

"Can I make a quick phone call?" Matt asked.

"Sure, after we get you back to the jail."

"No, right now. I need to call Lynn on her mobile phone and warn her."

"Who do you think you are, the president or something? Let me clue you in. You're nothing but a two-bit con man who finally got what was coming to him. We're not stopping so you can make a damn phone call! Jesus! You're a real piece of work."

"If they harm my wife, I'm going to hold you responsible!"

"Don't you threaten me, you son of a bitch!" the deputy screamed. "One more word out of you and I'm going to stop this car and personally beat the shit out of you!"

"Fine. Beat the shit out of me, but first, let me make a damn phone call—*now!*"

The deputy made a sharp turn into a gas station and slammed on the brakes. He opened the door and pulled Matt out. He was about to hit him when his partner said, "Let him make the phone call. It can't hurt anything."

The deputy glared at his partner. "All right. Make your damn call."

He pushed Matt toward a telephone booth. Matt was handcuffed so the deputy made the call and held the phone up to his ear. The phone rang and rang, but there was no answer.

"Damn it!" Matt screamed. "She must have shut off her cell phone."

"Okay, back in the car," the deputy said. "You got your phone call."

Matt reluctantly got back into the car. Tears began to stream from his eyes as he feared the worst. A dark, ominous feeling plunged him into the deepest depression he had ever known.

***

Hans lit a cigarette as the black Mercedes followed Lori and Lynn up the Dallas North Tollway. Lori insisted on driving and she was traveling fast wanting to get Lynn home where she could take better care of her. When they got to Beltline Road, they exited the Tollway and proceeded to the apartment. After they parked the car, they went inside.

Hans and his driver pulled up as Lori closed the apartment door. They got out, the driver ran around the back, and Hans slipped unnoticed in between two buildings. He carefully removed a screen, cut a hole in the window with a circular glass cutter, stuck in his hand, and unlatched the lock. Then he lifted the window and climbed inside the bedroom without making a sound. He could hear the two women talking as he stepped inside.

"I can't believe Matt's going to prison," Lynn moaned.

"Eighteen months will go fast. It really will."

"No, it won't. It will seem like an eternity. Why is this happening? It's not fair!"

"What are you going to do while Matt's in prison?"

"I don't know. I've got to shut down the practice. Dad has agreed to finish up all of Matt's cases that were in progress."

"Are you going to get a job?"

"Not right away. I'm just not in the right mental state to work. I can't concentrate on anything. All I can think about is Matt all alone in prison."

"At least he's in a federal prison and not Huntsville."

"Yeah, thank God for small favors."

"You ought to get a job at an ad agency or something."

"The bank, I'm sure, has blackballed me. I doubt any ad agency would touch me with industrial strength rubber gloves."

"I don't know. You've proven how good you are."

"Yeah, too good, as it turns out."

"Let's turn on the TV and see how the press is reporting the plea bargain."

"No, I don't want to go through that again."

"You need to know what they're saying so you can respond appropriately tomorrow. You know you're not going to be able to hide from this thing."

"I know. Okay, turn it on if you must."

Lori turned on the TV and flipped through several stations until she found the local news. After a few minutes, Matt's story came on.

"Local Dallas Attorney Matt Coleman pleaded guilty today in Federal District to bankruptcy fraud and conspiracy charges. The court sentenced him to 18 months in prison, 42 months' probation, and a $200,000 fine. Coleman, along with his wife, Lynn, orchestrated the meteoric rise of the Debt Relief Centers of Texas, who boasted the filing of more than four thousand bankruptcies in less than a year, costing banks and other financial institutions nearly a quarter of a billion dollars in losses."

"Today the Debt Relief Centers closed their doors, and in response, the Dow Jones Industrial Average rose 282 points in active trading. Senator Bennington, a member of the Senate Banking Committee, looking into bankruptcy reform, told a news conference today that the recent bankruptcy crisis underscored the need for a wholesale revamping of the bankruptcy systems. He criticized the current law for being so liberal and debtor-friendly that consumers have little to lose by filing. He said he would be urging the Congress to abolish alternative state exemptions, require most consumers to file chapter thirteen, and increase the scrutiny of filings to eliminate bankruptcy fraud and concealment of assets.

"In other news, Exxon-Mobil Corporation announced a huge oil discovery in the southern Caribbean. . . ."

Lori shut off the TV and gave Lynn a sympathetic look.

"We'll I bet in six months no one will remember the name, Matt Coleman. Hell, who knows? Matt might even get out on parole in less than eighteen months," Lori said.

"Brad doesn't think so. He says the government doesn't want Matt out on the street for a while until the current economic crisis has cooled down. It's not likely he'll get out early."

"Hmm. That sucks."

The bedroom door suddenly opened and Hans stepped out with a gun pointed at them. There was a crashing noise from behind them, and the back door burst open. The driver stepped inside and gave them a menacing glare.

"Oh, my God!" Lori screamed.

Lynn yelled.

"All right, ladies, we're going to take a little ride," Hans said.

Lynn looked around searching for a way to escape or a weapon that she might use to defend herself. But Hans had the door blocked, and bedroom windows would take too long to open. Hans would get to her or shoot her before she could get it open. She was trapped, and there was nothing she could do. Lynn looked sorrowfully at Lori. This wasn't Lori's battle, yet she had been caught up in it, and her life was in danger. Lynn became angry.

"Where are you taking us?"

"You'll see. Just stand up and walk normally to your car. Don't try anything or we'll kill you. We're just going to take you for a ride."

"I'm not going anywhere until you tell us where were going," Lynn said.

Hans smacked Lynn across the face hard with the barrel of his pistol. She staggered backward from the blow reeling in pain. Blood streamed from her mouth.

"Ah, you bastard!" she moaned as she ran her index finger around the inside of her mouth. "You broke my tooth!"

"Just shut up and do what I say or I'll put a bullet in your head."

Lynn glared at Hans and then finally started to move. Lori, looking pale and frightened, followed her. The four of them moved slowly to the car. Hans got in the back seat with Lynn, and Lori sat in the front passenger seat. The driver took off toward the Dallas North Tollway and entered heading north. They drove to Highway 121 and took it west until they got to a dirt road near the East Fork of the Trinity River. After driving down the dirt road a while, they stopped.

"What are we doing out here?" Lynn asked.

Hans gave Lynn a hard stare and then replied, "Shut up and get out of the car."

Hans got out and yanked Lynn out of the car. The driver got out to watch.

"What are you going to do?" Lynn asked as she fell to the ground outside the car. "Ouch. Damn you!"

"Haven't you figured it out yet?" Hans replied. "It's a shame that I have to do this to such pretty ladies, but we need to teach your husband a lesson."

"What do you mean? What are you going to do? Are you going to rape us?"

"That's not a bad idea, but we're not perverts."

"What are you going to do then?" Lori asked.

"It's very unfortunate, but you two are going to be involved in a terrible accident."

"No! You can't kill us," Lori said. "We haven't done anything."

"Leave Lori out of this!" Lynn said. "She had nothing to do with what Matt and I did."

"I'm sorry but, as they say, she was at the wrong place at the wrong time. There's nothing I can do."

"You bastards!" Lynn said. "I thought we had a deal. If Matt went to prison, you'd leave me alone. Haven't we been punished enough?"

"It's not my decision. I've got my orders. You two messed with the wrong people."

"Please don't kill us," Lori cried. "Please . . . no."

"Sorry, girls," Hans said as he slipped a thin rope around Lynn's neck and began to strangle her. She grabbed at the rope and desperately tried to get a grip but to no avail. Unable to get a hold of the rope, she stomped hard on Han's foot. He winced in pain and Lynn nearly broke free, but she was no match for Hans' massive body.

"Ahh! No! No! Please!" she mumbled as she gasped for air.

She continued to struggle for several long seconds until her body went limp. Hans let her go, and she collapsed lifelessly on the ground before his feet. Suddenly the door opened, and Lori began to run into the brush. The driver immediately took chase and quickly tackled her. Then he took a rag, stuffed it in her mouth, and held his other hand over her nose. She tossed and wiggled, trying to get free, but it was hopeless. The driver was much stronger and bigger than poor Lori, and it wasn't long before she gave up the battle.

The two men attached leg and arm weights on the girls with duct tape and threw the bodies in the trunk. After dark, they drove to a bridge over the Trinity River and dumped the bodies over the side. They splashed and quickly sank beneath the muddy water.

***

Matt was having trouble sleeping in his cell. He was worried and had trouble falling asleep. When he did fall

213

into a shallow slumber, nightmares would soon wake him. He didn't hear the guard walk up to his cell.

"Mr. Coleman, you've got a visitor," the guard whispered.

Matt jumped and sat up quickly. Fear swept over him.

"Huh? What is it? What's happened?" he said.

"Get dressed. There is someone here to see you."

"It's the middle of the night."

"I know, but it's important."

"What is it?"

"I don't know. Just come on."

Matt put on his pants, grabbed a shirt, and followed the guard. When he entered the visitor's room, he saw Bruce with a solemn look on his face. He sat down and looked him in the eye.

"What happened?"

"I don't know how to tell you this, Matt."

"What? Is Lynn okay? Tell me Lynn is okay!"

"I'm sorry, Matt. Lynn and Lori are missing."

"Noooo!" Matt cried as he grabbed the bars and tried to rip them from their mountings. "Those bastards! They've killed her."

"I'm so sorry, Matt. Maybe they'll turn up."

"Those sleazy assholes are going to pay! Oh God! Believe me they'll wish they never heard the name, Matt Coleman."

"But Matt, you don't even know who they are."

"I'll find every last one of the little suckers. I don't care what it takes, and I'll make them bleed. Believe me, they're going to pay! Goddamn them!"

# 19

Jason didn't mind the drive to the Federal Correctional Institution at Texarkana. It was summer, and East Texas was gorgeous this time of year. If it weren't for the fact that he was visiting his friend in federal prison, it would have been almost like a vacation. But each time he neared his destination, he would inevitably fall into a deep depression as he recalled the events that made this weekly trip necessary.

The authorities eventually found Lori and Lynn's bodies near Lake Ray Hubbard. A fisherman had been shocked and mortified when he thought he had caught a record catfish, only to discover he'd snagged a woman's torso. Jason thought back to Lynn's funeral. The image of Matt standing in handcuffs at her grave, tears streaming from his eyes, was still vivid in his mind.

Matt was beginning to adjust to prison life after several difficult weeks. Being an extremely active person, the sheer boredom of sitting hour upon hour with nothing to do was debilitating. Because of his education, he had been assigned to work in the library, but stacking books was not exactly challenging for him. Fortunately, as time went on more and more inmates became aware that Matt was an attorney and sought his advice and counsel about a myriad of problems. Most, of course, wanted him to help them with their appeals or counsel them on making parole.

Matt gladly assisted every one of them because it made the days go faster and his time in prison less miserable.

Matt looked forward to Jason's visit. Although he had frequent visitors, including Erica and me, Professor Swensen, and Bruce Pierson, Jason's visits were his favorites because he could talk freely to Jason without worrying about his reaction to what he said. When Erica and I visited, he had to be careful because we were against his plans to seek revenge against the bank. We were still trying to get the Senate Banking Committee to investigate MidSouth Bank, but after Matt's guilty plea and the return to normalcy on the bankruptcy front, there was little incentive for an investigation.

"Hey, how's it going," Jason said.

"Okay, now that you are here."

"Well, it's nice to see you too," Jason said.

"You know why I particularly like seeing you, other than for your charm and wit, of course, is because it means another week has passed. This is your eighth visit, so that means I only have seventy weeks left in this Godforsaken place."

"Yeah, I can't believe it's been over two months since the sentencing hearing," Jason said. "Thank God time flies."

"It's starting to get a little more interesting in here. I'm helping some of the inmates with their legal problems, unofficially of course. It's kind of neat wielding a little power from my jail cell."

"What kind of things are you doing?" Jason asked.

"Oh, a guy named Art, a few doors down from me was being divorced by his wife. She hired some big law firm to take poor Art to the cleaners. Boy, were they pissed when he filed an eight-page answer and counterclaim to their petition."

Jason laughed. "I can imagine."

"So you seem to be feeling better, huh?"

"Yeah, I'm not nearly as depressed as I was the last few weeks. I had a kind of religious experience this week."

"A religious experience?"

"Un huh. You know I was so angry at MidSouth Bank for killing Lynn and Lori, and I missed Lynn so much I was going insane. I think if I'd have had a gun I would have stuck the barrel in my mouth and pulled the trigger. Fortunately, it's tough to commit suicide in here. They don't let you have any rope or sharp objects."

"You really thought about committing suicide?"

"Yes, I'm ashamed to say I thought about it a lot. I mean, what's the reason for living without Lynn?"

Matt began to weep.

"I know, but she would want you to be strong," Jason said.

"You're right, and if I committed suicide, how could I punish them for what they did?"

"Matt, forget about the bank. If they get even a hint that you're out for revenge, they'll kill you."

"Don't worry. I've finally got it all figured out. The other day I was alone in the library, and a group of homos came to visit me. They insisted I join their group and they wanted to initiate me with a gang bang."

"Oh, shit!" Jason moaned.

"It wasn't a big surprise. Several inmates had warned me that it was coming. Their leader was a Chicano named Eduardo."

"So what did you do?"

"I had agonized over this confrontation many times in my mind. I thought of telling them I had AIDS or gonorrhea or some other dreaded disease but they knew I would be in isolation if that were the case. I had to come up with something original, something compelling if I was to retain my masculinity and self-respect."

"'So, what's it going to be, big shot lawyer. You going to join in the fun or do we have to tie you down,' Eduardo asked."

"'Listen. I don't have anything against gays, okay? But I'm not into homosexuality. Just leave me out of your games, if you don't mind.'"

"'But we do mind. You've got a cute ass. Besides, in a few months you'll be so horny, we'll start looking good to you. So why wait?'"

"'I don't think so.'

"I was petrified of being defiled by this gang of thugs. As they started to close in on me, I got sick to my stomach and nearly threw up. They started to touch me and stick their hands in my pants. I pulled away and pleaded with them.

"'Come on, you don't want to do this. I can be a valuable resource for all of you. I'm a lawyer. I can do your appeals and help you file lawsuits against the government. We can be a team, but if you rape me, then I'll just be a worthless piece of ass.'"

"'I always wanted to screw a lawyer," Eduardo said drawing laughter from his gang. "Bend over. I've been waiting for years to do this.'"

That's when I became so desperate I finally said something very rash—something that could get me in a lot of trouble. But I couldn't let them rape me.

"'Listen. I've got lots of money. I'll see to it that each of you have a nice chunk of change when you leave this place. Just leave me alone.'"

"'How much change?'"

"'Two hundred thousand.'"

"'Where do you have it stashed?'"

"'In a bank account in the Cayman Islands.'"

"'Pretty slick, Mr. Lawyer,' the leader said. 'The problem is there are ten of us, so that's only $20,000 each.'"

"'Well, you can have it. Take it all.'"

"'It's not enough. Besides, how are you going to get it to us?'"

"'I've got a friend on the outside. I'll arrange to get you the money. Just give me a bank account number, and I'll have the funds wired into it.'"

"'Listen. I like you, Matt. You got some spunk, but I don't believe you, and I don't have time to check your banking references.'"

"The men laughed."

"'Okay, you're right, but what if I can show every one of you how to walk out of this prison with not only the $20,000 in cash but also a credit line of $50,000 just waiting for you to spend. After it's all gone, you can file bankruptcy and never have to pay it back.'"

"'Get out of here. . . . Okay, guys, hold him down. Let's get on with this.'"

"'No, wait! I'm serious. In addition to the $20,000, I can show you how to clean up your credit and have $50,000 credit available to use as you please. You can also share the information with other inmates and take a cut of what they make. The potential profit is really up to you. It will take about a year to implement the plan but—'"

The leader held up his hand and said, "'That's half a million dollars. Do we look like idiots? No banker in this right mind is going to give an inmate credit.'"

"'Do you watch TV?'"

"'Of course.'"

"'Then you must know I doubled the bankruptcy filings in the Northern District of Texas and nearly caused two Texas banks to fail.'"

"'Yeah. So what?'"

"'I'm telling you I can pull this off. I've got a friend who is the best credit repairman in Texas. He'll clean up each inmate's credit and then we'll apply to a bank I know that will give a credit card to anybody with a pulse.'"

"'Don't you have to have a job to get a credit card?'"

"'I've got that figured out too. It will be a piece of cake getting the credit cards.'"

"So what do you get out of all this?'"

"My honor and dignity, plus a little revenge against the bank that's responsible for killing my wife and putting me in here.'"

"'Hey, Eduardo. Maybe he can do it,' one of the men said. 'Give him a chance, man."

"Eduardo gave the man a scathing look, then smiled and said, 'All right, you've got ten days to get this plan underway and convince me it's for real. Otherwise, your ass is mine.'"

"'Don't worry. As I said, it's a piece of cake.'"

"I must admit that was quite ingenious," Jason said. "If you can't baffle them with brilliance, buffalo them with bullshit, right?"

"But it isn't total bullshit. I'm pretty sure I can actually do it. I had a client who was an expert at credit repair. He showed me how to do it. Just think if MidSouth were to issue two hundred inmates five credit cards, each with a $5,000 credit limit. That's five million dollars. And if MidSouth Bank is stupid enough to give a bunch of inmate's credit cards, then they deserve to lose their money, right?"

"I don't know if I want to be involved in anything illegal."

"Don't you want to make Frank Hill pay for killing Lynn and Lori?"

"Sure, but five million dollars is nothing to MidSouth Bank."

"True. This is actually just a diversion to annoy Frankie Boy and give my dad and Bill Ross time to get evidence against him. Hopefully, they'll put him out of business permanently."

"So how do I fit in?"

"All I need is for you to buy a business and run it for me."

"What kind of business?"

"It doesn't matter, just something that's labor intensive. You need to have lots of employees."

"Why?"

"I'll tell you later. Just buy a business, learn how to run it, and when the time is right I'll tell you what to do."

"But buying a business cost money. As you know, I don't have a cent."

"I'll give you a hundred grand. You can use it as a down payment. Just be sure and buy a business you can run and break even so we can operate it for at least a year."

"This is bizarre. I hope you know what you're doing."

"Not entirely, but I'll figure it out. This is going to be so awesome. I just wish Lynn and Lori were here to see it."

"See what? I have no clue what you're planning to do."

"Something like this has to be held close to the breast. You're better off not knowing all the details. When the time is right, I'll explain everything to you. In the meantime, you'll have to trust me."

"Okay, Matt, but I hope I don't end up as your cell mate."

"That wouldn't be so bad, would it?"

"Funny man."

The guard indicated their visiting time was up. Matt stood up and smiled at Jason who was still trying to fathom how Matt had roped him into his scheme.

"One last thing," Matt said.

"What?"

"I'm going to need the name, address, birth date, and social security number of every congressman and senator plus their spouses and children."

"How am I supposed to get that?"

"I don't know. But I'm sure you'll figure it out."

***

Jason looked back at Matt, smiled, and waved goodbye. He turned, walked down a long corridor, and left the visitor's center. On the way back to Dallas, he thought about the business he was supposed to buy. He didn't know anything about running a business and wondered if he could pull it off. He wasn't sure what Matt had up his sleeve but knew whatever it was; it would be dangerous. Nevertheless, he felt he had no choice but to do as Matt wished. He had to help Matt get his vengeance.

When Jason got back to Dallas, he bought a newspaper and started looking through the classified ads for businesses for sale. Not finding anything that looked appropriate, he called a business broker he knew to ask him what he had available.

"What kind of business are you looking for?"

"Oh, I don't know. Something simple. I don't want to have to go through extensive training to learn the business. Something well established so I don't have to worry about losing my ass the first ninety days."

"How about a printing business?"

"Hmm. Doesn't that take years to learn?"

"Well, you could hire someone to run it."

"No, I want something I can run."

"I've got a convenience store."

"How many employees?"

"Seven."

"No, I need lots of employees."

"Why?"

"It's a long story."

"How about a lumber yard."

"Where is it located?"

"Tyler."

"How many employees?"

"Thirty-seven."

"What are they asking?"

"Nine hundred and fifty thousand."

"How much down?"

"Two hundred and fifty thousand and the owner will finance the balance."

"Offer them a hundred down and a note for six hundred and fifty thousand," Jason said.

"Don't you want to see the place?" the broker asked.

"Well, yeah. . . . Of course, after we see the place, if I like it, then you can make the offer."

"Good. I'll call them tomorrow and arrange a tour."

"Do you have any financial information on them?"

"Yeah, I've got a complete packet. I'll give it to you."

"Good, I'll study it tonight, and if I have any questions, I'll ask you them in the morning on the way to Tyler."

"Fine, then I'll be seeing you tomorrow," the broker said.

"Right."

Jason had no clue what he was doing, but he felt kind of excited being part of Matt's scheme, whatever it was. He couldn't wait to see the lumber yard and report back to Matt on what he had accomplished so quickly.

After touring the lumber yard, the next day, he drove back to Texarkana to see Matt. He was impressed with what he had seen, but he needed Matt's approval and the money if he was going to close the deal. After waiting quite a while in the visitor's center, Matt finally appeared.

"You're back awfully quick."

"You said to find a business, so I've done it."

Matt smiled. "That's what I like about you, Jason, you never pussyfoot around. What kind of business is it?"

"A lumber yard over in Tyler."

"Hmm. That should work. What's it going to cost?"

"I was going to offer $100,000 down and a note for $650,000."

"What's the asking price?"

"Nine fifty."

"Okay, that's good."

"What about the money?"

"Give me your account number, and I'll have my bank transfer the money."

"Can you do that from in here?"

"Sure, I'll go through the internet."

"Okay," Jason said and then pulled out his check book and tore off a deposit slip. "Here, take this. The numbers are on the bottom."

Matt took the deposit slip, smiled and then said, "Now don't take a long vacation when you get this money."

Jason laughed and replied, "I've always wanted to go to Tahiti."

"You can live in Tahiti after we pull this deal off."

"Or, if we don't pull it off, I could have the same accommodations as you."

"No, if we don't pull it off, we'll more than likely be dead. If the inmates don't kill us, the bank will see to it."

"Oh, great, Matt. You're a fun guy to be partners with."

"Well, seriously, I want to be honest with you. You'd be better off not getting involved in this deal. It's going to be extremely risky. If you want to back out now, I'll understand, and I won't hold it against you."

"You need somebody on the outside though, right?"

"Yes, but there are other people out there. I'll find somebody."

"Yeah, but could you trust them?"

"Not like you."

"Exactly, and I want you to pull this thing off, whatever it is. I don't want you getting killed."

"Thanks. I kind of like living myself."

Jason put his hand on the glass that separated them and said, "Partners then?"

Matt nodded, put his hand up against the glass and replied, "Partners."

# 20

I examined the black book that Bill Ross had given me. It was a pocket size Day-Timer with one page per day from November 2006 through February 2007. The initials on the black leather exterior were FLH, which I knew stood for Franklin Leonard Hill, the chairman, and CEO of MidSouth Bank. In addition to the two calendars, there was an address book brimming with addresses, telephone and fax numbers, email listings, and notes of all sorts. Obviously, Martha Simonton did work for Mr. Hill. Otherwise, how could she have obtained possession of this most interesting calendar?

I flipped through the pages of the book, wondering how I could unlock the secrets that I just knew were hidden inside. Bill had taken the calendar to Senator Goss in Washington, but he had declined to even look at it. He said Matt's confession had blown any chance of a congressional investigation into predatory credit card practices. Dejected, Bill had returned to Dallas and given the black book to me. I looked up as I heard Erica walk in.

"Hi, honey," I said.

"Any luck?"

"Not much. I did find an address of a woman who I think was Mr. Hill's secretary before Martha Simonton."

"How did you figure that out?" Erica asked.

"Well, I noticed several different people wrote in the book. It looked like Mr. Hill on a few occasions made his own almost illegible entries, but most of the time Martha Simonton would make nice, clearly printed entries. There was also a two-week period during which a third person made entries in the calendar. Since that was about the time Martha came to work for Hill, I assume his former secretary made the entries."

"What was her name?"

"Well, both she and Martha initialed any entries they made. Her initials were RW. I checked the address book, and the only one with those initials is Roxanne Witherspoon."

"So, what are you going to do?"

"I've talked to Bill Ross and told him to find her. He's probably halfway to Albany as we speak. Perhaps she knows something about MidSouth's conspiracy to destroy Matt."

"I bet she does. You've got to find her. She may be our only chance to get Matt a new trial."

"Bill will find her. Don't worry. In the meantime, I'm going to check out every name and number in this book. I'm bound to find something out that will help us."

***

After Bill's plane landed in Albany, he rented a car, drove downtown, and checked into a hotel. He ate dinner and then called Roxanne Witherspoon to arrange a meeting. She agreed to meet him in Lincoln Park the following morning. With several hours to kill, he decided to go to the local police station and see if he could make a friend. He figured he might need some information later on, so if he had a contact in the local police department it could be quite helpful.

After driving around downtown, he spotted a station, parked his car, and went inside. Two dispatchers were sitting behind a counter talking to some patrol officers. He went up to them and waited for one of them to get free.

"Hi, what can I do for you?"

"Oh, I just came by to say hello. I'm a police officer from Mesquite, Texas. I'm doing a little freelance investigation work, and I wondered if I could visit with one of your detectives a minute."

"Well, there's just one detective working tonight. Let me see if she's got the time to talk to you."

"Thank you. I really appreciate it."

The dispatcher rang the detective's number and conversed with her briefly. Then she looked up and said, "Detective Paula Sands will be with you shortly."

"Thank you."

Bill turned around and walked over to some benches and sat down. He was tired after the long flight from Dallas and was having trouble keeping his eyes open. Spotting a coffee machine, he went over to it and got a cup of coffee.

"I could use a cup, too," Detective Sands said.

Bill turned around and was pleasantly surprised by the tall brunette who was looking him over. She smiled pleasantly and extended her hand. He shook it.

"Hello. You must be Detective Sands."

"Yes, Paula Sands."

"Hi. I'm Bill Ross," he said. "How do you take it?"

"Black."

Bill frowned. "Really?"

"Yes. Is that so strange?"

"I guess not. My ex-wife liked it black too. She always had to be the tough little cop."

She frowned. "You have something against female cops?"

"No, in fact, I still love my ex-wife. We just couldn't live together."

"Oh really?" she said as she folded her arms and looked at him intently. "Why?"

"At first it was great. We obviously had a lot in common, but then I started to move up, and she didn't go anywhere. It wasn't right. She was every bit as good a cop as I was but, let's face it; most police departments have been dominated by men for decades, so a woman has a tough go of it."

"Tell me about it," Paula said.

"Yeah, you should know what I'm talking about. Anyway, she became resentful and started blaming the discrimination on me. She said I didn't stand up for her. Our relationship went down fast."

"I'm lucky here. We've got a very liberal police chief. He won't tolerate the least bit of sexual discrimination. I've actually moved up in the ranks at a record pace."

"You must be good."

"Of course."

Bill laughed, "And proud, too, I can see. . . . Are you married?"

"No."

"That's surprising. As attractive and personable as you seem to be, I would have thought men would be tripping over themselves to pronounce their love."

"No, quite the contrary. Very few men want to date a female cop. I guess I intimidate them."

"Then you won't mind if I buy you a drink when you get off work?"

"No, not at all."

"When would that be?"

"Eleven."

"Excellent. You know the city better than me, so where should we meet?"

"There's a place called Monty's Hideout on Broadway. I'll see you there at 11:30."

"Good."

Bill left and went back to his hotel to clean up for his date with Detective Sands. He couldn't believe his good fortune. Not only did he now have a contact on the force but also a companion for the night. After he showered, shaved, and brushed his teeth, he got dressed and left for Monty's.

Monty's place was obviously a police hangout. Several officers were still in their police uniforms drinking beer before they headed home. Paula wasn't there yet, so Bill got a booth and ordered a beer. Pretty soon she walked through the door and scanned the room. When Bill saw her, he waved, and she walked over to him.

"Sorry I'm late, but I got covered up in paperwork."

"Oh, God. I hate paperwork. You want a beer?"

"No, actually I'd like a gin and tonic."

"Ma'am!" Bill yelled to the barmaid.

"Can I help you, sir?" she asked.

"We need a gin and tonic over here."

"All right, I'll be right back."

Bill frowned and said, "God, I hate gin. I don't know how you can stand it."

"What do you mean? It's good."

"Ehh!"

"So, what brings you to Albany?"

"I'm going to interview a potential witness in a case I've got going back in Texas."

"What kind of case?"

"A murder case."

"Oh really? Have I heard about it?"

"Maybe. Did you hear about the two women brutally murdered near Lewisville, Texas and then dumped in the Trinity River?"

"The attorney's wife?"

"Right. Lynn Coleman."

"I thought the authorities closed that case?"

"The authorities have closed it, but Matt's mother and father, Erica and Rich Coleman, won't give up. They've got me on the case, and they spend every spare moment trying to get their son out of jail."

"So, can I help out?"

"I'm not sure I need any help, but I appreciate the offer. If something comes up, I'll let you know."

Paula smiled and said, "I'm glad you came by tonight. I'd be home alone watching Jay Leno if you hadn't."

"We'd both be home alone watching Jay Leno."

"Right."

"So, did you ever come close to getting married?"

"Yes, right out of high school my boyfriend asked me. I gave it a lot of thought, but I wasn't ready to settle down and have kids. You know what I mean?"

"Oh yeah, that's way too young to get married. You need to wait until you understand life a little better and have some money in the bank."

"Did you understand life when you got married?"

"No, and I didn't have any money in the bank either."

They both laughed, and their hands touched. Bill took the opportunity to take Paula's hand in his and squeeze it gently. She smiled and then sat up straight as the barmaid showed up with her drink. Bill reluctantly let her hand go and picked up his beer and took a swig.

After they had consumed too many drinks to drive home, they got a cab and went to Bill's hotel. They paid the driver and went up to his room.

The following morning Bill and Paula slept late. When Bill finally looked over at the clock, it was already 9:30.

"Shit, I've got to meet someone at ten."

Paula rolled over and said, "Go ahead, I'll still be asleep when you get back."

"You will?" Bill laughed. "Don't you have to work today?"

"Not until three."

"Good, I'll be back in a couple of hours, and we can have lunch."

"Okay," Paula said and then turned over and hugged her pillow.

Bill got dressed and caught a cab to where he had left his rental car. Then he drove over to Lincoln Park to meet Roxanne Witherspoon. She had told him over the phone that she was a short, middle-aged woman who would be wearing a gray business suit. After searching for several minutes, they found each other and took a seat on a park bench.

"You mentioned having something that belonged to Frank Hill," she said.

"Right, a Day-Timer. That's how I found you," Bill replied.

"So, what do you want from me?"

"You used to work for him, right?"

She took a deep breath and looked away. "I guess it wouldn't do any good to deny it."

"No, and let me say right off the bat that we have no interest in hurting you in any way."

She turned to him and frowned. "I shouldn't be talking to you. Are you sure you aren't under surveillance?"

"Absolutely. I fully appreciate how ruthless Mr. Hill can be."

She let out a deep chuckle. "You have no idea."

Bill noted the fear in her voice and wanted to reassure her. He said, "Anyway, to answer your question. I took every precaution to ensure that we would be alone today. You don't have to worry about your safety."

"I'm safe now, but if I help you, and I presume that's why you're here, how safe will I be then?"

Bill smiled. "Honestly, I don't know, but the fact that you agreed to meet me indicates you realize it's time to stop Frank Hill."

She nodded and said, "On that subject, we are in agreement."

Bill smiled and took a deep breath. He didn't know exactly where to begin, but he figured he should brief Roxanne on Matt's run-in with MidSouth Bank, Lynn's murder, and Matt's incarceration. She knew all about it.

"My retirement from MidSouth Bank couldn't have come at a better time. Matt Coleman had just started rocking MidSouth's boat, and I knew it was going to get ugly. I had been Frank Hill's personal secretary for about fifteen years and knew him to be a ruthless businessman. Frank took over as chairman after the bank was shut down by the FDIC in 1986. He headed a group of well-financed vultures who were picking up failed banks and thrifts in Texas, Oklahoma, and Louisiana for a song. The group divided the assets they had acquired between two entities, MidContinent Bank and MidSouth Bank. The performing assets went to MidContinent, and the nonperforming went to MidSouth. They gave Frank the nonperforming assets to deal with."

"What was he supposed to do with them?" Bill asked.

"Hunt down the persons financially responsible for the debts and do whatever it took to collect them. He loved his job."

"Was he successful?"

"Oh, yes. He was like a bloodhound on a rabbit. He would become obsessed with collecting an account. He'd hire private detectives to locate assets or get dirt on the people who owed the bank money. Then he'd threaten them with dire consequences if they didn't pay up."

"What about the Fair Debt Collection Act?"

She laughed. "He didn't care about any collection laws. He scared people. Once Frank Hill was in their face they wanted nothing else but to be rid of him, at all cost."

"It's just hard to believe that he could get away with being so ruthless."

"Well, the people did owe the money, and the feds were very interested in slamming the people responsible for the banking and savings and loan crisis. The government loved Frank Hill. He was their man, and he knew it. Once he had established his reputation in the financial community, anyone who got word that Frank was after them either arranged to pay it quickly or made plans to leave the country."

Bill shook his head. "So, how long did it take him to liquidate the bank's assets?"

"In about four years he had collected nearly 80% of the debts owed the bank, which was phenomenal compared to the national average. Then he became bored and started looking around for ways to aggressively invest all the money he had collected. The clear choice was subprime lending. Credit cards were where big money was being made. They had been around for some time and were gaining in popularity each year. They were stable and easy to administer as computers got more powerful and traditionally demanded a very high-interest rate. The only problem was the credit card industry was becoming more and more competitive."

"So what was his plan?"

"To concentrate on higher risk accounts that banks and even subprime lenders wouldn't touch. He went after traditional customers but also launched a strong marketing campaign on college campuses. He got lists of high school graduating classes and immediately sent them a credit card application. For the first time, a job wasn't a requirement to get credit. He figured mom and dad would provide the funding for the debt service on the card or, if not, the students would get part time jobs to pay back the cards. He once said he didn't care if they had to sell drugs to pay back the bank as long as it got its money."

"Is it true MidSouth sent credit card applications to persons who had just filed bankruptcy?"

"Oh, yes. He loved people who had already filed bankruptcy. He said they couldn't file for another six years, so he had plenty of time to milk them dry."

"With all these high-risk accounts wasn't there a high default rate?" Bill asked.

"Yes, but it didn't matter. MidSouth was making so much money that the 5% who defaulted didn't leave a dent in bottom-line profits."

"Until Matt came along?"

"Exactly. I remember the first board meeting after Frank got wind of Matthew Coleman's new Debt Relief Centers. Frank was very upset because MidSouth's credit card default rate had gone up 3% in just sixty days. This wasn't enough to put the bank in any danger, but it caused a 25% decline in profits for the quarter. He ordered an immediate investigation of Matt and the centers so that he could develop a strategy to terminate the threat to the bank."

"So, what was his plan?"

"I don't know. I retired shortly after that and Martha Simonton took over for me. Thank God."

"Before you retired, did Frank Hill take any direct action against Matt?"

"Yes, he contacted an old buddy from the service, Hans Schultz. He paid him $20,000 to pull some dirty tricks on Matt to discredit him. I overheard several conversations between them."

"The prostitute?"

"Right. That was one of them."

"What else?"

"When that didn't work, Frank was pissed, so he told Hans to get someone on the inside to set Matt up."

Bill scratched his head. "He must have got to Tom. Shit."

"That's right. The guy on the inside was named Tom."

Bill took a deep breath. "The pieces are now starting to fall into place."

"That's all I know. I was glad to get the hell out of MidSouth Bank when I did."

"Does Frank know how much you know?"

"I'm not sure. Most of the information I picked up came about inadvertently. He never directly confided in me, but I'm sure he suspects I know something. He stressed when I left that everything I learned while working for the bank was strictly confidential and there would be dire consequences if I ever disclosed anything."

"So, why are you talking to me?"

She gave me a long hard look. "The bastard killed my friend."

"Martha?"

She nodded. "I warned her about taking the job, but she didn't listen. She said I was overreacting—that all

CEO's were ruthless and played hardball. She just didn't understand that Frank was—" She looked away. A deep, pervasive sadness overcame her. She leaned over and started to weep.

"Frank was what?"

She slowly looked up at Bill and replied, "The devil himself."

Bill swallowed hard. He knew she was right. Frank Hill had no honor and no conscience. He had killed Lori and Lynn even after Matt went to prison to protect them. Bill shook his head in disgust. He prayed one day he'd come face to face with Franklin Benjamin Hill. If he ever got so lucky, he'd put a bullet through his heart—if he had one.

When Bill got back to the hotel, Paula was still asleep. He smiled, kneeled down, and kissed her on the lips. She opened her eyes and said, "What time is it?"

"Eleven-thirty. You gonna sleep all day?"

"Uh huh," she said and turned over and closed her eyes.

"Come on, aren't you hungry?"

"A little," she said rolling back over on her back exposing her exquisite breasts. Bill shook his head and sat down next to her. She noticed him focusing on her breasts, so she pulled up the sheet.

"You sure got lucky last night."

"I know. Now I don't want to go back to Dallas."

"Hmm. Do you have to go?"

"Yeah, but I have a feeling I'll be back to visit soon."

"I hope so. I don't like one-night stands."

"Me either."

"Did you find what you were looking for?"

"Yes, exactly what I was looking for—a critical witness who can help me get a good friend out of prison."

"Really?"

He nodded. "But I have a problem."

"What's that?"

"Her life will be in danger just as soon as our adversaries find out we've found her."

She sat up, holding her sheet over her breasts, and gave Bill a sympathetic look. "Hmm. That *is* a problem."

"So, I was wondering if you might keep an eye on her for me?"

She frowned. "Have you forgotten I'm a detective?"

"I'm sure you have a couple of friends who could split duty with you? Unless you get paid a lot more than I do, I'm sure you could use the cash. My client can afford to pay top rates."

She gave him a thoughtful look. "I guess I could arrange it. If it's important to you."

"It is. Very important."

She gave him a wry smile. "You're going to owe me, though, big time."

Bill pulled the sheets from her grasp and tossed them aside. He pushed her back on the bed and said, "Don't worry. I always pay my debts."

# 21

Matt was taken from his cell and escorted out of the main cell block into the administrative wing of the prison. The guard stopped in front of the warden's office and opened the door. Matt took a deep breath. He had waited almost two weeks for this appointment, and he was anxious to get on with it. The warden's secretary stopped typing, looked up and smiled at him.

"Oh, Mr. Coleman. I'm Melinda, the warden's secretary. I'm glad I'm finally getting to meet you. Come in. Sit down."

"Thanks."

"I followed your case in the newspapers. Why on God's green earth did you plead guilty? That totally blew my mind."

"Well, it's a long story."

"I bet. I think I know part of it."

"You do?"

"But we can't talk about it now."

The door opened to the warden's office, and a short, stout, gray-haired man walked out. Matt stared at Melinda, wondering what she knew and how she would have gained that knowledge. She looked back at him with a sympathetic smile then turned away and began typing.

"Mr. Coleman, come in," the Warden said.

Matt got up, looked back at Melinda one last time, and walked into the warden's office. The office decor was

World War II, with pictures of a B29 Superfortress, the Flying Tigers, and several Army plaques strategically placed on the walls of the room. The warden's desk was heavy oak and looked like it had been through a few battles itself. The warden motioned for Matt to sit, so he took a seat in a dark wooden side chair.

"Well, Mr. Coleman, my people tell me you've really whipped the library into shape."

"I've tried to make it more functional for the inmates."

"I'm afraid I can't honor your request for the Texas statutes on CD ROM, however. I just can't see how that is a necessity."

"It makes research a lot easier."

"I'm sure it does, but if you think I'm fool enough to make it easier for you guys to file lawsuits against me, then you've misjudged me," the warden said smiling.

"Well, I suspected you might feel that way, but I figured it couldn't hurt to try, right?"

"No, it never hurts to try," the warden said.

"Anyway, that's not why I wanted to see you. What I wanted to know is if it would be okay to start a Bible study group?"

"A Bible study group?"

"Yes."

"But that would be something the chaplain would do, not you."

"I know, but many of the men don't have a religious preference but would like to learn more about the Bible without the pressure of a clergyman present. This would be strictly an academic endeavor."

"I don't know. I can't believe very many inmates would want to study the Bible."

"Well, if your aim here is to straighten people out and make them good citizens, I can't see how Bible study would hurt. You know, I pled guilty and everything, but I was really innocent. There were threats to kill my wife if I didn't plead out."

"And you thought someone who would threaten to kill your wife would keep their word?"

"Well, I figured they were businessmen, and they'd honor a contract."

"You're pretty naive."

Matt hung his head. "Apparently so."

"So what's your point?"

"Well, if I have to spend eighteen months of my life behind bars, I might as well try to do something constructive. I think I can really get through to some of the guys in here. Since I'm a prisoner like they are, they'll listen to me. It's worth a shot, don't you think?"

"Okay. If I were to approve your proposal, how would you handle this Bible study group?"

"Oh, we'd have several meetings each week to discuss the various scriptures. I've already got a half dozen or so guys wanting to join."

"Is that right?" the warden said skeptically as he rubbed his chin pondering the idea.

"Uh huh."

He shook his head and frowned. "I don't know. This is a very unusual request."

Matt leaned forward. "Well, I don't think it's unreasonable."

The warden looked Matt straight in the eye and after a moment cracked a smile. "No, I guess not. . . . All right, I'll authorize it—two one-hour meetings per week. Let's see how that goes, and if there really is a lot of interest, then I may give you more time."

"You're welcome to join the group, Warden," Matt said beaming.

The warden laughed and replied, "No, I don't think so. I get all the Bible study I need at my own church."

"Okay, but if you change your mind let me know."

"Don't hold your breath," the warden chuckled.

"Oh, Eduardo Gomez will be helping me with the program."

The warden frowned. "You've got to be kidding."

"No, I'm serious."

The warden shook his head in shock as Eduardo Gomez was one of his most violent and feared inmates.

"Well, if you can convert that son of a bitch, then I'll owe you a debt of gratitude."

"I will. He wants to be saved. He's told me so."

"Damn, Coleman. Maybe there is hope for your little study group."

Matt nodded, turned, and left the warden's office. As he passed by Melinda's desk, he stopped and looked at her.

She smiled and whispered, "Don't worry. I'll be in touch."

He frowned in confusion and started to ask her a question, but she put her fingers to her lips and said. "Not now. Go."

As he left the office, he wondered again who this woman was and what she knew about his predicament. He opened the door and reluctantly left her. The guard who had been waiting at the door took him back to the library. While he was alone working on his curriculum for the Bible study group, his mind couldn't let go of the mysterious Melinda. Who was she? An admirer? A spy hoping to find out what he was up to? Finally, he decided it didn't matter, as he wasn't about to take her into his confidence. He finally put her out of his mind.

Once he had focused back on the task at hand, he called the chaplain and arranged to get fifty new Bibles. There was much work to be done to prepare for the first session. At lunch, he sat with Eduardo and one of his friends and they discussed the meeting with the warden.

"So, how did your meeting go?" Eduardo asked.

"It couldn't have been better. The warden said we could meet twice a week for now and maybe more later on, depending on the turnout. He was impressed that you were involved in the project."

He cracked a smile. "I bet he was. The turnout is going to be outstanding, man, I guarantee. It may be damn near 100 percent."

"I doubt that. Some guys just aren't religious no matter how lucrative it promises to be."

"So what do you want us to do?"

"Find me two groups of twenty-five guys that you know will want to join the program. We'll have one group on Tuesday and one on Thursday. I don't want any skeptics at this stage, just devout Christians. We'll cut out the chaff later on."

"Okay, man. Do you need any help before then?"

"Yes, I'll need some help getting the Bibles ready. Find two or three guys with good handwriting."

"Okay, I'll send them over this afternoon."

"Thanks."

The lunch buzzer went off, and the inmates lined up to go to their work assignments. When Matt returned to the library, two boxes were sitting on the floor. He opened them and discovered they were his new Bibles. After inspecting one of them carefully, he made some blank pages with tracing paper and glued them on written pages of his Bible.

He figured the new pages would not be noticed unless they were  inspected carefully, which was unlikely. Finally, he wrote an outline of the material he intended to discuss on the blank pages.

Later on that afternoon three inmates showed up and said Eduardo had sent them. Matt thanked them for coming and gave them their assignments of duplicating what he had done with his Bible. It took them several hours, but they finally finished just before dinnertime.

***

After dinner, Jason showed up for his weekly visit. He had worked hard on the task Matt had given him and was anxious to tell him about what he had accomplished. He had been waiting nearly twenty minutes when the guard finally led Matt into the visitor's room.

"So, how did the purchase go?" Matt asked.

"No problem, I'm now the proud owner of a lumberyard. I'm going to call it Quality One Lumber. As you advised, I put it in a corporation owned by a limited partnership. The general partner is Conventure, Inc."

"Conventure?" Matt repeated and frowned. "Oh, I get it, cute. So there's no way anybody can tie the corporation to you?"

"No. Conventure is owned by a Cayman Islands trust and the limited partners are all straight out of the phone book."

"I hope they don't all begin with the same letter."

"No, I mixed it up a bit."

"Good, everything is going as planned here. I've got my first Bible study group on Tuesday, and the warden said we could have two a week."

"What if any of the guards listen in or, God forbid, want to join the group?"

"I've already invited the warden."

"Oh, you're a real comedian. What if he had accepted?"

"Then we would have done some real Bible study."

"Seriously, the place will undoubtedly be bugged, so how are you going to accomplish anything?"

"At every session, we'll hand out Bibles. It will appear that we're actually studying it, but the real lesson will be hidden deep within the Old Testament. We'll also develop a religious code that will allow us to communicate without detection."

"So what do you want me to do now?"

"Just operate your business normally, but be sure you and only you take all personnel and credit inquiries."

"I understand. Do you really think we can pull this off?"

"Only time will tell, but if we do, there are going to be some very pissed off people at MidSouth Bank. . . . Which reminds me, you better find us a damn good place to hide out once I'm released."

"How am I going to do that? I wouldn't know where to begin."

"Don't worry about it. I'll get you some help from some of the guys in here. Maybe they can refer us to someone to fix us up new identities."

"I hope so because running this damn lumber company is going to keep me really busy."

"You've still got all the old personnel, right?"

"Yeah, most of them."

"Then just don't get in their way and everything should be fine."

"I hope so."

"Have you heard anything from Bill lately?"

"Yeah, he's up in Albany checking on an ex-employee of MidSouth who might be able to help us out with the Day-Timer. He's been there nearly a week, so I would expect to hear from him soon."

"Good, we need a witness to make this plan really work. I sure hope he finds her."

"Me too."

On Tuesday the first Bible study group met. The warden stopped by and shook his head when he saw twenty-five inmates packed in the small reading room. He smiled, whispered something to a guard and then left. Matt stood before the group and began the meeting.

"Thank you all for coming out today. It certainly is a tribute to all of you that you've interrupted your busy day to learn more about God."

The inmates laughed, and Matt continued, "So today I'd like to discuss some parts of the Bible that have a special meaning to me. I'm going to have some of the guys pass out a copy of the King James' version of the Bible for each of you. Be sure you find each citation that I give you and read it carefully. The Bible is the richest book that has ever been written. Each passage has hidden meanings and messages that you can miss if you don't read and consider them carefully."

Three inmates passed out Bibles to everyone. One inmate offered a Bible to the guard, but he refused it. Matt smiled at him and then said, "Let's turn to Matthew 7:7. This is one of my very favorite passages. 'Ask, and it shall be given unto you, seek, and ye shall find; knock, and it shall be opened unto you.'

"Now all of us are here in prison because we never understood what Jesus was telling us. He's saying here that whatever we want we can have if we believe in God and let him provide it. Now if that's true none of us should be here, right?"

"I hear you, brother," someone said.

"Who's in here for robbery?" Matt asked.

A lot of hands went up. Matt shook his head and said, "Well, if you'd believed what Jesus said and trusted in him, you could have got what you wanted without having to steal it, isn't that right?"

"How do you know that?" an inmate said.

"Well, I can only speak for myself, but I've always been able to get what I want just by setting a goal and working diligently for it. It takes patience, but if you really believe what Jesus says, he will always come through, and you'll get what you want."

"What are you doing in here then?" the inmate asked.

Matt smiled, "Good question. . . . Actually I'm in here because I pissed off some very powerful people." The inmates laughed, Matt smiled and continued, "I had asked God to make me wealthy, and he obliged, but at the time I didn't realize God had already given me the greatest gift a man could ask for. Her name was Lynn. She was my wife, and I loved her dearly. I should have asked for God to protect her, but instead, all I thought about was material wealth and the happiness I thought it would bring. Because of my selfishness, she was murdered, and I'm here alone rotting in prison."

The inmates were still. Matt continued, "So the point is, you should be careful what you ask for and make sure your motives are pure. Some of you have probably had similar circumstances."

The discussions continued for the duration of the time the warden had allotted. When it came time to close, Matt said, "I'd like you all to turn to Jeremiah 15:15 and study it carefully. It will introduce you to a concept that will be important in our later studies. Does anyone have any questions? If not, I'll see you next week."

The inmates got up and mingled for a while and then left with their Bibles in hand. Eduardo came by before he left and said, "Very inspirational, Matt. I think I'm going to like this study group."

"How do you think the men liked it?" Matt asked.

"The ones I talked to were very impressed. However, there are some that are still skeptical."

"Well, I can understand that, but as time progresses I hope they will become believers. We need as many as possible to join our cause."

"I don't think many will turn down what you have to offer," Edwardo said.

"Good. . . . Listen. I may need your help on another aspect of the program."

"Just name it, boss. I'll make it happen."

"Thanks. I've got to clean this place up and get back to my cell right now, but I'll touch base with you in the yard tomorrow."

"Cool, man, see you then."

Eduardo left, and Matt began cleaning up the library. When he was done, he reported back to his cell. He picked up a calculator, sat on his bunk, and began punching numbers. When he was done, he smiled and shut it off. After putting the calculator back on his desk, he fell back on his bunk and fell asleep.

The next morning after breakfast he reported to the yard as required every morning at 9:30. He scanned the area for Eduardo but didn't see him. He stepped down onto the grass and began walking through the inmates playing basketball, lifting weights, jogging, or just laying out soaking in the sun. Finally, he spotted Eduardo in the distance. He walked over to him and put his hand on his shoulder. Eduardo turned and smiled when he saw who it was.

"Hey, Matt, my man."

"How's it going?"

"You tell me," Eduardo said.

"Good, very good, but like I said, I do need your help with something."

"No problem. Just name it."

"You got any contacts on the outside that can set a friend of mine and me up with a new identity. When this thing comes down, I want to be somewhere where *nobody*, I mean *nobody* can find me."

"Sure, I know the best man in the state. He's over in Fort Worth. He can make a new man out of you."

"Really."

"Yes, fake IDs, passports. Hell, he'll even get you a new face if you want it. When he's done, nobody will recognize you."

"Hmm. I don't know about the face. I'm kind of fond of the one I have."

"Well, that's up to you, man. But it's safer to go with the whole program."

"I'll think about it, but I definitely need the fake IDs and passports."

"His name is Wally Wilkins. He owns a pawn shop downtown near Tandy Center, A-1 Pawn & Loan Company."

"Thanks, I'll have Jason get with him right away."

"No problem. Just let me know if you need anything else."

"I will."

Matt turned and walked back across the yard. He was feeling good. His plan for revenge was coming along great, and as an added bonus, he had earned the respect and admiration of almost everyone at the prison, including the warden. But his string of good fortune wasn't quite over. He found a note back in his cell.

*Matt,*

*You need to talk to a new inmate, Cecil Walker. I think you two will have a lot in common. Hope you are holding up okay.*

*An admirer*

Matt studied the note and wondered how it got in his cell. He wondered who Cecil Walker was and why he should talk to him. The handwriting looked feminine. He thought back and tried to remember if he had met any women since he'd been at the prison. The warden's secretary came to mind. She had been friendly to him and asked him why he had pled guilty. He wondered if she was his secret admirer?

Convinced he had figured out the source of the note, he racked his brain trying to make a connection to Cecil Walker. The name didn't ring a bell. He wondered how he could find him. He figured it must be important or Melinda wouldn't have taken a chance in sending him the message. He wondered how she did it anyway. Which guard was her messenger boy, and why was she so anxious to help him?

<h1 style="text-align:center">22</h1>

Jason took a deep breath as he got out of his car in front of the office for Quality One Lumber Company. It was a cool autumn day, and he wished he were fishing rather than going to work. He walked inside and smiled at the bookkeeper as he went by her desk.

"Good morning, Mr. Robinson," she said.

"Good morning."

As he approached his office, his secretary stood up and smiled. "Good morning, Mr. Robinson. Can I get you a cup of coffee?"

"Yes, thank you," he said as he walked by. He went into his office and sat down. After a minute his secretary showed up with a cup of coffee. He smiled and said, "I've got to go to Fort Worth today. If we get any calls for personnel references, just take a message. I'll deal with them when I get back."

"I could take care of them for you. I used to do that before you bought the company."

"It's all right, Margie. I prefer to handle it myself. You know, nowadays with so much EEOC litigation you've got to be very careful what you say to people who call for references."

"I guess you're right. How long will you be gone?"

"Most of the day. It's a long drive to Fort Worth."

Margie left the room and Jason opened his briefcase. He began fumbling through the mail he had picked up from the UPS Store and several other private mailbox companies they used. He looked at his watch and then locked the mail back up in his briefcase. As he was about to leave, Margie came on over the intercom.

"Personnel inquiry on line two."

Jason pushed the button and replied, "Thanks." He picked up the phone and said, "Hello."

"Hi, this is Jenny at MidSouth Bank. I need to verify employment?"

"Sure, who is it?"

"Michael Madsen."

"Yes, he works here."

"When did his employment start?"

"Ah. When does it say?"

"August?"

"Yeah, that sounds about right."

Jason pulled out a blank employment form. He wrote down the name Michael Madsen. He put down the address of the UPS Store, 2923 Troup Highway, #101, Tyler, Texas.

"What's his annual salary?"

"$26,000 per year."

"Okay, thanks."

"No problem."

Matt unlocked a drawer and pulled out a brown, expanding file. He put the employment form under "M" and then locked the file back in his drawer. Then he got up, picked up his briefcase, and walked out of his office.

It was a beautiful day, and Jason enjoyed the drive to Fort Worth. He drove along Highway 121 until he got to the Belknap exit and took it to Tandy Center. He parked in the mall garage and then walked to A-1 Pawn & Loan Co. As he opened the door, a bell rang announcing his arrival. He walked in and gazed at the racks and racks of junk for sale. A young girl was sitting behind the counter chewing gum and reading a romance novel. He went over to her and said, "Is Wally here?"

She looked up and gave Jason a once over. Then she stood up and said, "Wait a minute."

Jason nodded and then turned to take a second look at the merchandise that cluttered the store. After a couple of minutes a short fat man in a T-shirt walked in the room.

"You looking for Wally?"

"Yes, I was referred by Eduardo Gomez. He said you might be able to help me out."

"Eduardo, what's he doing these days?"

"Serving time at Texarkana."

"Oh, I wondered why he hadn't been around lately. How's his momma?"

Jason frowned. "His momma?"

"Yes, anyone who knows Eduardo would know his mother's name, right?"

"Ah . . . Yes, Rosa, I think."

Wally smiled. "Yes, quite a woman, Rosa. Come on back to my office."

Wally turned and walked in the back room. Jason followed him cautiously. The back room was more cluttered than the front and had a musty smell. After they entered Wally's room, he closed the door.

"So what do you need?"

"A group of friends and I will need to leave the country and disappear in the next few months. There'll be a lot of people looking for us. We've got to have foolproof identities."

"Up to something big, eh? Well, that shouldn't be a problem, but it will cost you. How many in your group?"

"Four or five, I think."

"We don't give group rates," he chuckled.

Jason shrugged. "How much will it be?"

"Five thousand apiece, fifteen if you want a new look."

"Five thousand is fine. We don't have time for plastic surgery."

"Well, then I'll need you and your friends to come by and give me your vital statistics and get your pictures taken."

"I can give you whatever information you need for all of us, and you can take my photo, but my friends aren't available right now, so I'll have to provide you with their photos."

"Well, I don't recommend that. The quality of the photograph is important. Do you have pictures with the negatives?"

"I don't know. Maybe. I'll see what I can do."

"Well, check and see. Otherwise, just bring me some good quality photos. I guess that will have to do. . . . I'll need half up front and half on delivery."

"How long will it take?" Jason asked.

"Three weeks."

Jason opened his briefcase and counted out the cash required. Wally smiled, took the money and stood up. He pointed to a blank wall and nodded for Jason to stand in front of it. Jason went over to the wall and put his feet on some tape marks on the floor. Wally went to a camera mounted on a tripod and looked in the viewfinder. He pushed a button, and the flash went off. He waited a few seconds and took another shot. When he was finished taking pictures, he wrote down the rest of the information he needed for the new passports and IDs.

"Okay. Just get me your friends' pictures, and I'll take care of your order. Check back in about three weeks. "

When Jason got back to the office, there was a message from Bill. He was back and wanted to meet. Jason called him and suggested they meet at a bar just outside of Tyler around seven.

At seven Bill arrived at the Red Rose Cantina. He went inside and looked for Jason but didn't see him, so he took a seat at the bar. Finally, at seven-fifteen, Bill arrived and joined Jason at the bar.

"How was your trip?" Jason asked.

"Wonderful," Bill replied.

"Then you found what you were looking for?"

"Yeah, and I fell in love."

"Oh God. Who is she?"

"A cop. Can you believe it?"

"Another cop? Wasn't your last love a cop?"

"Yeah, so what?"

"Well, you should have learned."

"She's different, and besides, I'm in the security business now, so we shouldn't have the conflicts my ex and I had."

"I hope you're right. . . . So, how's our witness?"

Bill told him the details of his meeting with Roxanne and what he had learned about Frank Hill.

"Perfect. Being Frank Hill's personal secretary for a lot of years, she can authenticate the Day-Timer and implicate Mr. Hill in Martha's murder."

"Exactly. So what's our next move?"

"I'm not sure. I've got to talk to Matt and Rich and see where they want to go from here."

"Do you have enough to go back to the senator?"

"Maybe. . . . How is Matt?"

"He's doing good. He's leading a Bible study group."

Bill laughed. "You've got to be kidding?"

"No, I'm serious. He's going to make everybody in the jail a devout Christian."

Bill shook his head. "Boy, is he full of surprises."

"Yeah, I don't know exactly what he's up to, but I can bet Frank Hill won't like it."

"What do you know?"

"I can't tell you exactly, but the heat's going to come down on him hard and fast. A lot of people will be after him and anyone he's been associated with."

Bill grimaced. "How much time does he have left?"

"About nine months, so we are running out of time. Matt is hell-bent on getting revenge and the only way he'll back off is if you can nail Frank Hill and MidSouth Bank before he's let out of prison."

Bill shook his head and said, "Okay, I understand."

"Good. Call me if you have any news."

After a few more drinks and friendly banter, Jason left and went back to his office. He looked at all the unprocessed mail and wondered what to do about it. He needed help, but who could he trust? Suddenly he had an idea. He picked up the phone and dialed information. The operator gave him the number of Cheryl Mason. Lori's sister certainly could be trusted and would love to nail her sister's murderers. He dialed her number.

"Oh, hi, Jason. I haven't talked to you in a while. What have you been up to?"

"Matt and I are figuring out how to get a little revenge on the men who killed Lynn and Lori."

"Good. How's it going?"

"Well, it's complicated and dangerous, but if you're interested, I could meet you tonight and explain it to you."

"I'm definitely interested in nailing that son of a bitch. Where do you want to meet?"

"I'm in Tyler. I'll meet you halfway. There's a Catfish King restaurant outside of Terrell. I'll meet you there at 8:30, okay?"

"I'll be there."

Matt had told Jason not to get anybody else involved, but there was just too much work for him to do. He figured Matt would be mad, but he'd get over it when he found out it was Lori's sister who was going to help. At their meeting, Jason explained what was going on, and Cheryl insisted she be allowed to help. The following morning Cheryl reported for work.

"Every morning you need to go to the mail boxes and pull out all the mail for the personnel office. Take it to the house. When you're done processing it, come to the office. In the afternoon you can process personnel files."

"What mail will be coming in?"

"Advertisements, solicitations, and credit card applications. Lots of credit card applications."

"What do I do with them?"

"You apply for every card you can."

"Who are these people?"

"Most of them are inmates at Texarkana, but there will also be some other people in the Washington, D.C. area. I can't tell you any more for your own protection. You'll also have to take any phone calls that come in from the banks and credit card companies."

"How long will I be doing this?"

"In about nine months we'll be ready to move."

"What happens then?"

"Hopefully you'll be able to watch Frank Hill's demise."

"Will I be in any danger?"

"Nobody knows you are involved, so I doubt you'd have anything to worry about. But if they did find out they might come after you and then you'd have to disappear. I'll make sure you get a nice severance package in case that happens."

"All right. Whatever it takes to get those bastards."

# 23

Hans entered the Beverly Hills Tanning Salon and Spa for a massage and sauna. It was a weekly ritual to help him cope with the stress of his job. He went up to the front desk and asked for Debbie. The receptionist escorted Hans to a booth and said she'd send Debbie in right away. Hans removed his clothes and climbed up on the table. After a minute a pretty redhead entered the booth. Hans looked up and smiled.

"Good morning, Hans."

"Hi, Deborah."

"I missed you last week."

"Yeah, I had to go to Houston again. I'm getting so sick and tired of my paranoid employer. Every day he's got another problem."

"Paranoid?"

"Yes. Do you know what paranoid is?"

"Yes, my mother is paranoid. She was driving me nuts, so I had to get her professional help."

"Hmm. You haven't seen paranoid until you've worked for a banker worrying about losing his money."

Debbie put some ointment on her hands and began rubbing Hans' neck and shoulders.

"Oh God, that feels good."

"Boy, you are tight today. They must really be getting to you."

"I don't blame them, I guess. There's a lot of money at stake."

"I hope they pay you well."

"They do. I can't complain."

Debbie began to move farther down Hans' back. As she was working, the door flew open, and Doug Barnes appeared looking very distressed. Hans sat up and covered himself with his towel.

"What are you doing here? Damn it! I can't get a moment's peace."

Barnes said, "You didn't answer your cell phone, so I had to come looking for you."

"I forgot to charge the battery last night. Sorry."

Barnes looked at Debbie and said, "Get lost."

Hans frowned at Barnes and said, "I'm sorry, honey. Give us a moment." Debbie turned and went into another office but left the door cracked.

Hans turned to Barnes and said, "What's up?"

"We may have a problem in Texarkana. We need you to check it out."

"What kind of problem?"

"Remember Matt Coleman?"

"How could I forget?"

"Well, he's up to something. He's organized a weekly Bible study group amongst the prisoners. Dozens of prisoners are getting involved. We're afraid he's trying to brainwash them like he did his bankruptcy clients."

"What could he possibly do in prison that the chairman would be worried about?"

"I don't know, but you need to find out what's going on. You can make contact with the warden. He's a friend."

"All right, I'm on my way. I'll report to you in a couple of days."

"Oh, there's some ex-cop named Bill Ross who's been snooping around up in Albany. He's a friend of Matt Coleman. The chairman wants someone watching him too. Find out what he's looking for."

"Right. No problem."

Barnes left, and Debbie returned. "Damn it. I'm sorry Debbie, but I've got to go." He walked over to where his pants were hanging and pulled out his wallet. He pulled out a fifty-dollar bill and handed to her.

She gave him a seductive smile and said, "You sure you don't have time for me to finish you off?"

"No, I've got to go now," he said as he was getting dressed. When he was done, he took her hand, squeezed it, smiled, and then left. When he was on the freeway heading for Texarkana, he tried to call the warden's office on his mobile phone, but nothing happened. He cursed to himself as remembered his battery was dead. At the next exit, he got off, got gas, and called the warden's office from a pay phone. He told Melinda, the warden's secretary, that he was on his way and didn't have time to waste. She said she'd tell him.

Melinda advised the warden and then got up and paced back and forth. Finally, she pulled out a requisition form and stuck it in the typewriter. A minute later she pulled it out, put it in an envelope, and told one of the guards to deliver it to the library. Matt was surprised when the guard handed it to him. He set it on his desk and thanked the guard for bringing it. When the guard left, he opened the envelope and discovered a note on the back of the form that read:

*Matt, Hans Schultz is on his way to see the warden. They obviously suspect you're up to something. If you are up to something, and I hope you are, you better be careful.*

*A Secret Admirer*

Matt smiled. He knew for sure now his secret admirer was the warden's secretary. She was the only one who had access to requisition forms. He didn't know why she was so fond of him, but it was certainly fortunate for him. He thought for a moment and then sent for Eduardo.

"Hey, I've got word MidSouth suspects something."

"Oh shit! I thought you said they wouldn't have any way of knowing what we were up to."

"They don't. They're just grasping at straws at this stage. All you have to do is alert your men to the possibility that someone might try to get information from them. It's imperative that nothing leaks out. We must convince Hans Schultz that our Bible study group is for real."

"How did you find out about this?"

"The warden's secretary warned me. Can you believe that?"

"No, why would she do that?"

"Beats me."

"It may be a trap. She could be trying to gain your trust, so you'll tell her what you're up to. You better watch out."

"That possibility has already occurred to me. I haven't told her anything, and I don't intend to."

"Good."

It was late afternoon when Hans finally was able to get a meeting with the warden. Melinda watched him intently as he waited for the warden to see him. After he went in, she switched on the intercom so she could listen in on the conversation.

"Mr. Schultz, what brings you all the way to Texarkana?"

"I'm curious about this Bible study group that Matt Coleman is organizing."

"Really, what's so interesting about that?"

"Well, I understand it is quite popular."

"Yes, it is. There are nearly fifty inmates enrolled. It's really quite amazing."

"Don't you think it's odd that so many men would be interested in studying the Bible?"

"Yes, very odd indeed. That's why I've taped every session."

"Really."

"Yes, and Mr. Coleman is one hell of a pastor, let me tell you. I think he's found a new profession. In fact, our chaplain has told me he has invited Matt to enroll at the seminary after he gets out of here next year."

"Do you really believe he's sincere?"

"It sure sounds like it to me. You're welcome to listen to some of the tapes if you'd like."

"Could I get a copy instead? I'll listen to it on my way to Dallas."

"Sure, no problem."

"So you don't think he's up to anything?"

"No, not really. I've had a guard at all his meetings and, as I've said, I've got everything on tape. I don't know what else I could do."

"Well, we just don't like the idea of Matt Coleman becoming so powerful even if it's within the confines of a prison. He's a brilliant man who may be looking for revenge."

"Then why is he still alive?"

"We didn't want him to become a martyr. He would have been even more of a problem had he met an untimely death. Of course, now it wouldn't matter so much. Most everyone's forgotten him, so if he suddenly were to be the victim of a bathroom squabble, who would care?"

"He's not doing anyone any harm. I think you should leave him alone. I really don't think he's a threat to you."

"Well, we'll see. Only time will tell."

"I'll keep a close eye on him and report anything unusual."

"Good, I've got to go to Albany for a few days. I'll call you when I get back."

"Fine, have a good trip."

The next morning Hans and one of his men boarded a Southwest Airlines flight to New York City on his way to Albany, New York. Before he left, a package had arrived with a detailed account of Bill Ross' activities over the previous few months. Hans examined the report very carefully during his flight. When he arrived in Albany, he checked into the same Holiday Inn where Bill was staying. He got a room just down the hall. He left his door ajar so he would hear Bill if he left.

Several hours later Paula emerged from the elevator and went to Bill's room. She knocked and Bill opened the door. They embraced and kissed passionately.

"Oh, I'm so glad to see you," Bill said after they came up for a short breath of air.

"Me, too," she replied and then kissed him again. After a few minutes, Bill suggested they go to dinner. At the same time, they got into the elevator, Hans opened the door to the stairs and quickly ran down them. They took Paula's car and found a quiet Italian restaurant and settled in to enjoy some fine cuisine. Hans waited in his car outside the restaurant.

They were seated at a table in the corner, and the barmaid came by and took their drink order.

"So, how's my witness?" Bill asked.

"Fine. I've had someone with her every minute since you left. Nothing has happened. It's been a pretty boring assignment."

Bill smiled. "Well, just hope it stays that way."

"When are you going to tell me who your client is and why Roxanne is so important to your case?"

Bill gave Paula a thoughtful look. Reluctantly he said, "I suppose I should fill you in. You have a right to know the danger involved in this assignment."

She looked at him expectantly. He took a deep breath. "My client is . . . was an attorney. He helped me out of a few jams, so we became friends. When he got in trouble, he called me to provide protection."

"From who?"

"Before I give you confidential information I should disclose who my client is just in case you have a conflict."

"Good idea. Who is it?"

"Matt Coleman."

"Matt Coleman? That doesn't ring a bell."

"Remember the bankruptcy crisis? Congressional hearings, banking irregularities---"

"Oh, *that* Matt Coleman."

"Right. . . . Hmm. I don't see why there should be a conflict. I've never worked for a bank. . . . I take that back. I did do security briefly one summer for a savings and loan."

Bill told Paula the story. She shook her head in disbelief.

Bill continued. "I know for a fact that Frank Hill had Matt's wife Lynn and her friend Lori killed. They also killed Martha Simonton, her son Michael, and a prostitute named Monica Sommers."

"He must have a lot to hide."

The barmaid came and left their drinks. Bill gave her a ten-dollar bill, she thanked him and left. Then the waiter came to take their orders.

"What can I get you?" he said.

"I'll have the shrimp scampi," Paula said.

"That sounds good. I'll take the same," Bill added.

"Thank you. I'll be right back with your bread," the waiter said and left.

Paula said, "If they are that powerful, how in the hell are you and I going to have a ghost of a chance of bringing them to justice?"

"Matt has a senator who says if we get the evidence he needs, he'll force a congressional hearing. We'll go to the press at the same time to be sure the evidence is not covered up."

"Still, if we don't time everything perfectly you and I will end up dead too."

"That's right. So if you want to pull out, just say so, and you can forget I ever mentioned this to you."

Paula took a deep breath, smiled and said, "Why couldn't I fall in love with a plumber?"

Bill's face lit up. "You've fallen in love with me?"

Paula smiled and said, "Why do you think I'm here? I've been miserable since you left me."

"That's nice. I'm so glad because I've been miserable too."

The waiter finally showed up with dinner. Paula and Bill ate quietly as they contemplated their predicament. After dinner, they went for a ride since it was a pretty night. When they returned to their hotel, they decided to have a drink in the bar before they went up to their room.

Hans watched them order a drink, then walked to the elevator, and went up to his room. He went inside, got a black bag, and walked across the hall to Bill and Paula's room. He pulled out some tools and began working on the lock. Soon the door opened. He picked up his bag and went inside.

Once inside, he went to the telephone, unscrewed the cap and fitted a listening device inside. He put the phone back together and walked over to a light fixture next to the wall. He placed another listening device inside the base of the lamp. When he was done, he went to the bedroom and planted a device in the clock radio. Then he closed up his bag and went back to his room.

In his room, he set up a small receiver, plugged in some earphones, and cracked the door so he would see when they returned. When they came back to their room, they were half-drunk, laughing and carrying on so that anyone in the vicinity could hear them. Bill unlocked the door and pushed it open. Paula entered the room, walked over to the bed and collapsed. Bill followed her and climbed up next to her.

"I think you've had too much to drink," Bill laughed.

"No way," Paula said. "I'm just starting to feel good."

"Really?"

"Yeah, come here. I've been wanting to hold you all night."

Bill climbed on top of Paula and they began kissing. Then Bill sat up and took off his shirt while Paula removed her blouse. In the other room, Hans put on his receiver and listened to their lovemaking. He closed his eyes as he listened to the bed creak and Paula moan. He began to sweat, so he grabbed a towel and wiped his brow. When they were done, there was little conversation before they fell asleep. Finally, Hans took off the headset, took a cold shower and sat on his bed. He looked at his watch and the radio alarm and then set it for six.

The next morning Hans got up when the alarm went off. He cracked his door, so he'd know if Paula and Bill were leaving. He ordered room service and waited. At seven-thirty there was still no sign of them, so he ordered more coffee. At nine-thirty Bill and Paula finally got up, took a shower together and called room service. Hans put on his headset and listened to their conversation.

Paula called the station to see if she had any messages. She hung up the phone about the time the waiter knocked on the door with their food. Bill opened the door, and the waiter wheeled the cart into the room. After he set up their places at the table, Bill gave him a tip and he left.

"Hmm. I'm starving," Bill said as he began to help himself to the food.

"Me, too, would you like some coffee?"

"Yes, please."

Paula poured Bill some coffee and then did the same for herself. She put the pot down and began to eat.

"This is the life, huh?" Paula said.

"Yes, it's nice to have other people wait on you," Bill replied.

"Too bad we can't take off somewhere for a month or two."

"Maybe when this mess is all over, we can go on a cruise. I hear they are great."

"Promise?"

Bill smiled. "Promise. But for now, we better get back to reality. It's after ten o'clock, and we've got a lot of work to do."

Paula nodded, took one more bite of her toast, and then got up to go. Bill took one last drink of his coffee and followed her to the door. As they were leaving the room, Bill noticed Hans' door was not fully closed. He stopped in his tracks for a moment and looked at Paula.

"What?" she said.

"I forgot something. I'll be right back."

He went back into the room and started inspecting every inch of it. Soon he found the bug in the phone and then the one in the light. He stepped outside and motioned for Paula to come in.

"Someone's been listening to us," he said as he held up the listening device to Paula.

"Oh, shit! What should we do?"

"Let's find out who the asshole's working for," Bill said as he pulled out a .357 Magnum from his bag.

Paula stuck her hand into her purse and pulled out a .38 Special. She checked to be sure it the cylinder was loaded and then looked at Bill. He nodded and then went to the right side of the door. Paula took the opposite side. Bill kicked the door open and slipped inside. Hans was sitting in a chair with his headset on playing with his receiver. When he heard the door bang open he grabbed his gun and started shooting at Bill.

Bill dove behind the bed as a barrage of bullets came his way. While Hans had his eye on Bill, Paula rushed in and started firing. He tried to return the fire but was hit almost immediately. Paula kept firing, hitting him several more times. He fell to the floor, lying motionless with his eyes open. Bill got up and went over to him.

"Is he dead?" Paula asked.

"Yes," Bill said, "and we better get the hell out of here before the cops come and we have to explain what happened. Come on."

"Wait," Paula said. "Get his luggage and his wallet. There might be something in there to tie him to Frank Hill."

Bill opened the closet door and pulled out a small carry-on bag. Paula got his wallet and a notepad from his pants pocket. As they were leaving, Bill kicked open the bathroom door.

"Shit!" he said.

"What?" Paula asked.

"He wasn't alone. There are two toothbrushes."

"Oh, God."

Bill put his gun away, grabbed the bag and started to leave.

"Wait. Shouldn't you get the tape?"

"Oh, right," Bill said, and then rushed over to the recorder and took out the tape. He unzipped the bag, threw in the tape, and zipped it back.

Several people had come out of their rooms to see what the shooting was all about. Paula held her gun behind her back so they wouldn't see it.

"Somebody shot that poor sucker. I'm going to call the police," Paula said.

The spectators ran past her and entered the room, allowing Bill and Paula to slip into their room unnoticed. They quickly packed up their things and left the motel. Bill got the car, and they drove off.

"Are you all right, Paula?"

"I don't know. I'm feeling kind of sick inside."

"Have you ever killed anyone before?"

"No."

"I haven't either. . . . I don't think we had a choice. It was either him or us."

"What do you think is going to happen now?"

"I don't know. It depends on how much he told his superiors about us."

"What about the police?"

"We need to take care of our business and then get the hell out of town. We better forget the airport. They'll be watching it. We'll drive to New York City, hang around for a few days until things cool off, and then catch a flight home."

"I'm scared, Bill. Do you think they know who I am?"

"We've got to assume they do."

"Oh, God! What am I going to do?"

"Don't panic on me now, come on. It's a good thing we killed the bastard. There's no telling what he overheard us say. We'd have been in a lot worse shape had we not discovered he was on to us."

"Now I can't go back to Albany."

"I'm sorry, Paula. It wasn't my intention to force you into this deal. I shouldn't have called you. Will you ever forgive me?"

"It's not your fault. I probably would have come even if you had leveled with me in the beginning."

"Really?"

"Yes, as I said, I was miserable without you."

"I'll make it up to you somehow, I promise."

"I know," Paula said.

"We better get Roxanne and bring her with us. If they overheard us talking about her, they'll send someone up to kill her."

"Right. Blanch is with her now. I'll call and find out where they are."

"Okay, let's get her and get out of town before someone spots us."

Paula pulled out her cell phone from her purse and began to dial.

"Hello," a voice said.

"Blanch? Where are you?"

"Outside a supermarket. Roxanne's doing her grocery shopping."

"Get her home. Have her pack a bag. We're leaving town."

"Really?"

"Yes, the heat just got turned up a notch. I'm gonna take the rest of my vacation and go with Bill somewhere to hide Roxanne and figure out what to do next."

"Okay, got it. See you back at the homestead."

Thirty minutes later Bill and Paula arrived at Roxanne's home. Her car was parked in the driveway, and the front door was wide open. Bill and Paula approached the door cautiously. Paula pulled her gun and slipped up to one side of the door, her back against the stucco. Bill walked in slowly.

A gunshot sent Bill to the ground for cover. Paula turned into the doorway and fired at the shooter, who was scampering into the kitchen. Bill moved down the hall to cover the back entrance to the kitchen while Paula followed the shooter's footsteps. Suddenly there was a loud crash in the kitchen. Paula and Bill rushed in, nearly running into each other. They looked out the back door and saw the shooter jump a fence and get into a late model Volvo. He peeled rubber and was out of sight before Bill and Paula could reach him.

"Shit. Where are Blanch and Roxanne?" Paula asked frantically.

"I don't know. Let's take a look inside."

They rushed back inside and started searching one room at a time. They stopped when they got to a bathroom door with several bullet holes in it.

Bill's heart sank. Paula gave him a distressed look and said, "Blanch?"

There was a tense moment of silence, and then they heard someone crying. Bill pushed the door open. Blanch was lying on the ground with her head in Roxanne's lap. She had been shot in the chest. Paula got on her cell phone and called 911 while Bill did CPR. In a moment they heard sirens in the distance.

Paula said, "Get out of here. Take Roxanne with you. I'll clean up here and explain what happened."

"But how will you explain it?" Bill asked.

"Don't worry. I'll think of something. Just get out of here, so they don't find you and Roxanne. Then we'll really have a problem. I'll catch up with you later. Call me on my cell in an hour. If for any reason you can't get through to me, meet me in Washington at the Watergate Hotel as soon as you can get there."

Bill helped Roxanne up, grabbed her bag and ran out to Roxanne's car. They got in and took off just before the ambulance and police arrived. Bill wondered what kind of a story Paula would come up with and whether her superiors would buy it. He prayed she'd be all right and he'd see her again soon.

***

When they were a safe distance away from the crime scene, Bill called me to fill me on what had happened.

"Rich. The witness is safe."

"Thank God," I said. "Get her to Washington as soon as possible. I think I've convinced Senator Goss to see us. He's interested in the Day-Timer."

"Well, I may have some additional evidence too. I've got Hans Schultz' wallet and suitcase. I haven't had a chance to go through it, but there might be something in there that would be useful."

"How did you manage that?" I asked.

"We caught him eavesdropping, and he pulled a gun and started shooting. Paula killed him."

The news of Hans Schultz' death gave me pause. He had no doubt killed Lynn and Lori. I was relieved he was dead, but there was no joy in my heart. The man responsible for their death and my son's incarceration was still at large. There would be other goons just like Schultz as long as Frank Hill had position and power at his disposal. He had to be stopped. He had to be punished, and he had to be humiliated in front of the whole world so others like him would get a message. Their days of ravaging and pillaging the American people were over.

"Another demon falls into the pits of hell."

"Yeah, unfortunately, he had a friend," Bill said, "who shot Roxanne's bodyguard. I hope she's still alive."

"Is Paula okay?"

"Yes, thank God."

"Well, call me when you've had a chance to look through Schultz' things."

"I will. I've already found something you might find useful."

"What's that?"

"Frank Hill's private cell phone number."

I laughed in sheer joy. "Oh yes. I've wanted to give that bastard a piece of my mind."

<h1 style="text-align:center">24</h1>

Frank Hill stared intently at the latest copy of the *Houston Chronicle* spread in front of him. His attention was focused on a news story buried on page 14 about a cop who had been killed in an exchange of gunfire when she surprised a burglar in an Albany, New York residence. The article went on to say that a detective in the neighborhood heard shooting and rushed to the scene. The burglar took off, but it was too late for Blanch Nicholson, an eight-year veteran of the Albany police department.

Hill tossed the newspaper aside and started pacing. He picked up his cell phone and checked it for messages. He set it down, and it immediately began to ring. He picked it up eagerly.

"Hans. Where in the hell have you been?" he yelled.

"Sorry, Frank. This isn't Hans. Your little terrorist puppet is dead."

Schultz scowled "Who is this? How did you get my number?"

"This is Richard Coleman."

There was a moment of silence in which I could feel Hill thinking. *Hans is dead. That means Roxanne is still alive. I should have killed her years ago. Damn it!*

"Mr. Coleman. I don't know how or why you got my telephone number, but I think it is highly inappropriate for us to talk—you know, with your son in *prison* and everything."

"Listen, Frank. I'll make it brief. . . . I know you set up my son and killed my daughter-in-law. I just wanted to warn you that MidSouth Bank is about to take a hit that's going to knock it on its ass."

"What are you talking about?" he said.

"That's all I can say. You just better watch your back because you're about to get your ass kicked."

"You son of a bitch! You don't scare me. There's nothing you can do to MidSouth or me, but since you've had the audacity to threaten me, I'm going to see to it that you crash and burn. Trust me."

I laughed. "I don't think so. We're on to you, and so are the feds. Your days are numbered. Have a nice day." I said and hung up the telephone.

Hill just stood there for a moment breathing heavily, then he went to his desk, pressed his intercom and shouted, "Hazel, get me a new cell phone with a new number and cancel my old account." He picked up his regular telephone and dialed a number.

"Let me talk to the warden," Hill said. The receptionist asked who it was and upon hearing it was Frank Hill said she'd put him right through. There was a long silence then the warden came on the line.

"Yes, Frank. How are you?"

"Not worth shit."

"Oh," the warden said. "What's wrong?"

"Word has it your preacher friend is up to no good."

"What do you mean? I haven't noticed anything unusual going on."

"Well, you better take a closer look because *informed sources* say he's about to do some serious damage to MidSouth Bank."

The warden gasped in amazement, "But, I don't see how he could possibly hurt your bank from prison."

"I'm telling you he's up to something and you better find out what it is and fast, or I'll cut off your little annuity." Frank scowled.

"Okay, calm down. I'll get right on it."

The warden had been receiving $500 a week which came in the form of a deferred annuity. He told people it was from his former employer but in actuality, it was money paid by MidSouth for him to keep a close eye on Matt Coleman. There was also an understanding that if Matt became a problem, one phone call would be all it took to end the problem—permanently.

"Good. Has he had any unusual visitors lately?"

"No, just the usual. His parents, his attorney, and his friend Jason."

"Jason?"

"Yeah, Jason Reynolds. He comes once a week religiously."

"Is that right? Well, the next time he visits let's put a tail on him for a few days and see what he's up to."

"Okay, and in the meantime, I'll take a closer look at his Bible study group and see if there is more to it than meets the eye."

"All right. Call me immediately if you find anything out."

Hill hung up the phone and leaned back in his big executive chair. The call to him had rattled him so much he couldn't keep his mind off Matt. *What the hell is he up to?* He doubted Matt or anyone could possibly hurt him, but he couldn't take a chance of anything going wrong at the bank. His position as chairman was the source of all his wealth and power, and he loved having both. So, he decided to send a couple of men to Dallas and another contingency to Albany, New York to help Hans' partner find Bill and

Roxanne. He wondered what else he should be doing. Suddenly he hit the intercom button.

"Hazel, get Senator Bennington on the line."

He sat at his desk biting his fingernail as he waited. A voice came over the intercom. "The senator is on line three, sir." He picked up the phone.

"Senator?"

"Yes, Frank. How are you?"

"You tell me," he muttered.

"Excuse me?"

"There hasn't been any talk of investigating MidSouth Bank, has there?"

"Why, no. I assure you that issue is dead. Why do you ask?"

"Richard Coleman called me and warned me something big was coming down. I don't know if he was just trying to scare me or what."

"If there was something in the works, he certainly wouldn't have called to warn you about it."

"Right, it's probably just a bluff, but he sounded so confident it unnerved me a bit."

"I'll ask around and see if there is anything on the horizon, but frankly I doubt it."

"Thanks, Senator. Sorry I bothered you."

"No trouble."

Frank hung up the phone. He picked up a pencil between his fingers and started tapping it slowly at first, then faster and faster. Finally, he took the pencil in both hands and broke it in two. He got up, went to his bar and poured himself a scotch. He guzzled it down and poured another one. He was about to pour a third when he slammed the glass down on the counter and exclaimed, "Damn you, Coleman!"

**25**

The DART train pulled up to the West End Station. Jason got aboard and took a seat. It was mid-afternoon, and the train was nearly empty. Just as the doors began to close, a middle-aged man in a blue suit squeezed through the doors and sat down across from him. They looked at each other nervously.

"So, you must be Jason Robinson," he said.

"That's right," Jason replied. "And you would be George Mathias, right?"

"Correct."

"So, what's this all about? Why did you want to see me?"

"I'm here to give you the biggest story of your life," Jason said.

He looked at him skeptically. "Really? I've heard that before."

Jason shrugged. "I bet you have."

Mathias sighed. "So, why me?"

"Because you're well known, respected, and I think we can trust you."

"How do you figure that?" Mathias chuckled.

Jason frowned. "I don't know. I guess it's because I read about you going to jail last year rather than revealing a source. That to me indicates integrity and loyalty."

Mathias smiled. "Well, in this business you have to protect your sources. . . . So, what kind of story do you have?"

"It's a little complicated, but we're about to blow the whistle on some very powerful people. If they knew what we were up to, they'd kill us all without giving it a second thought."

"Really? So where do I fit in?"

"We have a senator who will help us if we can deliver certain evidence to him to produce for Congress. The problem is preserving that evidence. The minute these people find out what's coming down, they'll do whatever it takes to destroy the evidence before it can be delivered."

"I see. So what do you want me to do?"

"We want to show you and a couple of other reporters the evidence so you all can study it and see that it's real. Then you'll write a story about it that will come out simultaneously with its delivery to Congress. That way Congress won't be able to bury it. You see these powerful people have a lot of influence in Congress too."

"You're talking about MidSouth Bank, right?"

"Exactly."

"Oh God. . . . Does this have something to do with Matt Coleman?"

"How did you know?"

"I did my homework. You have a history with him."

"That's true. He'll be getting out of prison soon."

"Huh. . . . So where did you get this evidence?"

"Do you remember a lady and her son who were executed in a parking garage at the Hotel Continental a year or so ago?"

"Yeah, vaguely."

"That was Martha Simonton. She was the secretary to the chairman of MidSouth Bank."

"I don't remember that connection," Mathias said.

"Somehow the identities of the victims were altered," Jason said.

"Really?"

"Yes, Ms. Simonton saw the Senate Banking Committee hearings on TV and wanted to help Matt Coleman and Professor Swensen. She contacted Professor Swensen, they met, and shortly after that she and her son were killed by a man named Hans Schultz. Schultz worked directly for Frank Hill at MidSouth Bank."

"Whoa. That's pretty intense," Mathias said. "And you can prove this?"

"Yes, but I can't tell you exactly how right now. What I would like to do is meet you in Washington, D.C. and show you and two of your colleagues the evidence just before we meet certain Senate officials."

Mathias stroked his chin while he pondered the proposition. Jason watched him intently for a moment and then said, "We need to know if you're in or out. There are lots of reporters who would love this story if you're not interested."

He shrugged. "All right, I'm game. When will this all take place?"

"In seventy-two hours. Check in at the Watergate, and we'll be in touch with more instructions. Bring two other reporters with you."

"That doesn't give me much time."

"We can't delay any longer than that. It's too dangerous."

"Okay."

"Oh, there is one condition to your participation in this venture."

"What's that?"

"You can't discuss this with anyone, including your boss, your photographer, or even your wife, prior to the meeting. We know Frank Hill has some influence with your newspaper. You can't give them any time to quash the story."

"Don't worry. I'll make sure the story gets printed."

***

After the meeting with Mathias, Jason drove back to Texarkana to see Matt. He had missed the previous week's visit and was anxious to find out how things were going.

The jailer opened the door and let Jason into the visitor's center. He walked to his usual booth and sat down and waited for Matt. Soon he saw him come through a door and walk toward him. He was smiling when he sat down.

"Hey, I'm glad to see you. I missed you last week," Matt said.

"I know, I'm sorry I didn't make it, but you wanted me to take care of the press, right?"

"Right, how did it go?"

"Well, we've got three papers and a TV station ready to jump on the story the minute we give them the word."

"Did they give you any hassle?"

"Well, they're a little skeptical, but they know they can't afford to miss this if it turns out to be real."

"Do they understand that they must keep this confidential until we say it's okay to print?"

"Yes, I explained that to them, and they seemed to understand."

"Good, I'm glad that loose-end has been tied down.

"Me too."

"So, how's the lumber business?"

"Not bad, we actually made a small profit last month. I think things are stabilizing," Jason said.

"Can you make it another ninety days?" Matt asked.

"Yeah, we'll make it. I've become good friends with the banker. I'm sure he'll work with me awhile longer."

"They've got a lot at stake. They better. . . . How's the personnel department doing?"

"Cheryl has been very busy. She must get fifty to a hundred calls a day."

"Really? How's she holding up?"

"Very well. I told her the more calls she got, the better your plan was working. The girls Eduardo rounded up for us have been life savers. Three of them are helping Cheryl, and the other nine are helping me process credit cards."

"That's good."

"Where did Eduardo find the girls he sent over anyway?" Jason asked.

"I think they're some of the inmates' wives and sisters mainly. He assured me they would work hard and keep their mouths shut."

"How can he be so sure?"

"I don't know, but so far everything he has told me has been gospel," Matt replied.

"That's good."

"Yeah, so far we've been able to keep a lid on this thing, and I want to keep it that way. I've only got little time left, and I'm a free man. We've got to be very careful from now on. We're so close to victory we can't let anything derail us now."

"I know," Jason said.

"Are the projections holding up?"

"Yeah, we're averaging one new card a week per applicant just like you figured."

"Amazing, isn't it?"

"Yeah. So how's your Bible study coming?"

"We have thirty-six here in our congregation and one hundred and forty-four more in other institutions around the country."

"Damn, how do you keep up with them?"

"On the internet. The warden's secretary arranged for me to have access since I run the library. Dad set up a website where I can post and view messages without the warden screening them. We use codes and encryptions to ensure privacy."

"So how many more do you think you'll get signed up?"

"I don't think we'll get too many more. There are a certain number of guys who just don't trust anybody; then there are the skeptics and, of course, there's a few who consider themselves to be honest, if you can believe that."

"Yeah, right. Some people just can't deal with reality, can they?"

"No."

"So do you have enough, you think?"

"Uh huh. I picked out twelve who will be getting out of prison about the same time as I do. I call them my disciples. Each will have the ability to start his own flock on the outside, if necessary."

"Oh really?" Jason laughed. "God, you are ruthless."

"Yeah, I don't know how long it will take to sink MidSouth Bank, but we plan to keep the heat on as long as necessary. He who lives by the sword will die by the sword," Matt said with a faint smile. "The day of reckoning is at hand."

"Amen," Jason replied.

# 26

Bill was worried about Paula. He had left her in a very difficult situation. It was all over the news that Blanche had died, and he wondered how she was going to explain what happened. He doubted she would tell the truth as that would compromise the witness. Not only would Frank Hill's goons be looking for him and Roxanne but so would every law enforcement agency in New York, not to mention the FBI. Bill jumped when his cell phone rang.

"Paula?" he said.

"Yes, it's me."

"Thank God! Are you okay? I've been so worried about you."

"Yes, I'm fine. It was a little sticky here, but I managed to get myself unglued."

"Where are you?"

"I'm at the airport. Where are you?"

"I don't want to say over the telephone. I'll just meet you tonight where we discussed earlier. You can fill me in on what happened."

"Okay."

"God, I'm so glad you're okay. I've missed you."

"Me too."

"I better get off the line. Be careful."

"I will. See you soon."

Bill flipped his cell phone closed and looked at Roxanne. She smiled at him, but he could see the worry in her expression. He had decided to drive to New York as he didn't want to hang around the airport waiting for a flight. They had parked Roxanne's car in a public garage and rented a car to take them to Washington so it would be more difficult for anyone to spot them. Still, Bill was uneasy. He knew that Frank Hill would be doing everything in his power to find them and that one careless move could be fatal. At 8:15 they checked into the Watergate Hotel.

When they got into their room, Bill called the front desk and asked if Paula Sands had checked in. They said she had and connected him. They talked, and Paula said she would be right up. As she left her room, she spotted a man at a drinking fountain. When she walked by, he started after her and followed her into the elevator. Instead of pushing the button for the floor Bill was on, she pushed the button for the lobby.

Once downstairs she walked into the bar and took a seat. The man who had been following her took a seat at a table a few feet away. A bartender came by, and she ordered a drink. She wondered how she was going to lose the guy. As she was pondering the situation, she spotted two more suspicious men, one near the elevator and another at the front desk. They were standing around, looking, and waiting. She got on her cell phone and called Bill.

"I'm afraid I've led them to you."

"Oh, shit. Where are you?"

"In the lobby at the bar. You better find another place to hide out. Don't tell me where it is. I don't want to know. Just get out of here fast before they find out what room you're in."

"Damn it. Are you going to be okay?"

"Yeah, I'll hang around here for a while, then go back to my room. Call me if you need me to do anything. I'm sorry we can't be together."

"Me too. Be careful."

Bill looked at Roxanne and said, "We've got to get out of here fast." Roxanne threw her clothes back in her suitcase, and Bill picked it up. He opened the door slowly and peered out. The coast appeared clear, so they walked quickly to the stairs. As they were halfway into the stairwell, the elevator bell rang, and the door opened. Two men jumped out and saw the door to the stairwell closing. They came after them.

Bill and Roxanne descended the stairs quickly. They could hear their pursuers just one flight behind them. Bill wondered if there would be more men at the bottom of the staircase. He elected to exit the stairwell on the second floor and go through the mall to avoid them. When they broke out into the mall, they began running to an escalator going down to the street, but when they started to descend they saw two more men at the bottom of the escalator.

"Damn," Bill screamed, taking Roxanne's hand. "This way."

They ran down another corridor as four men gave chase. Luckily they reached another elevator bank, and the door to one was just closing. They slipped inside. The elevator went down, and the four pursuers ran to the stairs. Bill and Roxanne quickly exited the elevator and ran to a door leading to the street. As they went outside the four men came bounding out of the stairwell. They reached the door just as Bill and Roxanne were getting into a cab. By the time the four men had hailed their own taxi, Bill and Roxanne were gone.

Bill looked at Roxanne. She was as pale as skim milk and shaking. He said, "Are you all right?"

She forced a smile and replied, "I guess. I've never been chased before. It's kind of scary. Do you think they would hurt me if they found me?"

Bill nodded. "I'm afraid they'd kill you if they had the chance. That's why we can't let them find you."

"What's going to happen now? Why are we in Washington?"

"We've got a meeting tomorrow with Senator Goss. If he likes you as a witness, then he'll convince the chairman of the Senate Banking Committee to convene a meeting of the committee to consider starting an investigation of MidSouth Bank."

"Where are going to stay tonight?" Roxanne asked.

"I know a place in Georgetown that is out of the way and should be safe. I'll call Senator Goss in the morning and switch our meeting place since we don't want to go back to the Watergate."

"I'm so scared, Bill. What if they find us?"

"They won't, I promise. But just in case I don't plan to go to sleep tonight."

She laughed. "I don't think I'll be sleeping either."

They checked into a bed-and-breakfast in Georgetown and settled in for the night. Bill wondered how Paula was doing. He wanted to call her but was afraid a cell phone transmission might give away his position. Instead he sat in an overstuffed chair next to a window where he wondered if they'd be found

# 27

During the preceding few weeks, most of Matt's disciples had been released and gone home to wait. On Good Friday Matt had a prayer meeting with one of his Bible study groups. At the conclusion of the meeting, he addressed his flock.

"Well, I'm going to be leaving here today, brothers. I wish all of you were coming with me."

"Amen," someone said. The other inmates laughed.

"We've all accomplished a great deal in the last year since we started studying the Bible. It's been hard but rewarding work. Now it's time to reap the harvest of our labors. I think it's only fitting to sing one final hymn before I leave."

Matt pointed to one of the inmates and said, "Brother Bob, would you lead us?"

Bob stood up and began to lead the small congregation.

"Onward Christian Soldiers,
Marching as to war,
With the Cross of Jesus,
Going on before."

As they sung, Matt smiled at them, waved, and then left the room. As he was leaving, he saw the warden and the chaplain waiting to say goodbye.

"Well, Matt we'll miss you around here," the warden said. "You've done a tremendous job with these men. My superiors wanted me to ask you if you'd like to go to work for the department."

"You're offering me a job?"

"Yes, you could set up programs like you've done here all over the country."

"Matt smiled and replied, "That's mighty tempting, warden, but I've got other plans."

"Well, if you change your mind just let me know."

"There'll always be a place in the seminary for you, Matt," the chaplain said. "You've got a God-given gift to heal men's souls. You should use it in the service of the Lord."

"I'll give that some thought, Reverend. Thank you for the kind words."

"Well, goodbye then," the warden said and extended his hand. Matt smiled and shook it warmly. Then he shook the chaplain's hand and left.

Jason and Cheryl arrived before ten to pick him up. It was a bright but crisp morning in East Texas. The sky was clear, and there was a light northerly wind. At precisely nine a door from the main cell block opened and several inmates stepped out as free men. Matt was the last to leave.

"Hello, Jason. Hi, Cheryl."

"Hello, Matt," Cheryl said. "How does it feel to finally be free?"

"Wonderful, but let's get the hell out of here. I'll feel better when we're a hundred miles away from this place."

"Come on, let's go then," Jason replied.

The three friends left the building and walked to Jason's car. They got in, and as they drove away, Matt took one last look at the walls that had surrounded him for eighteen months. He took a deep breath and smiled.

"Now I'm starting to feel good," he said. He raised his hands and yelled, "Hallelujah! Thank you, Jesus!"

Cheryl turned, smiled, and said, "Are you ready to kick Frank Hill's ass?"

"You betcha," Matt replied.

"Good, because we've processed 3,232 credit cards and all your friends are ready to do some heavy shopping."

"How long do you think it will take them to max them out?" Jason asked.

"Not long, a week or ten days I would imagine. . . . Just enough time for us to get to our hideaway."

"I wish I could be at the weekly board meeting to hear their reaction when they realize they've taken a 16-million-dollar hit."

They all laughed.

"Actually," Matt said. "The credit card scenario is plan B. I would prefer to have Congress conduct an investigation of MidSouth. If they did, I'm sure Frank Hill would be ousted as chairman and eventually indicted for murder. He would be publicly humiliated and would lose everything."

"But why not take MidSouth's money too?" Jason said.

"Once we take a dime from MidSouth, we become fugitives from the law and would have to hide out the rest of our lives. I'm prepared to do that if need be, but I would prefer to get my revenge without destroying the rest of my life."

Jason nodded. "You're right. Hopefully, your Dad and Bill will be able to convince Congress to go after Hill."

"I hope so, but if they can't then Plan B is ready to go."

"Do you think losing sixteen million dollars is enough to break MidSouth Bank?" Jason asked.

"Actually, no. That's why I set up eleven more operations just like ours in various other prisons around the country. A hundred and seventy-six million ought to do it, don't you think?"

"Yeah, I guess so," Jason chuckled.

Finally, they all settled down, and Matt leaned back and closed his eyes. He felt more relaxed at that moment than he had felt in eighteen months. Jason looked in his rearview mirror and smiled. Then he noticed a car following them.

"Oh, shit!" Jason mumbled.

Matt sat up and said, "What?"

"Someone's following us."

Matt turned around and looked at the silver Lexus following a hundred yards behind.

"How do you know they're following us?" Cheryl asked.

"I don't know for sure, but we can certainly find out."

Jason pulled onto the shoulder and slammed on his brakes. The Lexus slowed down and passed very slowly. A half mile down the road it pulled off the road and stopped.

"See, what did I tell you!" Jason said.

"Frank Hill must be worried about your release," Cheryl said.

"I can understand that. I guess I should have anticipated they'd follow me, but we've got to lose them somehow. They can't know where we're going."

"If I had a gun we could drive by really slow, wave, and then blow out their tires," Jason suggested.

"Right, and they'd blow out our brains," Matt replied.

"Yeah, I guess you're right. Why don't we go to the lumberyard? We can park out front, go inside, and then sneak out the back in a delivery van."

"Good idea. Get moving."

Jason hit the accelerator and sped past the Lexus. Just as soon as they had gone by, the Lexus took up the pursuit. When they got to the Tyler cutoff, they went south to where the Quality One Lumber plant was situated. They parked in front and went inside.

Jason's secretary smiled at them as they walked through.

"I thought you were taking the day off," she said.

"I just forgot to get something out of my office," Jason said. Matt smiled at her as they went into Jason's office. After a minute they came out.

"We're going to borrow a cargo van," he said. "We've got to move some stuff from Cheryl's apartment."

"Oh, okay."

"We'll bring it back tomorrow morning."

"Fine. I'll see you then."

They all left out the back door and hustled over to the cargo van. They got in and Jason drove it out through the back of the lumber yard and onto a surface street. They drove for a while looking back to see if anyone was following them.

"It looks like we lost them," Jason said.

"I wonder how long it will take them to figure out that we ditched them," Cheryl asked.

"Probably ten or fifteen minutes," Matt replied.

Jason pushed the pedal to the floor. "I better step on it then."

"When we get to Canton, let's take a detour through the countryside. We'll go over to Kaufman and come into Dallas on Highway 175. If we stay on the freeway, they might catch up to us."

"Good thinking," Jason replied.

At Canton, they got off the freeway and headed south through the lush countryside. It was so beautiful they nearly forgot they were fleeing the country. When they finally got to Dallas, it was just after lunch. They pulled into a Burger King drive-thru and got some hamburgers. Cheryl dashed inside for a minute to go to the bathroom, and Matt and Jason got out to stretch their legs.

It was after two when they got to South Arlington to an office warehouse. They parked the car in the back and went inside. Wally was seated at a desk with three manila envelopes.

"Okay, Matt, you're Martin A. Monroe. Cheryl, you're Cathy B. Monroe and Jason, you are now John T. Walls."

"Okay, whatever you say," Matt said.

Wally handed each a packet and said, "Inside you'll find Texas drivers' licenses, passports, two credit cards for identification, a birth certificate and in yours, Matt, a marriage certificate for you and Cheryl."

"Excellent," Matt said.

"We've also provided you with luggage. Inside you'll find clothing, toiletries, etcetera. You should have everything you'll need for the trip to your hideaway."

"Is the place we're going nice?" Cheryl asked.

"Yes, I think you'll find it quite nice. It was purchased from the estate of a drug lord who was assassinated by a rival organization."

"Hmm," Cheryl said. "What about Bill and Paula?"

"They're working Plan A," Matt said. "If it works out, we won't have to go into hiding, and we'll be able to come back to Dallas, and they'll join us there. If Plan A doesn't work out, they'll join us at our hideaway."

Wally got up from his chair and indicated it was time to leave. He said, "There's a small private airfield not too far from here. We're going to fly you to Kansas City. Then you'll take a commercial flight to Chicago. From Chicago, you'll go to Vancouver, and from Vancouver, you'll fly to Mexico City. Then you'll disappear."

"Good. When do we leave?" Matt asked.

"Right now if we're going to keep on schedule."

"All right then, let's go."

"Right this way."

Wally led them to a blue conversion van and opened the door. They got in and took off down the road. After a ten-minute ride, they entered a small airport and drove up to a private hangar. They got out and went inside. Two pilots collected their luggage and loaded it on the plane that was parked inside. When the plane was ready Matt, Cheryl and Jason climbed aboard. They were about to close the hatch when they heard tires screeching. They looked up and saw two men running toward them, and a half dozen cars could be heard surrounding the building.

One of the men began shooting at the plane as they cranked up the engine and tried to taxi out to the runway. Wally was in the line of fire and took a bullet in the leg.

"Ah!" he screamed as he went down on one knee. "Get out of here!" he yelled.

Matt went to him and tried to drag him aboard, but he refused. "The plane is full. It won't take off with me aboard. Get out of here! Go!"

Matt reluctantly jumped on the plane. A bullet nearly hit him. He closed the hatch, and the plane began to pull out of the hangar. One of the cars pulled up in front of the hangar trying to block the plane, but the pilot managed to squeeze by barely missing the front bumper. Six men began shooting frantically at the plane, but they failed to do serious damage as the plane picked up speed.

One of the cars raced down the runway. A man leaned out and took shots at the plane as it was lifting off the runway. One of the bullets pierced a window and narrowly missed the pilot but soon the plane was out of range, and Matt and his friends were safe.

28

Paula, Bill, Roxanne, and I met Senator Goss and two staff members, George Mathias, three other reporters, and a camera crew at the local NBC studio. Bill had Roxanne tell them about her relationship with Frank Hill, explain the Day-Timer and the secrets that it contained, as well as what she personally knew about Hill's plan to set up Matt for the bankruptcy fraud charges. When she was done, he let the others question her.

Senator Goss was impressed with her testimony but indicated it still wasn't enough to convince the Senate Banking Committee to reopen the investigation against MidSouth. I had anticipated this would be the case, so I brought another witness. He was very reluctant to cooperate until I told him Hans Schultz was dead.

"Senator," I said. "I've got another witness that can corroborate Roxanne Witherspoon's testimony."

"Really? You didn't mention that in your phone call."

"I didn't have a definite commitment at the time, so I didn't want to say anything in case it didn't pan out."

"I see. Well, do we get to talk to this mystery witness?"

I nodded and motioned for Paula to bring him in.

Paula brought Tom Hartsfield into the conference room, and he took a seat at the end of the long conference table. I introduced him and told them he was once Matt's office manager for the Debt Relief Center. The court

299

reporter swore him in. The cameramen filmed the interview.

"Mr. Hartsfield," I said. "Were you contacted by a Hans Schultz while you were employed by the Debt Relief Centers?"

"Yes."

"What was the purpose of the contact?"

"To give me instructions on how I was to set up Matt Coleman so that he could be implicated in a bankruptcy fraud case."

"Why did he think you would participate in such a scheme?"

"Because he said he would kill my son if I didn't."

"And why are you coming forward now after Matt has already been convicted?"

"Because the man who threatened me, Hans Schultz, is dead and you convinced me it was safe to speak out now. You said I would be provided protection."

I turned from the witness and addressed Senator Goss and his staff. "So you see, Martha Simonton has linked Hans Schultz to Frank Hill. She testified Schultz was his errand boy, enforcer, or whatever you want to call it. Now Tom Hartsfield has tied Hans Schultz to extortion, perjury, and fraud. And we are confident that further investigation will link Hans Schultz to the murders of five women and a boy, Lori Keys, Lynn Coleman, Martha Simonton and her son, Michael, and Monica Sommers. We are certain each one of these murders was orchestrated by Frank Hill, and we implore you to do something about it before Frank Hill kills again."

"What concerns me," Senator Goss replied, "is that Roxanne Witherspoon never really saw Hans Schultz with Frank Hill. She only believed he was working for him. This is a critical link in your evidence, and it's very weak. I don't think I can ask the committee to reopen the investigation just on speculation that Hans Schultz was working for MidSouth or Frank Hill."

"Don't you think it's enough to warrant further investigation?" I asked.

"Yes, and I will forward this evidence to the FBI for further development, but I can't recommend the committee to convene hearings at this time."

The meeting broke up, and Senator Goss agreed, off the record, he would present the evidence to the committee and try to get them to reopen the investigation, but he was doubtful they would grant his request.

I warned him that Frank Hill had contacts in the FBI so referring the case to them might be a waste of time. The Senator assured me, however, that he would take it high up in ranks of the FBI where Frank Hill couldn't possibly have any influence. In the meantime, we were told to stay in Washington for a few days in case he got lucky and was able to set up a hearing. The members of the press were asked not to go public with what they had heard for seventy-two hours, at which time they were free to run any stories they liked.

I wondered how we could prove Hans Schultz was working for Frank Hill. Roxanne had told Senator Goss that Hill had a discretionary advertising account which he drew upon to fund his operations. Whenever he needed money, she would cut a check for cash and expense it to radio or TV advertising. Everyone knew the advertising account was Frank's spending money, so no one ever questioned how the money was used. Frank often gave money to Doug Barnes, and she believed it ended up in Hans Schultz' pocket. I needed to find someone who could link Hans to Doug Barnes.

Jason called later that afternoon to let us know that Matt had been released from prison. He told us they had been followed and were worried about making it to the airport safely. I told him we had come up short on evidence and so far hadn't convinced Senate Banking Committee to reopen the MidSouth investigation. He said they were on their way to South America and would call again when they arrived. I wished him good luck.

# 29

The plane flew north toward Kansas City and the weary group settled in for the long flight. Matt reclined his chair and pulled a Bible from his carry-on bag. He said, "'Put on the whole armor of God, that ye may be able to stand against the wiles of the devil.'"

"'For we wrestle not against flesh and blood, but against principalities, against powers, against the rulers of the darkness of this world, against spiritual wickedness in high places.'"

"'Wherefore take unto you the whole armor of God, that ye may be able to withstand the evil day, . . . '"

Everyone stared at Matt in silence. Finally, he smiled and said, "That's one of my favorite passages. It's from Ephesians. I thought it was appropriate for this momentous occasion."

"It was inspiring, Matt, but what are we going to do now?" Cheryl asked.

"Nothing. We've done all we can right now. The ball is now in Senator Goss' court. If he fails, then perhaps the forces we have unleashed against the MidSouth bank may yet be lethal."

"It will hurt them sure," Jason said, "but without the evidence coming out and a congressional investigation the bank and Frank Hill will survive and just get stronger."

Cheryl shook her head and said, "Well, you've done more than anyone in the last twenty years to expose the crime being committed against the American consumer, Matt. I think you should be proud."

Matt looked at Cheryl and smiled. "Thank you, Cheryl, but nothing short of the total destruction and eradication of MidSouth Bank and all other predatory banks will ever make me feel proud."

Cheryl embraced Matt and gave him a peck on the cheek. Matt smiled and hugged her warmly.

"I wonder how Wally made out," Jason asked.

"He's probably dead," Cheryl said

"I doubt it," Matt said. "I imagine they kept him alive to pump him for information."

"What if he tells them our plans?" Jason asked.

"We're screwed then," Cheryl replied.

"I don't think we have to worry about him talking," Matt said.

"Why wouldn't he?" Jason asked.

"Eduardo told me he was a real professional," Matt replied. "He had a lot of pride in the services he provided. He knew one day this could happen and he knew that he was a dead man whether he talked or not. . . . No, I'd be willing to bet my life that he didn't talk."

"You just have," Cheryl added.

Matt shrugged.

"Doesn't the pilot have to file a flight plan?" Jason asked.

"I asked him that, too. He said it wasn't mandatory. A lot of pilots never bother to file one," Matt replied.

"Well, I guess we'll find out when we get to Kansas City if you're right about him," Jason said.

Several hours later the plane made its approach to a small airstrip outside of Kansas City. Everyone breathed a sigh of relief when they landed, and no one seemed interested in them. They rented a car and drove to Kansas

City International Airport, getting there just in time to catch their flight to Chicago. It was a packed flight, so they had to split up. Matt and Cheryl sat together since they were pretending to be husband and wife.

"I feel terrible about Wally. He did such a great job getting us out of the country." Cheryl said.

"I know, I wish we could have brought him along," Matt said. "It's too bad we didn't have a bigger plane. I know I could have pulled him aboard."

"You did all you could."

"Do you think Frank Hill knows what's going to happen?"

"No, he just figures if they kill me they'll stop whatever's coming down," Matt replied. "What they don't know is that it's out of my control now. Even if they did kill me, it wouldn't matter."

"I wish you could communicate that to them so they'd quit chasing us," Cheryl said.

"I think we lost them. Wally was pretty smart sending us to Chicago and then to Vancouver. They probably have the Mexican border pretty well covered, but I doubt they'd figure we'd go to Canada."

"I'm exhausted. I'm going to take a nap," Cheryl said.

"Good idea, I'll probably do the same thing after we get airborne."

Cheryl laid back and closed her eyes. Then she took Matt's hand and leaned her head on his shoulder. Matt froze up for a moment and then remembered this was his new wife, at least in theory. For the first time, he noticed how attractive she was and how long it had been since he had held Lynn in his arms. He took a deep breath, smiled, slipped his arm out and put it around Cheryl's shoulder. She squirmed a little bit to get comfortable and then fell asleep. As the plane took off into the heavens, Matt wondered if Lynn was watching. He looked out the window at the fluffy white cumulus clouds surrounding the plane and whispered, "Honey, they're going to pay. Believe me, they're going to pay!"

"Huh," Cheryl said without opening her eyes.

"Nothing, go back to sleep."

# 30

Bill Ross flew into DFW Airport and rented a car. It was his last lead, and he was afraid it wouldn't pan out. The warden's secretary told Matt that he needed to talk to an inmate named Cecil Walker. Matt had tried to locate Walker before he was released but had been unsuccessful. Bill hoped that Cecil Walker would talk to him. He didn't know how he would react when a stranger came to visit him. When he got to Texarkana, he went straight to the visitor's center and put in a request to see him. Two and a half hours later Bill was directed into a visiting area and told to go to booth eleven. He sat down and waited.

"Mr. Walker, I'm Bill Ross, a private investigator."

"Okay, so what do you want with me?"

"Well, we got a tip that you had some information that might be helpful to our investigation."

"So what are you investigating?"

"MidSouth Bank and its chairman, Frank Hill."

"I don't know anything about them."

Bill took a deep breath wondering if he was the victim of a practical joke. He pulled out a notepad and flipped a few pages.

"Okay, I'm going to read off the names of some people involved in our investigation. If you've heard of any of them, let me know."

"Why should I help you?"

"You don't have to, of course. But if you do know something, we'll need you as a witness, and they'll have to

307

send you to Washington, D.C. for God knows how long. They'll probably keep you in a hotel somewhere while you testify."

Walker smiled. "And when I get back here, how long 'till I get knocked off for having a big mouth?"

Bill took a deep breath. "Listen, I don't know how you fit into the puzzle I'm trying to solve, but if you lead me to the missing piece, there will be ten thousand dollars immediately wired to any bank account you name."

Walker raised his eyebrows. "Okay, you got my attention. Let me hear the names."

Bill looked down at his notepad and said, "Martha Simonton," Walker shook his head no. "Roxanne Witherspoon?" He responded with another negative nod. "Matt Coleman."

"I've heard of Coleman. He used to be in this prison, didn't he?"

"Right. Do you know anything about him?"

"No, not really—just that he's planning some big scam against that bank you mentioned. MidSouth I believe."

Bill listed a half dozen more names, and Walker shook his head no. Then Bill asked him about Doug Barnes.

"Yeah, I've heard that name. My girlfriend knew him."

"Really? Who's your girlfriend?"

"Debbie Ralston. She's a massage therapist at Beverly Hills Spa & Massage in Dallas. One of her customers was a guy named Hans Schultz. He came in for a massage a couple of times a week, and they would talk. One day he was in the middle of a massage when this Barnes guy shows up. They tell her to get lost, but she's curious as to what's so important to interrupt her work, so she doesn't go off too far. She listens and hears them talking about your friend, Matt Coleman, and how he's up to something. Barnes is really upset about it and insists Hans go look into it right away."

"So, your girlfriend saw Hans Schultz and Doug Barnes together discussing Matt Coleman?"

"Exactly."

"Thank you, Cecil. You're just what we need to put Frank Hill out of business. . . . I'm curious though, what are you in here for?"

"Theft. I helped sell the contents of a hijacked eighteen-wheeler. I was on drugs at the time and desperate for money."

Bill nodded sympathetically. "Do you know the warden's secretary?"

"Sure. I was assigned to janitorial duty in the warden's office for a couple of months. I got to know her pretty well."

"You must have talked a lot?"

"Yeah, she's a very friendly lady."

"Thank God for that," Bill said, feeling exhilarated as the case against Frank Hill and MidSouth Bank finally came together.

"You don't happen to know her connection to Matt Coleman, do you?"

"What do you mean?"

"Well, she seems to like him a lot."

"Oh, yeah. She mentioned that. His firm filed bankruptcy for her sister in Dallas—said it was the best thing that ever happened to her."

Bill chuckled as he took down Walker's wife's bank account number so he could wire him his reward. A wave of relief washed over him as the final piece to his puzzle was now in place.

# 31

It was a cold, drizzly day in Houston, and Frank Hill was upset. He was tired and wanted to get home, but his helicopter had been grounded. Now he'd have to waste two hours sitting in Houston traffic before he got home. He hit the intercom button on his desk.

"Leslie, get me Monique on the phone."

"Yes, sir."

Frank went to his closet and got his coat. The intercom buzzed, so he went over to it and pushed the reply button.

"Yes."

"Monique is on one."

"Good," he said and picked up the phone. "Monique, honey, hey, I'm going to be in traffic a few hours tonight, can you send somebody over. I hate that long lonely drive."

"Sure, anything for you, Frank. I'll have someone in your limo when it picks you up."

"Good. You're a life saver."

Frank took the elevator to the basement garage. As he stepped out onto the sidewalk, a limousine pulled up. The valet went over and opened the door. As he climbed in his eyes lit up as he saw twin girls dressed in tight red dresses and black stockings. Their dresses were pulled up high giving him an eyeful. He climbed in eagerly and sat between them. Smiling broadly, he opened the lid on the bar.

"How about a drink, girls?" he asked.

"Vodka for us," one of them said.

He grabbed the Vodka and poured a glass for each of them. Soon Frank was undressing one of the girls and fondling her breasts. Suddenly the phone rang. Frank reached for the phone and picked it up.

"Yeah."

"Frank, turn on the TV—Channel 3," Barnes said.

"What?"

"Channel 3. We've got serious trouble."

Frank turned on the limo's TV set. "This is Diane McClure with the six o'clock evening news. In Washington, today congressmen and senators were dismayed when they and members of their families received hundreds of credit cards in the mail. The cards, each with a credit limit of $5,000, were issued by MidSouth Bank of Houston. MidSouth Bank, a subprime lender, suffered severe financial setbacks two years ago when Dallas bankruptcy attorney Matt Coleman opened up its Debt Relief Centers of Texas.

"In a news conference today Senator Goss called for an investigation of MidSouth and its chairman, Frank Hill, citing mounting evidence of wrongdoing by the Texas banker," McClure said.

The camera went to Senator Goss' news conference.

"These credit cards to members of Congress and their families are the last straw," Senator Goss said, holding up a fist full of credit cards. "If Frank Hill thinks he can buy his way out of trouble, he's in for a rude awakening."

"Senator, what about reports that Senator Bennington received large campaign contributions from Frank Hill?"

"You'll have to ask him about that," Senator Goss replied.

The screen went back to Diane McClure at the studio.

"And Senator Bennington *was* asked about the alleged campaign contributions as he left his office today."

The screen went to Senator Bennington's office, where he has just come out the front door. A mob of reporters surrounds him.

"Senator Bennington. Did you and your family members receive credit cards from MidSouth Bank?"

"Yes, and I'm sending them right back. I didn't ask for them and frankly, I'm quite perplexed as to why we got them."

Another reporter said, "Is it true that you received substantial campaign contributions from Frank Hill?"

Senator Bennington shrugged, "Well, he has been a supporter but—"

"Is that why you opposed any investigation of MidSouth Bank?"

"No. No. . . . I'm sorry. That's all for today. I have no further comment at this time."

Senator Bennington looked around nervously and then pushed his way through the crowd. The camera zoomed in on him getting in his limo and driving off. The screen flipped back to the studio and Diane McClure.

"Coincidentally," McClure continued. "Matt Coleman was released from prison today. It is unclear whether the events on the Hill today and Coleman's release are related, but it's a little hard to believe that they're not. Diane McClure here for Channel 3 News."

The car stopped, and voices could be heard outside. The driver's door opened and then slammed. Frank looked up in a half stupor wondering what was going on. The girls scrambled to find their clothes and put them on.

Annoyed by the news report and delay in getting home, Frank opened the passenger door and found himself face to face with two police detectives. They pulled him out of the car and stood him in front of Agent Radcliff.

"Franklin Benjamin Hill?" the officer asked.

Struggling, he said, "What do you think you are doing?"

"You're under arrest for the murder of Lynn Coleman and Lori Keys. Put your hands in the air, sir."

Frank reluctantly raised his hands and said, "What's your name? Do you know who I am? I'll have your badge before morning."

"I don't think so, sir. I'm assisting these officers in executing a valid arrest warrant issued less than two hours ago. . . . You have the right to remain silent. Anything you say can and will be used against you in a court of law. You have the right to an attorney. If you cannot afford an attorney one will be provided for you. Do you understand these rights?"

"Don't worry. I've got the best attorneys in the state. I'll be out on bail in twenty minutes."

"Well, we'll see."

The officers put Hill in a squad car, and took him to the federal building. At a bond hearing an hour later the magistrate denied him bond due to the multiple murder charges and likelihood that he would try to escape.

***

The following day financial stocks took the largest nosedive since the great depression. Rumors of the imminent appointment of a special prosecutor to handle not only MidSouth Bank but other banks suspected of predatory credit card practices fueled the crash. But the mood of the country was not of panic but more of hope. For by the grace of God a vicious cancer that had been growing in America had been detected and for the first time was under treatment.

# EPILOGUE

After Matt's release from prison, thousands of newly released inmates around the country enjoyed the bounty provided by thousands of new credit cards issued to them by MidSouth Bank. Soon MidSouth was declared insolvent and shut down.

It took nearly five years to conclude the dozens of investigations and trials associated with the prosecution of key officers of MidSouth Bank and seven other institutions which later became targets of the special prosecutor. In time Matt Coleman and Bill Ross became household names as the facts behind their efforts to expose MidSouth Bank became known.

Matt's trip to South America violated his parole and cost him another six months of incarceration. He took his additional time in stride. He had accomplished his goal of putting Frank Hill out of business and waking up the American people to the threat of excessive credit and predatory credit practices. But memories were short, so he knew he would have to do more.

While in prison, Matt realized God had called him, so instead of reestablishing his lucrative Debt Relief Centers he returned to Dallas and started a nonprofit foundation in a restored mansion on Swiss Avenue. He called it the "Lynn Coleman Foundation." The clinic had the same purpose, to help consumers rid themselves of debilitating debt, but diverted all its profits to a ministry devoted to stopping the rampant spread of materialism which he believed was largely responsible for the high divorce rate and the decline of the family as a dominant force in America.

A local radio station provided Matt with air time for a weekly talk show, and he frequently preached at several local churches. His reputation and influence grew, and eventually, his weekly talk show was syndicated nationwide. Matt never remarried.

# About the Author

William Manchee

William Manchee makes a living as a consumer lawyer practicing in Dallas, Texas with his son Jim. Originally from Southern California, he lives now in Plano, Texas. Writing is his passion and his novels are in the genres of mystery, science fiction, and suspense. His works to date include the Stan Turner Mystery series (11 volumes), the Rich Coleman novels (3 volumes), the Tarizon Saga (5 volumes) and stand-alone novels, Uncommon Thief and the Prime Minister's Daughter. He's also written a non-fiction work for small business owners, Go Broke, Die Rich.

Other Works by William Manchee

<u>Stan Turner Mysteries</u>
*Undaunted*
*Disillusioned*
*Brash Endeavor*
*Second Chair*
*Cash Call*
*Deadly Distractions*
*Black Monday,*
*Cactus Island*
*Act Normal*
*Deadly Defiance,*
*Deadly Dining*

<u>Rich Coleman Novels</u>
*Death Pact*
*Plastic Gods*
*Unconscionable*

<u>Science Fiction</u>
*Tarizon: Desert Swarm*
*Tarizon: Shroud of Doom*
*Tarizon: The Liberator*
*Tarizon: Civil War*
*Tarizon: Conquest Earth*

<u>Romantic Suspense</u>
*The Prime Minister's Daughter*
*Uncommon Thief*

<u>Non Fiction</u>
*Go Broke, Die Rich*